No Hiding Place

By

Kevin O'Hagan

2019

**Grosvenor House
Publishing Limited**

This book is published by
Grosvenor House Publishing Ltd
Link House
140 The Broadway, Tolworth, Surrey, KT6 7HT.
www.grosvenorhousepublishing.co.uk

This book is a work of fiction. Any resemblance to
people or events, past or present, is purely coincidental.

A CIP record for this book
is available from the British Library

ISBN 978-1-78623-563-3

Dedication

For my incredible grandchildren. Enjoy and embrace every moment of your lives.

Acknowledgements

To my wonderful family that inspire and encourage me in ways they don't even know. Thank you for being there.

To my rock, Tina, my wife who has always supported all my ventures and been there for me in the good and bad times.

To Lauren, my daughter, for editing and initially proofreading the book. Thank you for your honest feedback, advice and believing in my writing.

Finally, to all the fantastic authors out there. Your incredible tales, plotlines and characters have inspired my desire to write and attempt to stand on the shoulders of giants.

Kevin O'Hagan, June 2019.

Prologue

The man stood on the porch steps of the ancient stone fisherman's cottage high on the cliffside and looked out at the sea view before him which stretched to the far horizon. The early morning mist was clearing, and he spied a small fishing boat out on the waters. The air was cold. September was drawing in and the summer was well and truly on the wane.

He heard the familiar ring of the windchimes in the light breeze hanging outside the front door. He briefly regarded the weather-beaten sign carved from wood above the doorframe displaying the name of the cottage: *Seaspray.* This is where he called home... for now.

He sipped from his mug of hot black coffee. It was good and strong just how he liked it. His head felt fuzzy. A result, no doubt, of the half a bottle of bourbon he had drunk the previous evening. God bless *Jack.*

He knew he should cut his drinking down, but it helped blot out the bad memories and helped him sleep most of the time... unless the nightmares came. And they came frequently these days.

He walked down a short pathway and opened an old wooden gate. The paint had long since peeled from it. He noticed a sheen of condensation on the iron latch.

A sure sign that autumn was around the corner. The gate and surrounding fence of the garden could do with a coat of paint. One day maybe.

He made his way to a cliff pathway which led down to small shingle and pebble beach. Not another soul was on the beach when he reached it, except for a few seagulls and terns scavenging for anything edible tossed up by the tide.

He approached 'his' rock and sat down on it. It was a large smooth stone ideal for sitting on, so it had become his seat. He sat here most mornings at sunrise and sometimes at night as the sun set.

He put his coffee mug down on the ground, stretched his arms above his head and yawned. He felt the tightness of his skin over the old scars on his torso and left shoulder. They were no longer painful in the physical sense. They were healing remarkably well. He was getting stronger day by day. But the mental scars after six months or so since the shootings were still very much raw.

He closed his eyes against the rising sun and visualised her face. Beautiful and smiling. The full lips and white teeth. The flawless Mediterranean skin. The long dark hair falling around her shoulders. He could smell her perfume. Fragrant and subtle with a faint aroma of lemons.

This is how he wanted to remember her. Needed to remember her. He had to blot out the blood, the sightless eyes. The death.

His breathing became heavy. He felt the panic rising. He opened his eyes and gazed out towards the fishing boat. It was getting a little nearer. He breathed deeply, and the feelings of panic subsided... for now.

A sudden noise from behind startled him and he reached for the knife on his belt. Then, he relaxed as Skipper, his black and white Jack Russell, came trotting towards him. He hugged the dog and smiled. He had reared him from a pup. The animal had been a welcoming present to his new island life from an old friend.

Skipper had become a faithful companion. He had to be. There wasn't anybody else he trusted in his life. Not now, not after what had happened.

Somehow, he had cheated death and for some reason, he was given another chance when others close to him had not been as lucky. But he sensed the past was still trying to catch up with him. Even at this remote location at which he found himself, he could not fully relax.

Although he knew that he was safe here for now, he could not shake off the feeling that somebody soon would find him and then there would be no hiding place. He realised he would have to move on soon and keep his trail cold.

The man drained his coffee cup and stood up. With one final look out to sea, he turned and headed back towards the cottage.

Another day had dawned on the Welsh island of Graig o Mor for Tony Slade.

PART ONE

Chapter One

Six Months Earlier

He could see lights. They were blurred, but he could see them. He could also hear voices, but they were fading in and out of his consciousness like a bad radio signal. His head felt like it was stuffed with cotton wool. He felt the sensation of being rapidly pushed along on something.

He was lying on his back. His body felt numb and it had a light floating sensation to it. He could occasionally pick up fragments of conversation. He heard words such as blood loss, trauma, gunshot and operate, but he could make no sense of their meaning. The voices had an echoey, dreamy sound to them.

He could now register a door crash open and another babble of voices. He came to a stop and felt himself being lifted onto what he surmised was a table. He felt a prick of a needle to his arm and then the voices faded and blackness descended. That was the last that he could remember.

When he next awoke, it took him several minutes to orientate himself. His vision was blurred and it took him a few moments to focus his eyes properly. The first thing he saw was Jesus on the cross. Was he in heaven? Fat chance. Not with his track record. As his vision cleared, he realised that he was looking at a wooden crucifix on a plain white wall.

Then, he was aware of a mask over his face. It made him feel like gagging. He could also see other tubes running from his right arm and the left side of his chest to plastic bags filled with clear fluid and blood. A machine to his right constantly bleeped. A green light moved across it. His left arm was in an elevated sling. He realised now that he was in a hospital bed and that somehow, he was alive.

As he coughed on the obstruction over his nose and mouth, a nurse rushed forward towards him. She gently removed it and monitored the bleeping screen checking on his blood pressure, heartrate and breathing. She smiled and walked off. Soon, she came back with a tall distinguished looking Asian man in a white coat. The man checked a clip board at the bottom of the bed and then he smiled.

"Welcome back to the land of the living, Mr Slade. My name is Doctor Arjun Varma. I performed the surgery on you."

Tony's throat felt like sandpaper. He croaked that he would like some water. The doctor nodded to the nurse who filled a glass, popped a straw into it and assisted Tony to drink it.

"Just sip it, no gulping it down now."

Tony detected a soft Irish lilt to her voice.

The water tasted like nectar and soothed the dryness.

Doctor Varma moved closer to the bed.

"Well, Mr Slade, you had us worried for a little while, but the operation seems to have been a success. You have been here for two days. We have kept you sedated, but this was more a precautionary procedure on our part.

You sustained three bullet wounds. Two of which passed through your body. One shattered your collarbone, but with no major underlying problems. The same can be said of the one that passed through your chest wall.

It was the third one that gave us problems because it nicked your lung causing partial collapse. But the lung tissue is not as dense as blood, solid organs or bone, so there is less damage to it, which is fortunate for you. You appear to be healing well, all things considered.

You also have a minor head wound from what looks like a fall. It required stitches.

You are a lucky man considering the incident you were involved in."

At this this moment in time, Tony did not feel particularly lucky.

Doctor Varma continued.

"You now need plenty of rest. We will regularly monitor you and hopefully, we can get rid of all these tubes as soon as possible. The one in the side of your chest may have to stay a few days until we are sure that your lung is inflating properly and that there is no infection present. I will be back later. In the meantime, I will leave you in the capable hands of Nurse O'Neill."

He went to move away and then paused.

"From examination, this isn't the first bullet wound you have received. Army?"

Tony nodded in response.

"I noticed the tattoo on your upper left arm. Parachute regiment, I guess?"

Tony stayed quiet.

Dr Varma smiled faintly and moved away towards another bed. He had dealt with enough patients in his time with unusual wounds to know not to question him too much. His job was to patch up and heal, not judge.

Tony looked towards the nurse. She was busy fixing his blankets.

He estimated her to be in her early fifties. She was an attractive lady, but her face showed the strain of long hours on the ward. Her black hair was flecked with grey.

"Is this intensive care?" he asked Nurse O'Neill. His voice was almost a whisper.

"Indeed it is, Mr Slade and you will be in here a few weeks I shouldn't wonder."

"Tony. Please call me Tony if I am going to be in here for a while."

"Fair enough. I am Nurse O'Neill."

"Have you got a first name?"

"Yes, I have. Thank you. But to you for now I am Nurse O'Neill. I never like to get too close to my patients just in case they suddenly drop off their perch, so to speak."

Tony smiled. "Wow. Well, thanks for your candour, Nurse O'Neill."

With a small wry smile playing on her lips, she helped move Tony to a more comfortable position. The pain was intense and he gritted his teeth as he managed to obtain a seated posture.

"May I have some more water, please."

She poured more for him.

"The oxygen mask is there if you feel the need for it. It really depends on how quickly your lung is healing.

You are fortunate that you are a fit and healthy man. This should make your recovery easier."

"Where am I?" asked Tony.

"You are at Southmead Hospital in Bristol. You were brought in by ambulance just over two days ago. Do you remember what happened to you?"

For a moment, there was blankness.

Then, it all came rushing back to Tony like a runaway train. Annette, Robbins. Sat in the coffee shop. The shootings. The chaos, noise, blood and screams. He remembered another man with a machine gun pistol, just randomly spraying the shop with bullets. Just like a scene out of a Tarantino movie.

He saw Robbins and his goons die and... Christ, Annette. Beautiful, fragile Annette. He remembered her lying on the floor, her sightless eyes staring at him.

Tony looked towards Nurse O'Neill and suddenly, clutched her arm. This startled her.

"The rest of the people in the coffee shop. Do you know if anybody else survived?"

"I can't really say. From what I have gathered from the news, eight people died and six or seven more were hurt. Others were treated for shock, that kind of thing. Why? Were you with somebody?"

Tony remained silent.

Nurse O'Neill' carried on talking.

"Apparently, a stranger just walked in and opened fire. So tragic. Police are considering the possibility of a terrorist attack. You were just in the wrong place at the wrong time. The world had gone mad."

"Was anybody else brought in here the same time as me?"

Nurse O'Neill thought for a second.

"A few people for superficial wounds, but they have now been discharged. You are the only long-term recovery. Unfortunately, the others died. You are big news, Tony Slade. The media are clamouring to find out who you are and get your story. They know there is a survivor of the shootings, but don't know who it is. For now, we are keeping them at bay."

Tony closed his eyes to blot out the images in his head. It did not work.

A few days ago, he was ready to embark on an exciting adventure with the women he loved and leave his violent and lonely past behind. But fate has a way of strangling your hopes and dreams at the last minute.

To lose Annette was the cruellest of blows that he had ever received.

He had lost comrades in the army in Northern Ireland, the Falklands and other places whilst in action, but this was not the same. Annette had been an innocent party and wanted no part of the violent life in which she had become entangled.

He was feeling a hurt deep inside that he had never experienced before.

Tony Slade was a hard man and had seen more violence and bloodshed than most, but he was struggling to deal with this loss.

Fuck the media. He wanted no part of the circus that was about to begin. He needed to stay anonymous as long as possible.

Part of him now wanted to rip out the wires and tubes and to say be damned to the world take me to. What is my life now without the women I loved?

But another small part of him, the survivalist in him, wondered why he was not dead with the rest of them.

Why was he still alive? He had a distinct feeling that the situation in which he had found himself was not yet over. There had to be a reason. He needed peace and quiet to contemplate this.

"I am sorry. I am tired. I would like to sleep now," he said.

Nurse O'Neill put the glass of water down on the bedside table.

"Of course, I am sorry to prattle on. My friends are always telling me I could talk for England. I will leave you in peace."

Before she walked off, Tony asked, "Have the police come to see me?"

She turned back. "Yes, they were here earlier, but you were unconscious and we told them to leave. We said we would contact them when you came around and were well enough to answer questions. I am sure they will be back very soon. They were most insistent about talking to you as soon as you came around."

She noticed a look of concern cross his face.

"But there is no hurry for that just yet, is there? You just rest and get your strength back. You have been through a lot."

"How did they find out my name?"

Nurse O'Neill came closer to his bed.

"When you came in here, it was most unusual that you weren't carrying any form of identity on you. Then we took off your watch and found out your name."

Tony smiled weakly and sank back on his pillow.

The watch.

It had been a gift from his section when he left the army. It was a beauty. A Traser pro watch. It was a paratrooper edition with the cap badge insignia on the face. He always wore it, but in doing so, he had forgotten about the inscription engraved on the back.

To Corporal Anthony Slade from 2 PARA.

No doubt the police would have already sniffed out who he was. It was not an ideal situation.

His thoughts were interrupted.

"Have you any next of kin, Tony? A wife? Family member? Anybody you need to let know that you are here?" asked Nurse O'Neill

"No one," Tony answered.

She didn't push it.

"Okay, I will let you rest. I am just outside. If you need anything, press the button by your bedside."

Once alone, he went back over the incident in the coffee shop that had brought him here. The police were sniffing around which was not good. He needed to have a solid story to keep them off his back. He needed them to think that he was just a normal punter having his morning coffee when this terrible thing happened.

There was no obvious direct connection between Northern gangster Kenny Robbins and him. Even if the police up in Newcastle got involved, none of Robbins' crew were going to say anything.

All he needed to do was play dumb. Like Nurse O'Neill presumed, he was just in the wrong place at the wrong time.

Shit, the gun. His gun. He had forgotten about it. He remembered shooting Rudi, one of Robbins' minders, and then things began to get hazy as the bullet wounds he had sustained drew him into unconsciousness.

They must have found it. It would have his fingerprints all over it. The police will want to know why. He had to get his thoughts straight and be ready for their questioning.

But whenever he went through the incident in his mind, he kept coming back to Annette. She was gone. A beautiful light snuffed out in a few moments of madness. He had loved her. Maybe she was the only person he had ever truly loved.

Tony had questioned himself on many occasions if he really knew what love was. But in meeting Annette, that beautiful forbidden fruit, he felt he did find it, if only fleetingly.

But it was over. His one moment to change his life was gone. It was done. He would cherish the brief memories of their time together, but he had to move on now.

He had to once again harden his heart and become Tony Slade the paratrooper, the fighter, the warrior, the survivor. To get himself out of this mess, he had to be wily and clever.

He had to find a way to disappear for good. He knew the police would dig and look for a connection between him and Tyneside gangster Kenny Robbins. They would eventually find out that he had been working for him, which would ultimately lead to a trail of violence and death.

He also knew that even though Robbins was dead, his empire went on and his loyal 'subjects' would, no doubt, like to tie up any loose ends that may come back to incriminate them.

Tony Slade, being a possible would-be media darling given the chance, certainly made him one of those loose ends needing attention. He had a bad feeling it would not be long before not only the police would come looking for him, but others that would not be asking questions. No, they would be coming to kill him.

To have a hope in hell of surviving, he would have to move fast. But at this moment, that was impossible lying here in this hospital bed. He was not yet fit enough to move.

Tony felt vulnerable. He would have to hope and pray that he was safe in here for now. He needed to come up with a plan, but he was tired and his body ached. He felt himself slipping into sleep.

Tony Slade may be out of the trees but not the wood.

Over the next few days, Tony gradually felt more human. As promised, the tubes and monitors went and he could eat solid food.

Although he still felt weak and sore in his body, his mind was regaining its sharpness as his medication was gradually reduced. He could sit up in bed and in a chair. He even took trips to the bathroom unaided.

He was told he would soon be moving out of I.C.U and into a side room on a ward. That was encouraging news for him.

He had found his personal effects in a plastic bag in the bedside cabinet. Wallet, car keys, mobile phone and, of course, his watch. His clothes had been binned. He did still have his shoes. Tony needed some new clothes as soon as possible if he was to get out of here.

At present, he sported a pair of oversized blue pyjamas ,courtesy of the hospital's laundry room, to replace his gown. The pyjamas were not very flattering, but unlike the gown, they did cover his modesty.

The press was still trying hard to get an interview with him, but so far, that had not happened, but a local newspaper had somehow found out his name and some background information on him. One of the headlines read *Ex- Army hero caught in crossfire of maniac.*

The main tabloids had now picked up on this and many were camped outside the hospital looking for a scoop.

Tony cursed under his breath and threw the offending newspaper across the bed. Somebody in the hospital must have leaked information for a few quid. The newspaper and TV media were like vultures. Nothing was sacred.

His name was out there for the world to see, including Robbins' cronies. They now would know that Tony Slade was still alive and that was not good news.

He also knew the police would be calling any time soon. They had called every day, but so far, the nursing staff had kept them at bay.

He needed to be on the ball when they came asking their questions.

Before they did, he needed to make a phone call.

Chapter Two

Days passed without any incident until one morning Tony woke up with a start. He heard a commotion coming from outside his room. There was some sort of argument going on. He could hear Nurse O'Neill and Doctor Varma in a heated discussion with another couple of male voices.

He then saw a face that he did not recognise look through the small circular window in the door to his room.

He was now out of I.C.U and in a quiet side room recovering well. Tony had started physiotherapy and was beginning to get his strength back. It would not be long before he could get out of here.

The door suddenly opened and in walked two men. Tony instantly knew they were police.

Nurse O'Neill came in behind them looking flustered.

"Ten minutes is all the time you can have with the patient. He needs rest," she said.

The older of the two men replied. "Yes, okay. I understand, Nurse. Now kindly let us get on with our business."

Nurse O'Neill looked towards Tony. "These gentlemen are police officers. They wish to talk to you."

Tony nodded.

Nurse O'Neill left with a look of concern on her face.

"I will be back in ten minutes."

The police officers said nothing and waited for her to leave.

Both men then approached the bed. Tony appraised them.

The older man, he estimated, was in his late-fifties. He sported neatly cut grey hair and a beard. He wore a smart grey suit. Tony noticed a small crescent shaped scar above his left eye.

The other man was younger. Probably early thirties. He was 6ft plus, heavy built. He looked like a rugby player. His jet-black hair was gelled back and he sported designer stubble. Tony had him earmarked as a smarmy bastard.

The older man introduced them.

"Hello, Mr Slade, my name is Detective Chief Inspector John Wyatt and this is Sergeant Steve Richmond. We are from Bristol CID, Bridewell Station."

Tony remained silent.

"Glad to hear you are on the mend. We would like to ask you a few questions if we may?"

Wyatt had a broad West Country accent.

"Fire away, Chief Inspector. No pun intended," replied Tony.

Neither of the policemen smiled.

"We would like to hear your version of what happened in the *Alpha Coffee House* in relation to the shooting."

Tony pushed himself up on the pillows and grimaced as he did so.

"Well, it is all pretty hazy, I'm afraid. I can't really remember more than I was sat by the window reading

the newspaper and enjoying a cup of coffee when the
door burst open and a fucking lunatic came in and just
opened fire all over the place."

"Have you ever seen this man before?" It was
Sergeant Richmond who asked the question.

"No. Never saw him before. Like I said, I was just
minding my own business. It all happened so fast."

"What about any of the other customers? Did you
know them. Were you there alone?"

Tony composed his words carefully.

"I knew some of the staff, but as for customers, no.
They were just punters like me. I was alone and was not
really taking much notice of anybody else."

Wyatt spoke again.

"What were you doing in the coffee shop, Mr Slade?"

"I told you, reading the paper and having a
coffee."

"No. I mean, what were you doing here in Bristol? If
I am not mistaken, that is a Geordie accent you have.
You are a long way from home. We checked and you are
a resident of Newcastle.

Tony smiled.

"I didn't realise us Northerners had to check in with
the police if we made a trip down to the West Country.
Do I need my passport?"

Richmond cut in.

"Don't be a smart ass. Just answer the question."

Tony sighed.

"I was looking for work. A friend told me he might
have something for me in Bristol. He was going to meet
me in the coffee shop and let me know."

"As I said before, that's a long way to come for
work," said Wyatt.

"Well, sometimes beggars can't be choosers. I have no ties, so I go where the work is."

Wyatt contemplated Tony's answer.

"Did your friend show up?"

"Thankfully, no. I don't know what happened to him. A stroke of luck for him really."

Richmond cut in again.

"Staff at the coffee shop told us that you had been coming in there for a few weeks. How come?"

Tony regarded him. He was right about his assessment. Richmond was a smarmy bastard.

"Well, my diary wasn't exactly full, so I came down early for a little holiday and do a bit of sight-seeing."

"So, what do you think of Bristol, Mr Slade?" asked Wyatt.

"It was wonderful until all this happened."

Wyatt looked at his notebook.

"What is the name of your friend who promised you the job?"

Tony had anticipated this and had managed to phone Doug Jacobs earlier that morning.

Jacobs, an old army buddy, was the person who had organised passports for Annette and him to get out of the country and away from Robbins. That was the real reason that Tony had come to Bristol. Doug assured Tony if the police came sniffing around, he would back up his story.

Initially, Doug had been surprised to hear Tony's voice.

He had been away on business in the States and had called at Tony's flat with the passports before he caught his flight, but Tony had not been there.

Doug had been concerned about his absence, particularly as he had not been answering his phone. He left for the States worried about his old friend.

Then, he had read a snippet of English news in the *US Today* about the death of Tyneside gangster Kenny Robbins and others in a random shooting in *Alpha Coffee House* in Bristol. Doug had known that was where Tony had been spending his time waiting for his documents. The penny had dropped.

Up until then, Doug had not known if Tony was alive or dead. On returning to Bristol yesterday morning, he was awoken early by his mobile phone ringing. It had been Tony.

He told Doug the whole crazy story. Doug was glad that his old friend was alive and promised to help him in any way he could.

"His name is Doug Jacobs. He is an old army buddy."

Wyatt nodded and wrote down the name.

"Do you have a number for this Jacobs?"

"I can't remember it off the top of my head and my phone's battery has died," Tony lied.

Wyatt regarded him, searching his face for a trace of mistrust.

"I will try to get it charged later," Tony added.

"No worries. We will track him down," replied Wyatt.

He suddenly changed tact.

"We have done a bit of background on you, Mr Slade. You are an ex-para trooper. You have certainly seen some action in your time. Northern Ireland, Falklands."

Richmond piped up.

"Yeah, right little Rambo, according to your records. Bit of a hard man is our Mr Slade. A boxer and Jujutsu expert. Just the kind of person a man like Kenny Robbins liked working for him."

He left the question hanging in the air and regarded Tony with a smirk on his face.

Tony said nothing.

Wyatt cleared his voice.

"Do you know Kenny Robbins?"

Tony regarded Wyatt.

The Chief Inspector's icy blue eyes bored into his.

"I know of him. Everybody in Newcastle does. He owns a lot of businesses up there."

Tony's own gaze never left Wyatt's.

"Wouldn't you say that it is one hell of a coincidence that you happened to be sat next to him and his friends in a coffee shop in Bristol?" It was Richmond again.

"Who says I was sat by him?" asked Tony.

"You were found next to his body."

The smirk was back on the sergeant's face.

'What? And that is your evidence? Fucking hell, once this lunatic started shooting, people were diving for cover everywhere. You could have ended up next to just about anybody. That doesn't prove that I was sat next to him or that I knew him."

"Come on, Mr Slade. Do you really expect us to believe this wasn't a planned meeting?"

"I don't expect you to believe anything. That's how it happened. End of story."

Both Tony and Richmond locked stares.

The policeman was just about to speak again to push his point home when Nurse O'Neill came in through the door and interrupted him.

"That's it, gentlemen. Ten minutes is up. Time for Mr Slade to rest now."

She regarded the scene and could feel the tension in the air.

"Gentlemen, I really have to insist that you leave."

"Okay, Nurse. We are going. But we will be back very soon," said Wyatt.

Tony smiled.

"Don't worry, Chief Inspector. I won't be going anywhere."

Both men walked towards the door. Wyatt paused and turned back to Tony.

"One last thing. Did you carry a gun into the coffee shop, Mr Slade?"

Tony raised his eyebrows in mock surprise.

"A gun? Shit, no. That's against the law, isn't it? Why do you ask?"

"This Crane character that opened fire with the Uzi wasn't the only person carrying a firearm. Robbins and his two cronies were also carrying guns."

Tony felt a trickle of sweat run down his back.

"So?"

Wyatt continued.

"So, Robbins and his boys were shot with multiple bullets from the Uzi, which ties up with the evidence, but one of them also had massive trauma to his neck inflicted. Ballistics tells us the wound came from a Glock handgun."

Tony remained quiet.

"Strange because Robbins was carrying a Browning 9mm and so were his two sidekicks."

Tony swallowed hard. His throat felt tight as he asked the question.

"Was a Glock found at the scene?"

Richmond answered.

"No, there wasn't, which makes this even more puzzling."

Slade could sense the policeman wanted to push this matter, but once again, Nurse O'Neill intervened.

"That will do for the day, gentlemen. Please, I won't ask you again."

Chief Inspector Wyatt raised a hand.

"Okay, we are going. We will leave it there for now. Goodbye, Mr Slade. We will be back within the next day or so."

Both policemen left.

Tony reached for a glass of water on his bedside table. His mouth was dry.

Nurse O'Neill regarded him.

"Everything alright, Mr Slade?"

Tony sipped on his water. He felt a slight tremor in his hand. He gripped the glass tighter and breathed a sigh of relief.

"Only time will tell, Nurse O'Neill. Only time will tell."

She regarded him. "Rosie. My name is Rosie."

Tony smiled.

"Does that mean I am in your good books?"

"Only time will tell, Tony. Only tell will tell."

Since the police left, Tony had found it hard to rest. His mind was running around in circles going over the conversation they had. Where the hell had the gun disappeared to?

He had felt sure that they would have found it. He could recall shooting Robbin's minder, Rudi, and then lying back on the floor, drifting towards unconsciousness because of his own wounds and the Glock slipping from his fingers.

So, where had it gone?

There was nothing else to connect him to Robbins. Anything they found would be tenuous.

When he started working for Robbins, he had been given a throwaway, cheap burner mobile to contact Robbins or any of his firm.

On leaving Newcastle and hitting the road to Bristol, he had destroyed it. His own mobile would not carry anything incriminating if the police took it to check his phone records. So, without the gun, the police were just fishing. Yes, there was a lot of coincidences, but no evidence to suggest Tony was up to anything unlawful.

Tony thought about the car he had driven to Bristol and the one that he hoped would still be parked in the quiet side street five minutes from the coffee shop. The car that contained in the boot around a quarter of a million pounds that once belonged to Kenny Robbins. It had been liberated from the bastard. Not by Tony. By a friend. A friend Robbins that had murdered.

It was a long story, but Tony now had inherited the money and it was to have been Annette's and his getaway money to a new life. But not anymore. Robbins had found out what they had been up to and tracked them down in Bristol.

Tony was to have met Annette in the *Alpha Coffee House* and then leave the country, but Robbins had got to her first. When she entered the coffee house, Tony's heart had soared, but when he saw Robbins behind her and his two huge minders, Rudi and Errol, he knew the game was up.

As Robbins instructed him to leave with him, the door had sprung open and this crazy looking young man had run in and just randomly opened fire with an Uzi machine pistol.

Everybody in his path was getting hit with bullets, including Robbins and his thugs, but also Annette and him.

Clinging onto life, Rudi, the big blonde minder, had levelled his gun and blasted the man killing him instantly with a head shot and then he had turned his gun on Tony.

Tony, who was already badly hurt, managed to fire his own gun and kill Rudi with a shot to the neck and that was all he could remember.

It was one big fucking mess. Tony had reluctantly worked for Robbins for some time and had got the job of chauffeuring his women Annette around. That is how their affair had begun.

But other serious stuff had gone down and Tony could not afford for the police to dig too deeply. Otherwise, a whole hornet's nest could open. He thought of the money lying in the boot of the Audi. Nobody knew about it. Now it had to be his ticket to disappear for good.

He needed to get out of this hospital bed soon and get to the car in case a nosey neighbour might clock the fact that it had been parked in the same spot for some time and call the police to remove it. He could not afford for it to be towed away and impounded. Fuck, he could not lose that money. Not after all he had been through. With Annette gone, there was nothing else left for him.

Since leaving the parachute regiment, he had been in and out of meaningless jobs. Nobody gave a damn about his military experience. It counted for nothing. He felt that he had been chucked on the scrap heap. But he was not alone. A big percentage of ex-military, especially those from the '80s and '90s had been totally neglected by the government.

He had always felt that he had a huge glass box around him with a sign on it saying *Only break open in time of war.* Outside of this, he was faceless.

Every other week, he had read in the newspaper about many ex-vets being treated horrendously. He had read only recently that an ex-SAS veteran of the Iranian Embassy seize in London in 1980 was now penniless and left homeless because the local council would not help him. It was disgraceful.

Fuck it, the money in the car would give him a cushion to live a decent life. He was nearing sixty years of age and the thought of standing on another pub door or driving a parcel delivery van filled him with dread.

Also, there was no way the police were going to pin anything on him in relation to that scumbag Kenny Robbins. The incident in the coffee shop had been unavoidable and he had only done what he needed to do to save his life, but he knew with his patchy background that the police would not believe him. If they were looking for a scapegoat, he would do nicely. After all, any other suspect was dead. Tony Slade had become a wanted man.

Seeing out the rest of his days behind bars was not an option. Tony Slade was still alive and he was going to survive. That was one of the many things the army had taught him.

Chapter Three

The next day, Nurse O'Neill informed Tony that the police were back and needed to talk to him again. He agreed.

Before she left the room, she stopped and asked.

"Are you a bad man, Tony?"

Tony smiled.

"I am sure, Rosie, that if you asked around enough, you would find somebody to say I was."

Rosie nodded. "What do you say?"

Tony's face became serious.

"No, I am not a bad man, but I have made a few bad choices in my life."

It was Nurse O'Neill's turn to smile.

"Haven't we all, love. Haven't we all."

She left Tony alone.

DCI Wyatt and Sergeant Richmond soon appeared.

"Well, good morning, Tony. Can I call you, Tony?" asked Wyatt.

Tony nodded. "Feel free. What can I do for you today?"

Wyatt pulled a chair up to Tony's bedside. Richmond chose to stand.

"We have been looking into your past, Tony. I contacted a colleague of mine in the CID up in Newcastle. He did a bit of digging for me. Since your army days, there isn't much record of any employment. A few jobs here and there and then lengthy periods of no record of you."

"Jobs for ex-military seem to be far and few between. That's what brought me here to Bristol, as I told you."

Richmond piped up.

"There are various reports of you working the doors of pubs and clubs in the area. Is that correct?"

Tony eyed the younger man. He still did not like his attitude.

"That's right. Needs must and all that. It was the best option for me, but it was better than signing up for the police force."

Richmond smirked.

"Very witty. Paid your taxes, have you?"

"The wage was pin money, not enough to declare."

Richmond continued pressing.

"I heard the money isn't bad."

"Yeah, it's great, Richmond. I spent it on huge luxuries such as food and rent. I had to put the roller and the holiday to the Maldives on the backburner."

Wyatt intervened.

"Alright, alright. What we are suggesting is that we know Kenny Robbins liked to employ down on their luck ex-military just like yourself. What I am asking is have you ever worked for him? And think carefully before you answer this question, Tony."

Tony looked Wyatt directly in the eye.

"I have worked more clubs and pubs in the North East than I can remember. I take my wages directly from the manager at the end of the night. If any of those establishments had any connection to Kenny Robbins, I wasn't told nor was I aware of it."

Wyatt again studied Tony's face for any sign of guilt, but could detect nothing immediate. He had dealt with many criminals over his lengthy career and was used to finally breaking them down or seeing through their lies.

A few years ago, he had cracked the case on the Bristol serial rapist John Mulholland. This man had evaded police arrest for over two years, but Wyatt got him in the end and got the all-important confession.

Presently he did not have enough on Slade; only that he was in the same coffee shop as Kenny Robbins when the shootings began and that they were both from the North East. Nowhere near enough evidence to detain this man. But he sensed that Tony Slade knew more than he was telling.

Wyatt stood up.

"Okay, Tony. I am going to leave it there for now. I will be trying to get to the bottom of this case and for some reason, I feel that you may have a few clues about it that you are not revealing. So, no doubt I would like to be kept informed of your movements when you finally leave the hospital. And please do not go back up North until you have popped in to see us. Understood?"

Tony nodded.

"That's providing we aren't back with fresh evidence before that," chided Richmond.

Tony ignored the comment.

"Can I ask you something, Chief Inspector."

Wyatt nodded.

"Go ahead."

"The guy with the Uzi, do you know who he is and why he did it?"

"Yes. His name was Colin Crane and according to the manager of the shop who survived the shooting,

Crane was an unstable disgruntled ex-employee who came back to exact his violent revenge. No doubt looking for his fifteen minutes of fame. We investigated his background. He had been in and out of jobs most of his adult life. Minor convictions for drug use. Adopted. A bit of a loner. Nothing really to suggest that he was capable of what he did."

Tony nodded, but did not show that he had already heard of Crane before.

"Have you ever thought maybe we were all in the wrong place at the wrong time when this incident happened? I was an innocent party who just so happened to survive. If I had died, would you still be pursuing such a tentative lead between me and Robbins? Surely, your main priority now is to investigate how somebody like Crane could get away with committing this crime and see if you can stop similar ones happening in the future rather than wasting your time with me?"

Richmond came closer to Tony's bed.

"Nice speech, Slade, but you don't fool me. We are looking into Colin Crane and talking to the authorities. But you are a little side issue that we would also like to deal with."

Tony smiled.

"You really are uptight, Richmond. Aren't you getting any at home these days?"

Richmond's face darkened.

"Fuck you, Slade. I am going to nail your ass. That's a promise."

Wyatt intervened.

"That is enough, Sergeant. Time we were going."

He gestured for Richmond to head to the door.

"Maybe you are right, Tony, about what you just said, but I am a very good copper and I can assure you that I will be conducting this investigation thoroughly. I don't like loose ends. I do not like dead bodies in my city. If you are hiding anything, I will find it. Colleagues of mine like to refer to me as the *Old Bloodhound* and for good reason. Bye for now. I wish you all the best with your recovery."

Then, they were gone.

Tony lay back on his pillow and breathed a sigh of relief. For the moment, it seemed that he had got them off his back, but he knew a pair of coppers like that would be back. They were determined to keep on probing and that prick of a sergeant seemed to have it in for him.

Nurse O'Neill suddenly appeared with a tray in her hand.

"Dinner time, Mr Slade. Do you want to eat it in bed or sit out on your chair?"

"I will sit out on the chair please, Nurse. I am feeling a bit better again today."

Nurse O'Neill smiled.

"Well, that is good news because Doctor Arjun informs me that your physiotherapy is going well."

That was music to Tony's ears.

"Really. That's great news. I will soon be out of your hair."

"Aye, you probably will. Something tells me you have more lives than a cat. Right, let's get you in that chair before this dinner goes cold."

As Tony forked his food into his mouth, he thought over what Wyatt had mentioned, especially the part about the manager of the coffee shop surviving the attack.

Kim was alive. That was one piece of good news in this tragedy.

This lunatic Crane had literally been gunning for her since his sacking from the *Alpha Coffee House*. How ironic that the person that he had really come looking for had survived.

Although his heart was heavy for the loss of Annette, in the brief time he had known her, Kim had become a good friend and he was so glad that she was okay. When he got out of here, he would try and track her down.

He pushed his plate away and sipped on his water. The menu had offered a beef lasagne or steak and kidney pie. He had opted for the lasagne. Now he wished he had not. It was just a flavourless lump on the plate. The dessert masquerading as banana and custard did not look a whole lot better. God, how he craved for fish and chips and a few shots of whisky.

He thought back home to Newcastle and a little fish and chip place called *Krispies* that he used to call into at least once a week when he worked on the doors of clubland. *Krispies* was renowned for the best cod in the city. His mouth watered as he thought about it.

Well, he would have to find another great fish and chip place, as going back up North was not an option. But where was he planning to head? Getting out of the country would be a mission, as the police would, no doubt, put the word out to the airports or ports if he suddenly did a runner. How the hell had he suddenly become public enemy number one?

Wyatt and Richmond certainly had him down as a marked man and they were not finished with him by a long chalk. But this was not the main concern. He knew that somebody in the Robbins' criminal empire would come looking for him sooner rather than later and want some answers from him. Answers that he did not fancy hanging around to explain.

When he left Newcastle, Robbins was in the final stages of selling off his businesses to a Dutchman named Bergkemp. Did he still go through with it? Maybe the Dutchman pulled out after the shooting? Who knew? But the one thing he was sure of was that he did not want to wait around to find out.

He reached into his bedside cabinet and retrieved his mobile phone and dialled Doug Jacobs' number. Frustratingly, it went to answerphone. After the bleep, he left a message asking Doug to come in and visit him tomorrow. He needed to talk urgently.

As he hung up, Nurse O'Neill came into the room. She surveyed his plate.

"Is that all you have managed to eat, Tony Slade?"

Tony held his right hand up in mock submission.

"Sorry, Nurse. I am just too full to enjoy any more of these culinary delights."

She shook her head and picked up the tray.

"I want an improvement tomorrow."

Tony laughed.

"What? In my eating or the food? No chance of a kebab is there?

Nurse O'Neill left without another word.

Come visiting time that evening, Tony was surprised to be informed that a Miss Walters was here to visit him.

Tony did not know a Miss Walters. He asked if she was from the press, but was told no. So, out of curiosity, he agreed for her to come in.

As soon as the blonde-haired woman walked in, he knew who it was.

Chapter Four

Tony could not believe his eyes, but the blonde-haired lady was Kim Walters, the manager of the *Alpha Coffee House* where the shootings had taken place. She was alive and, to all intents and purposes, she looked well.

"Kim. Christ, I can't believe it. Come here," said Tony.

Kim's face broke into a smile and she moved across the room to embrace him. Tony winced with the pain in his shoulder.

"Oh shit, sorry. I forgot. Are you okay?"

"Hell yeah. Just a bit sore still. But I am doing fine."

"Well, well, well. Tony Slade, the mystery man, still living and breathing. Last time I saw you, it looked for all the world like you were bound for the afterlife."

They both laughed and regarded each other. Then, Tony's face became serious.

"Kim, I am so glad you are okay. What a fucking terrible thing to happen. I mean, Crane just walking in like that and playing Rambo. It's hard to believe and I have seen some shit in my time. I know you said he was pissed at you, but fuck, this was something else. Thank Christ you are okay. I didn't know if you survived or not."

Tears came to Kim's eyes. She was a strong woman, but something like this would leave its mark forever.

"It was all so surreal. I was just turning around from preparing a coffee, as the shop door burst open. I immediately recognised Crane and then I saw the gun. For a brief second, our eyes met and I knew he had come for me. Maybe sublimely, I knew that he would be back. But I never in my wildest dreams thought it would be like this.

Everything then just seemed to go into slow motion. I just reacted and ducked down behind the counter as he opened fire. Bullets flew all around me, but miraculously, I wasn't hit. From behind the counter, I could then make out the exchange of different gunfire and then it all stopped. I could then hear screaming from some of the customers and moaning from the wounded or dying.

When I thought it was safe, I rose up from my hiding place and surveyed the shop, it was like a warzone. Bodies were strewn everywhere. There was a heavy acrid smell in the air of gun smoke and I could see blood everywhere. So much blood. It was terrible. I couldn't stop shaking. I just stood there until somebody started shouting for the police. It shook me back into life and I rang the emergency services.

I then walked over to the table you had been sat at. All those people that had come in and sat down with you were dead, including that beautiful lady."

Tony closed his eyes for a moment. The pain of losing Annette was still raw, no matter how much he tried to put it from his thoughts. Kim could sense this.

"I am sorry, Tony. I suspect she was special to you?"

Tony just nodded in response. Kim continued.

"I saw you lying there so still. You seemed to be bleeding from everywhere and I couldn't tell if you were breathing or not. It was hard to take in and process all the carnage. What I do know is whoever those people were with you, in a roundabout way, they saved my life because one of them must have shot Crane before he got to me. Whatever their motives were, I don't know and frankly, I don't care, but I do know that is why I am here now."

Tony reached out and took her hand. It felt cold. It was trembling.

"Those men were bad men, Kim. Just the same as Crane. I guess karma brought them there that day at the same time."

"What about you, Tony? Where do you fit in? Are you also a bad man?"

Tony looked at the concern etched across her pretty face.

"You're the second person in the last few days to ask me that. What do you think?"

"I don't know, Tony. I always sensed from the first day you came into the *Alpha* that you were in some sort of trouble and I guess now that it involved the lady."

Tony remained silent.

"I do know that when I found you on the floor, you also had a gun in your hand."

Tony's heart skipped a beat, but he remained calm.

"The gun, Kim. Where is it? The police have been here asking awkward questions."

"Why were you carrying a gun, Tony?" she asked.

Tony swallowed hard.

"Look, Kim, there is a hell of a lot you don't know about me and it is probably better that you don't. When I am fit enough, I will be gone, and you won't ever see me again. My life has been a chequered one. I am no saint. I personally see myself as essentially a good guy who has had some bad breaks in his life. I needed the gun for insurance. I got involved in a very dangerous situation. I wasn't planning on using it, but if I didn't, I would be dead. But I can't tell you any more about it, as I am not sure that the situation is over yet."

He detected fear in Kim's eyes.

"You have nothing more to fear, Kim. Crane is dead. But for me. Well... the less you know, the better."

Kim was quiet for a moment, as if she was thinking over his words and deciding what to say. She then spoke.

"I took the gun, Tony. I don't know why. I did it on impulse. I heard the police sirens getting closer and I just picked it up. I guess I knew that you weren't a bad guy."

"Thank you," replied Tony.

Kim was silent again and Tony realised how difficult this must be for her. Finally, he broke the silence.

"What did you do with it?"

Kim seemed to come back to the present.

"I hid it in the stock room until the police and paramedics had left. I then took it and later that night very discreetly dropped it into Bristol Docks. It is gone forever."

Tony breathed a sigh of relief.

"Jesus Christ, Kim. You just might have saved my ass. I don't know what to say?"

Kim smiled sadly.

"You don't need to say anything. It is done. I just wanted to come and visit you and to tell you what happened. I now want to forget about the whole thing and try to move on. But it is going to take time. That is why I am leaving Bristol tonight and heading back home to Nottingham."

"Nottingham? I didn't realise," said Tony.

"There is a lot you don't know about me as well," replied Kim.

Tony smiled and held up his hands in mock surrender.

"Go on, please."

Kim continued.

"I left Nottingham two years ago. I am a qualified nurse by trade, but I got fed up and ground down by the NHS cuts and the long shifts. So, I just quit and walked away from all the stress. Back when I qualified, I really wanted to make a difference, but, in the end, I realised I couldn't.

I also got involved with a fellow colleague at the hospital I was working at, but he turned out to be trouble. He got heavily hooked on using prescription drugs after a knee injury obtained through rugby.

He began to make life difficult for me. I hated his mood swings and then he began to get violent, so I left and came down to Bristol on an invitation of a friend. I ended up working in the *Alpha* and the next thing I knew, I was manager. It was okay. Easy work really, no stress."

She paused and smiled wryly.

"Well, that was until recently. Anyhow, I have decided to go home and give the nursing another go. Helping those poor people in the *Alpha* made me think long and hard about myself."

Tony nodded.

"If you think it is the right thing to do, then good for you. But remember, Kim. It doesn't matter how far you run, the memories are inside your head. They will go with you."

Tears formed in Kim's eyes again.

"I know, Tony. I have started seeing a counsellor. It has helped. I will have to learn to get over it. I am not running away, but I can't stay close to where all this shit started. It is too painful."

"I understand, pet. I have been there and done it enough myself."

"Anyway, I feel that my life was spared as a sign for me to get on and do something better and more fulfilling in the world."

For a moment, they were once again silent, both reflecting on the fact that they had been spared.

Finally, Kim spoke.

"So, what about you, Tony? Where do you go from here?"

Tony reached out for his glass of water and took a sip.

"Now, that's a good question. But one better off unanswered."

Kim leaned in and gently kissed his lips.

"Still the man of mystery, eh? Well, take care, mystery man. I won't forget you in a hurry. I wish you all the best wherever you go."

Tony smiled.

"You too, Kim. Have a great life and make that difference. Also, thank you again. I really mean it, pet."

She smiled and nodded in acknowledgement.

Kim walked towards the door. She turned and regarded him one last time and then she was gone.

Tony leaned back in bed and replayed the conversation he had just had with Kim. She was going to find things tough. Most people will go through life mercifully never being exposed to the horrors of violent death and just as well. It leaves its scars forever. He hoped that she would cope. It would not be easy.

Tony had to harden his heart on more occasions than he cared to remember. He had dealt with death in one shape or form in the army for many a year. You never forget; you just try to learn to live with it the best you can. One day at a time. Even after all these years he would wake up from some nightmare from his past.

This made him think again of Annette and the emptiness he felt inside right now. Life was strange. A few weeks ago, he was on top of the world looking forward to a life with a woman he truly loved and now he had nothing. He felt numb and that was not just down to the medication and painkillers that he was taking.

It was only his primal survival instincts that kept him going and wanting to get out of this hospital. Whilst he was here, he felt like a sitting duck. He hated to feel this helpless and being reliant on other people.

But he was a fighter. Always had been since a kid. He had to climb back from the brink. If his life had been spared for a reason, then he sure as hell was not going to give it up lying in a hospital bed.

Tony tried to rationalise his present position. The gun was not an issue any longer thanks to Kim, so he felt that the police would not be a problem anymore. Yes, they may have an unsubstantiated link between Robbins and him, but that was all it was. No matter what their suspicions may be, they had no hard evidence.

The press was still clamouring to get to him to hear his story. The hospital had been great in fending them off. They had his name. He knew that much had been leaked out. It would not be long before a story would be formalised for the tabloids with or without his permission.

Chapter Five

Next afternoon, Tony returned to his room helped by his physiotherapist Hettie Brown. She was a tough no-nonsense African Caribbean. She was a large lady and Tony could attest to her strength, as she had manipulated his body in some weird and wonderful positions that he never knew he could get into.

His arm was out of the sling and the collarbone was on the mend. The bullet wounds also seemed to be healing well. He now had to get full mobility back in his upper body and work on his cardiovascular capacity to see how the injured lung was holding out.

Hettie seemed pleased with his progress.

"Same time tomorrow then, Tony. You did well today." She nodded and left the room.

As Tony made his way over to his chair, he heard another person coming into the room and turned as quickly as he could to be greeted by the larger than life figure of Doug Jacobs carrying a big bunch of flowers and a bag of grapes.

"Shape up, soldier. Stand up straight."

Tony grinned.

"If I could, I fucking would. I feel like a ninety-year-old."

Doug laughed.

"Hell, now me, I feel like a twenty-one-year-old, but the Missus won't hear of it."

Both men broke into laughter and embraced.

"Steady, big man. I am still sore here, you know," said Tony.

"Shit, Tony. You are alive, aren't you? Stop bitching. Where shall I put these flowers?"

Tony gestured to an empty vase on the table.

"I think I will leave that to the nurse. Flower arranging was never my strong point."

Tony sat up on the bed.

"Are those grapes for me too or are you just feeling peckish?"

Doug placed them down on the table with the flowers and sat down into the bedside chair.

It had been some while since Tony had met his old friend face to face. In recent times, all their contact had been done by phone.

He now regarded him. He certainly was looking older. His hair was now grey and thinning and he was probably carrying fifteen pounds extra weight, but he looked healthy enough. The disability of having a prosthetic leg did not seem to faze him in anyway. He moved okay for a big man.

Doug took a handful of grapes and looked at Tony.

"Well, fuck me, Tony. I thought you had finished with being in the wars. Obviously not, judging from this latest escapade.

I was in the States and just happened to see a bit about it in the tabloids. I saw your name. At first, I couldn't believe it, but then it made sense, since you didn't pick up your passports and papers from my flat.

It seemed as if you had just vanished from the face of the earth.

You weren't kidding when you told me you were into something heavy. You care to enlighten me a bit more, buddy?"

Tony nodded.

Over the next half an hour, he related the whole story of his involvement with Tyneside gangster Kenny Robbins and how, by chauffeuring his woman Annette around, they had both fell in love.

He went on to tell Doug about the plan they hatched to run away together and escape to another country; hence, Doug's help with the fake passports and credit cards.

Then, he told him about Robbins finding them in the coffee shop and was about to administer his own brand of revenge when this crazed ex-employee of the shop, Colin Crane, just burst in and started a random killing spree.

A firefight had ensued resulting in the death of Robbins and his two minders along with Annette tragically. Tony was also shot and left for dead and had finally woken up here in hospital.

Doug listened in silence hardly being able to take on board this incredible tale. When Tony had finished, his old friend puffed out his cheeks as he expelled a lungful of air.

"Jesus Christ, Tony. That is some story. Fuck, you are lucky to be alive."

Tony smiled ruefully.

"So, everybody keeps telling me. It sure doesn't feel like it."

Doug reached over and touched his friend's arm.

"I am truly sorry for your loss."

Both men were silent for a moment. Then, Doug spoke.

"So, what can I do for you, Tony? What do you need?"

Tony leaned in closer to Doug.

"I need to get out of here and as far away as possible as soon as possible. I have had the police sniffing around me and the press are clamouring for an exclusive. I can't let anybody else know where I am. I have a feeling that Robbin's firm will know that I am alive and come looking for me."

"Why do you think that? Maybe they think you were all down in Bristol on business and just all got caught up in the random shooting. Just a tragic accident."

Tony shook his head.

"I don't think so. I imagine Robbins would have told somebody else his plans and whereabouts in case something did go wrong. He has a few loyal men like Andy Roth, for example. He is one of Robbin's trusted enforcers. A right psychopath. I believe he will want to avenge his boss's death."

"But you mentioned about some Dutch bloke. Bergkemp, wasn't it?"

Tony nodded.

Doug continued.

"You say he was wrapping up a deal to buy Robbins out. If that's the case, I suspect he wouldn't want to get his hands dirty with this lot."

"I agree with you, Doug. I don't think for one-minute that Bergkemp would want to be looking for me. He is probably totally unaware of the situation. Either the deal was signed and sealed, and he now owns Robbins' empire or if it hadn't been done, I should imagine when he found out about Robbins' death, he was on the first plane back to Amsterdam feeling that he had a close shave."

"So, what are you worried about then, my friend?"

"It's Roth. I met him once at Robbins' offices. I could tell straight off that he was a dangerous bastard. I can just sniff a person like that out. He operates on his own agenda. Robbins and him went way back. Just for his own sick pleasure, he would hunt me down in his spare time and waste me and then go home and sleep like a baby."

Doug took this information in.

"Well, you still have the fake passport, credit cards etc. Get yourself on a flight out of here. I can arrange it. Just tell me where you want to go."

"That's just it, Doug. With Annette gone, I don't know where I want to go. I need time to think and make my next move, plus I don't know if I am up to a plane ride just yet."

"So, what then? Even if I get you out of here, you can't stay in Bristol. If what you say is right, this Roth character will have read the newspapers and know you are here in this hospital. It won't be long until he comes calling."

Tony grabbed Doug's arm.

"I fucking know that, Doug. Every time the door opens in here, I think the mad bastard is going to walk in.

I just need to disappear somewhere for a while until I heal. If I then must go back to Newcastle and hunt Roth down myself and end this, I will. I have nothing to lose, but I want to do it on a level playing field and not just be laying here in bed like a fucking dummy when he does turn up."

Doug noted the anger, but also the fear, in his friend's voice.

"Okay. Okay. I get it. Look, there is somewhere I may know. It is a bit of a godforsaken place, but it is not out of the country. There is somebody who lives there that may help an ex-army lad, but I need to make a few phone calls."

Tony leant back in his chair.

"Alright, Doug. Do it as soon as you can and get me out of here. I don't care how desolate this place is. If I can keep a low profile for a while, then that will do me for now. I just feel like a sitting duck here."

Doug rose up from the bed and patted Tony on the shoulder.

"Leave it with me. I will get on it now and get back to you as soon as possible. Okay? Look, I may need to grease a few palms."

Tony immediately thought of the money in the boot of his car.

"It's okay. I have access to money when I get out of here. Is all my stuff still at your flat?"

"Yes, mate. Just as you left it all."

"Can you bring me some clothes in?"

"No problem, Tony. I will come back visiting time this evening with some."

Tony seemed satisfied.

"Okay. Thanks, Doug."

Doug nodded in acknowledgement and walked towards the door. Tony called out to him.

"Just out of interest where is this place I am supposedly going to?"

Doug's face broke into a grin again.

"It is a little island in the British Channel named Graig O Mor."

Tony looked puzzled.

"Never heard of it."

"That's a good thing then because most people wouldn't have a fucking clue where it is. That could be a blessing for you."

With that, he turned and left the room with a promise that he would contact Tony soon.

Tony suddenly felt tired and he lay back on his bed and stared at the ceiling. Within minutes, he was asleep.

Chapter Six

Andrew Winston Roth, aka 'Psycho' Andy, sat in the lounge of the *Black Horse* public house near Eldon Square, Newcastle upon Tyne.

He nursed a pint of Newcastle brown ale as he scanned *The Sun* newspaper.

In recent weeks, the papers had brought another story on the shootings at the coffee shop down in Bristol every day.

Why had it happened? How could it have happened here in the UK? How did this man Crane avoid detection? Where did the firearm come from? Who was this shady character Robbins? Why was he in the coffee shop? Who was this Tony Slade? What was his connection to it all?

The questions just kept coming, but there were not too many forthcoming answers at the present. The police seemed to be dragging their heels and there was not much apparent evidence.

The story gradually unfolded about the shooter, Crane, the death of North East gangster, Kenny Robbins, and the sole survivor of the shooting, Tony Slade.

Andy Roth knew all about the circumstances of this accident, as he had driven his boss, Kenny Robbins, down to Bristol that day along with Robbins' two personal minders, Rudi and Errol.

They had all made the trip to find that no good piece of shit Slade and Robbins' missus, Annette. They both planned to run off together, but the boss had found out.

Roth had waited in the car outside the *Alpha Coffee House*, whilst the others had gone inside to surprise Slade. Then, all hell broke loose. Guns started blazing like the fucking Alamo.

When Kenny Robbins did not appear, Roth knew something had gone terribly wrong. He was just about to get out of the car to check when he heard approaching police sirens. He knew he could not afford for the law to find him there, so he drove off back up North.

Over the next few days, the media was all over the story and he had learnt that Kenny Robbins was well and truly dead. He was gutted. They had gone back a long way.

Roth had served time in prison with Robbins. Both had been convicted for GBH when they were younger men. They had hit it off instantly and became friends. They watched each other's back in the harsh prison environment.

Kenny had saved Roth's life when a fellow inmate with a grudge against him went looking to stab him whilst he showered. Kenny had been on to this and had caught up with the man just as he was going to plunge his home-made shank into Roth's back. Robbins had grabbed the man in a chokehold and lifted him off the floor with his immense strength and strangled him unconscious.

The incident was over and done, but then Robbins witnessed for the first time that Andy Roth might not be the 'full shilling' when he picked up the disregarded knife and stabbed the unconscious man to death.

Roth had disposed of the blade down the shower drain and washed himself clean of the victim's blood and walked back to his cell as if nothing had happened.

The crime was never solved. The dead man was an Edmond Sturridge. He was a nasty piece of work. He had been a violent drug dealer, so nobody was going to mourn his death and the authorities were not going to dig too hard into his death.

When Roth and Robbins were released, they kept in touch and as Kenny's criminal empire began to build, he employed Roth as an enforcer. In time, Roth's reputation as being a savage and unhinged individual with a penchant for torture proceeded him.

If Roth was on your case, you better beware, as he did not take any prisoners. He was ferociously loyal to Robbins because of him saving his life in their younger days.

If you crossed Robbins and Roth was on your trail, you had better understand that this man was relentless. He would track you down to the ends of the earth like a fucking Terminator.

Roth had had a hand in helping sniff out Tony Slade's little caper. That was why Robbins had him drive that day to the *Alpha*.

Roth took a sip of his beer and closed the paper.

At present, the Kenny Robbins' empire was in limbo. The Dutchman Bergkemp who was in line to buy the business had not put pen to paper and had hurriedly gone back to Holland.

Robbins' two most senior members of the firm, Danny Ewan and Joe Walsh, along with lawyer Charles Gibson, were trying to sort things out.

Roth had gone to them expressing his wishes to go back down to Bristol and dispose of Slade. He knew which hospital he was in courtesy of the media. He wanted to put the bastard out of his misery.

Ewan and Walsh had told him to hang fire, as the police were all over everything at present and they could not afford any more heat by getting rid of their number one witness.

They made it clear to Roth that when the dust settled, rest assured, they would deal with Slade and until then ,they did not want him going off half-cocked on a one-man vendetta.

Roth was told to be patient and the time would come. The one thing Roth was not good at was being patient. He wanted Tony Slade's ass right now.

Ewan and Walsh both knew how unpredictable Roth could be. With Robbins now dead, he was a loose cannon.

Times had changed from the days of the 'old school gangsters'. There was a new breed of villain on the streets, but Roth was stuck back in the past. It was an eye for an eye with him and he was not subtle about how he went about his brand of retribution.

You only used men like Andy Roth when the situation you were in was extreme. Apart from that, you left well alone.

But both men knew because of his close ties with Robbins, it was going to be hard to keep the leash on him. They decided that they would have to keep a close eye on Roth until the business was more stable and the police interest had died off.

Kenny Robbins had been a smart operator. Along with his lawyer, the wily Charles Gibson, they felt that the police would find nothing, and the Robbins' empire would rise from the ashes once again, but it would take a bit of time and they could not afford any more unwanted attention coming their way.

For the time being, it seemed that Roth had heeded their words, but they knew deep down that he would not stay patient for ever.

Andy Roth left the *Black Horse* and walked down the road towards the Chinese takeaway. He had not eaten all day and his stomach rumbled.

He noticed the black 4x4 Mercedes Benz parked across the road and the two men sat inside watching him.

Babysitters, eh. So, he was being watched.

The occupants of the vehicle had been hired by Ewan and Walsh to keep an eye on Roth and his movements.

The men's names were Eddie and Billy McQueen. They had been flown in from Spain. Their brief was surveillance on Roth and if he got out of hand, then to eliminate him. The McQueen brothers were good at that sort of thing.

They had both been hardcore gangster enforcers in their home city of Glasgow before moving out to Spain some years ago to avoid impending charges of suspected murder.

The dead body of a well-known Glasgow nightclub owner and entrepreneur, Robert Lennox, had been found in a city hotel room. He had been shot once through the head. The murder held all the marks of a gangland execution.

Because of their reputation and gangster connections, the McQueen brothers were one of the first suspects the police interviewed. Initially, they did not have any substantial evidence against them, other than an eyewitness at the hotel who said that he had seen two men matching their description outside the room of Lennox just after midnight when he was on the way to his own room after leaving the bar.

However, the word was that the police were building a stronger case based on some more new evidence case against the McQueen brothers. Strong enough for them both to decide to get out of the UK.

A private plane charter had allowed them to slip back over to home soil for the first time in a while to do a little job. Well, everybody had to make a living, so they reasoned.

Roth sunk another pint of ale in the *Crown* before deciding to find some food. Whilst he had been drinking, he had come to a decision.

Fuck Ewan and Walsh and fuck the two wankers in the 4x4. He was going to Bristol first thing in the morning to finish Slade off. He would then take an extended vacation abroad. He owed it to his boss and nothing and no-one was going to get in his way.

Chapter Seven

Tony had slept well for once and woke feeling positive. After talking with Doug the previous day, he had felt his spirits rise a little. He knew Doug was true to his word and he would get him out of the hospital.

He got out of bed at first gingerly, as he had become used to some form of pain or discomfort in the past weeks, but he was surprised to feel more mobile today. He decided to take the short walk to the toilets.

Nurse O'Neill was at her desk on the phone as he passed by. She looked up and saw him.

"Hold on one moment, please," she said into the phone.

"Good morning, Tony. You okay there walking on your own?"

Tony flashed her one of his best smiles.

"Never better, Rosie. Don't worry, I am only going to the toilet. I thought I would leave the charity walk from Land's End to John O'Groats another day or two."

Nurse O'Neill rolled her eyes and went back to her phone call.

Tony then saw Doctor Arjun Varma approaching him along the corridor. He was with another doctor and both were discussing information that Varma had in a file he was carrying.

When he saw Tony, he stopped.

"Ah hello, Tony. It is good to see you up and about. You have made remarkable progress. The wounds are healing nicely, and the collarbone is fusing properly. Physiotherapy is also going well, so I have been informed. A week or so and you will be out of here."

"Well, that's great news, Doctor. Thank you."

Doctor Varma nodded and he and his fellow doctor walked on.

As Tony reached the door of the toilets, he glanced back up the corridor at the disappearing doctor and thought *I plan to be out of here sooner than that, my friend*.

When Tony came back out of the toilets, he almost collided with a young woman who was running down the corridor. She had a look of concern on her face and had been so preoccupied that she had not seen Tony until the last minute.

"Shit. I am so sorry. I didn't see you there. Please forgive me. I seem to be a little lost."

Tony regarded the women. He estimated her to be in her mid-thirties. She had chestnut brown hair cut in a pageboy style. She had elfin like features and large brown eyes. She wore blue jeans and a loose-fitting floral blouse. Her face was slightly flushed, a result, he presumed, of her running.

Tony smiled.

"It's okay. No harm done. Where are you looking for? I pretty much know this place inside out. I have been in here so long."

The woman seemed to relax a little.

"I am looking for Ward 12. My grandfather was taken ill earlier today, and I was told he was to be found there."

"Well, you are in luck. My room is right by Ward 12. If you can bear to shuffle along with me for a few moments, I am heading back there now."

"Well, thank you. That is very kind of you."

The woman extended her hand.

"My name is Susie Rawlings."

Tony shook her offered hand.

"Tony Slade. Pleased to meet you. Shall we?"

He pointed up the corridor.

They both began to walk together.

"So, what happened to your grandfather?" asked Tony

Susie seemed to hesitate for a moment.

"He had a fall. He is in his mid-eighties and very frail. I think he may have broken his hip."

"I am sorry to hear that, but he is in the best place now and I am sure he will be well looked after," answered Tony.

As an afterthought, he added.

"Are you sure it was Ward 12 he is in?"

Susie nodded.

"Yes, why do you ask?"

It was now Tony's turn to hesitate. Susie saw this.

Tony continued.

"It's just that Ward 12 is for trauma wound victims, not fractures or breaks."

"Oh right. I am sure I was told Ward 12. Maybe I will just check seeing I have come this far. I don't fancy a trek all the way back to reception if it isn't necessary."

Tony smiled.

"No problem. I just thought I would say in case you get to the Ward, and your Grandfather isn't there."

They carried on walking.

Susie then asked.

"You said trauma wounds. You mean stabbings, shootings, that kind of stuff?"

Tony nodded.

"Yes, that kind of thing."

"I hope you don't mind me asking what happened to you?"

Tony thought about what his answer should be and decided it would not do any harm to tell Susie.

"I was shot."

Susie's eyes widened

"Shot. Jesus. That's terrible."

"Yeah, it wasn't the best day of my life."

Susie suddenly stopped walking.

"Are you the guy shot in that massacre at the *Alpha Coffee House*?"

"Unfortunately, yes. But I would appreciate it if you didn't go shouting it from the rooftops."

"Shit. No. Of course not. I used to go in the *Alpha* weekly myself. It so happened I was out of town when the shooting occurred. Otherwise, I may well have been in there. It doesn't bear thinking about. According to the newspapers, you were the only survivor from the people shot?"

"Yes, that's right apparently," answered Tony.

"Wow. That's spooky."

"Why do you say that?"

Susie looked at him with concern in her eyes.

"Well, don't you ever wonder why you didn't die. I am into fate and all that sort of stuff. Have you thought about that before?"

Tony was not sure where this conversation was heading.

"No, not really," he lied.

They carried on walking in an awkward silence.

They now neared Ward 12.

"Well, here we are. That board on the wall with the names written on it will let you know where your grandfather is. What is his name?" asked Tony.

There was no answer.

Tony looked at Susie.

She was holding something up in her hand.

He felt a sinking feeling in his stomach as he saw it was a press pass. That now explained her questions.

"Sorry, Mr Slade, for the fairy story, but I have been trying to get in to see you for days. Please can I have just ten minutes of your time?"

Tony was angry that he had been taken in so easily.

"Go away, Miss Rawlings. That is if it is your real name."

"Yes, of course it is. I work for the local newspaper *The West Country Express*."

Tony backed away towards his room.

"I don't care who you work for. I am not talking to the press."

Susie came towards him.

"Just ten minutes. Tell me your side of the story. Up to now, all the tabloids have been speculating. They know your background. Military service etc., but they don't know what happened in the coffee shop."

"Good. They don't need to fucking know. Now go before I call for security."

Susie looked at him pleadingly.

"Did you know the shooter? What about crime boss, Kenny Robbins? Did you work for him?"

"Goodbye, Miss Rawlings."

"Why don't you want to let the public know your story? What harm can it do? Unless you are hiding something. Is that it? Maybe I should just go away and write that."

Tony glanced up and down the corridor and with speed belying his injury, he grabbed Susie by the blouse with his good arm and dragged her into his room shutting the door. He then released her. He saw fear in her eyes but also defiance. Susie reached in her handbag.

"Don't you fucking touch me. I have CS gas in here."

Tony moved away from the door.

"You don't say. I bet you also have a grenade launcher as well."

"Come any closer, Mister, and you will find out."

Tony held up his hands.

"Relax. I am not going to hurt you, but I can't have you shouting the odds in the corridor. There are too many prying ears."

Susie slowly eased her hand back out of the bag.

"So, you will talk to me then?"

"Look don't get excited. There is nothing to tell. I was in the shop having a coffee, this lunatic walked in and shot the place up, including me. I survived; others didn't. End of story. That is it."

Susie nodded.

"Okay, Tony. That is fine. But there are rumours that you were connected to Kenny Robbins who died in the shooting and you were there with him. Is that true?"

Tony glared at her.

"That is all bollocks. I don't know any Robbins. Now get the hell out. We are done here."

Susie held her ground.

"What are you frightened of, Tony? Who is it that you don't want to know that you are in here? Are you still in danger?"

Tony said nothing.

"Damn it, Tony. I can help you if you tell me."

Just then, the door opened and Nurse O'Neill stood there with the medication trolley.

She surveyed the scene. She had already heard raised voices before she entered. She was astute enough to sense something was not right.

"I don't know who you are, Miss, but it is not visiting hours and Mr Slade needs his rest and his medication. I am going to have to ask you to leave."

Susie glanced from Tony to Nurse O'Neill and back again.

"That's okay. I was just going. Maybe I can come back again, Tony?"

Tony smiled grimly.

"I wouldn't bother. You have got all that you are going to get."

Susie walked towards the door. Before she left, she dropped a business card onto the medication trolley.

"Just in case you change your mind."

Nurse O'Neill stood back and let her out. She then came into the room.

"Well, well. I leave you alone for ten minutes and all hell breaks loose. The press, I take it?"

Tony nodded as he sat down into his chair.

"Clever cow, got in here under false pretences. That doesn't boost my confidence in the hospital security."

Nurse O'Neill nodded.

"I understand that, Tony. Staff cuts and general lack of finances have made security a little thin on the ground. Unfortunately, that is out of my control, but I will have a word and hopefully, make sure it doesn't happen again."

Tony smiled.

"It's okay. It's not your fault, Rosie."

She smiled.

"Time for your medication."

Out in the car park, Susie Rawlings jumped into the passenger side of a blue Ford Focus. A red-faced overweight man in his thirties sat in the driver's seat. He glanced across at Susie as he started the engine.

"Well, did you manage to get anything on Slade?"

Susie opened her handbag and produced a small hand-held tape recorder.

"Enough to get started. But I know he is hiding something, and I will get to the bottom of it."

The man nodded and drove towards the exit.

As the Ford Fiesta went out of the car park, a black Mercedes C class drove in. Behind the wheel was Andy Roth. He had set out at the crack of dawn to reach Bristol. The pair of clowns in the 4x4 were both sleeping like babies when he left. Fucking amateurs.

No doubt they now realised they had lost him, which explained the half a dozen miscalls on his mobile from Joe Walsh and Danny Ewan. It would not take them long to figure out that he had headed to Bristol. Never mind, he would be done and gone from here before they arrived.

The car's satellite navigation system had brought him off the M4 onto the M32 and joined the B4469, which brought him to Southmead Hospital.

He had made decent time. The thought of hunting down Slade had made the journey fly by.

Roth parked up. He reached across into his glove compartment and his hand found what he was looking for. Time to pay the patient a visit.

Chapter Eight

Andy Roth pulled the black baseball cap tight down on his head as he strolled into the hospital on the dot of 2.00pm. Visiting time.

He had parked discreetly in the car park as near to the exit as possible. His car had a set of false number plates, so he would not be traced easily.

Roth was smart enough also to disguise his features as much as he could from the hospital CCTV cameras.

He entered through the front doors and glanced across to the security desk. It was not manned. Perfect.

He went to the hospital shop and purchased a bunch of flowers. He then made his way to reception and told the receptionist that he was here to visit Tony Slade. The receptionist informed him that only close family members could visit at present. Roth coolly told her that he was his brother, Steven Slade. He was told that Tony was on Ward 12 in side room 2B on the third floor. Roth thanked her and headed for the lift.

Once inside, he pressed the button for number three. He then checked his inside jacket pocket and smiled as he felt the rubber coated handle of the combat knife. It was a RUI Mohican Mk 11 fixed bladed knife. It had a razor-sharp stainless-steel blade coated with titanium. Its sole purpose was to kill.

Andy Roth liked knives. He had a vast collection from Bowies and K bars to the famed Fairbairn Sykes dagger and Gerber Mark 1 and 2 to the modern designs like the Mohican.

UK hospital security was pretty much non-existent. You could walk in 99% of the time and never be challenged, let alone searched. That was good news for Roth.

On the second floor, half a dozen people got into the lift and Roth blended into the background waiting to exit at the next level.

Tony was just finishing off his exercises with physiotherapist Hettie Brown. He was feeling stronger every day. The road to recovery was not going to happen overnight, but he was getting there on a physical level.

He still had trouble sleeping and was having reoccurring nightmares. But this had been part of his normal existence before the shooting. Tony Slade had seen many horrors of war. Generally, he handled the dark moments well, but recently, those moments had been coming thick and fast.

Doctor Varma had explained that it was normal to experience this after gunshot trauma. Tony knew himself that this was true. After tours of Northern Ireland and the Falklands, as well as action in Africa, he had seen the physical and psychological results of a fire fight.

"That was splendid work again, Tony. You are becoming my star patient," said Hettie.

Tony smiled.

"It's all down to you, Hettie, pet. I will miss these sessions when I eventually leave."

Hettie let out a snort of derision.

"Of course you will, Tony."

Hettie knew her patients had a love hate relationship with her. Some saw her as their saviour; others as the devil reincarnated.

"Same time tomorrow, my man. Sorry we were running a little late today. We have cut into your visiting time."

Tony headed towards the door.

"Don't worry about that, Hettie. I don't expect a whole host of visitors to be queuing up outside my door."

Hettie looked sad for a moment.

"Your parents passed on?"

Tony nodded.

"No wife, kids, brothers, sisters?"

Tony was thoughtful for a moment.

"No, just me. Married to the army, you see. Queen and country."

"Any regrets?" asked Hettie.

Tony smiled wryly.

"Dozens, pet, dozens, but you can't turn back the clock. See you tomorrow, Hettie."

Hettie nodded understandingly.

"You okay to get back to your room, sweetie?"

Tony threw up a mock salute.

"An old soldier never loses his direction. I am all good, thanks."

Tony headed towards the lifts.

He was in B block of the hospital and needed to get back to A and then up to the third floor. He had been offered wheelchair assistance, but he had refused it. He needed to walk and get his fitness back.

Hettie Brown watched Tony leave. She could understand his situation only too well. She too was alone. Her parents had been dead for many years. Both succumbed to cancer in their sixties. Her only sibling had been her sister, Clara, who had died tragically in a car accident back in their parent's birthplace of Jamaica five years ago whilst on holiday. There was not a day that went by when Hettie did not think about her.

Hettie had not married. She had given her life to the medical profession and caring for people. A worthy cause, no doubt, but she still went home to an empty flat at the end of the day and a microwave meal for one.

The ringing of the phone brought her thoughts back to the present.

She picked it up.

"Hettie Brown speaking."

On the line was a young nurse from Ward 12 named Teresa Wicks.

"Hello Hettie, this is Teresa. I was wondering if Mr Slade is still with you?"

"No, Teresa. He has just left. Is everything okay?"

"Yes, it is fine. It's just that he has a visitor here asking for him. His brother."

"Well, he shouldn't be too long getting back. He left me about five minutes ago."

Teresa thanked her and hung up.

As soon as Hettie put the phone down, the realisation hit her. Tony had just told her moments ago that he did not have a brother.

She instantly went back to the phone and pressed the extension for Ward 12. It was engaged.

Andy Roth thanked the young nurse for telling him that Tony would be back soon. He watched her walk away and followed the sway of her hips in her tight nurse's outfit. Very tasty. Any other time, he may have chanced chatting her up, but not today.

He slipped back into Tony's room. He checked that his knife was still in place. A habitual ritual that weapon carriers had. He sat in a chair by the door and waited. He would have the element of surprise when Slade came in. The bastard would not know what hit him. Roth was looking forward to using his knife on him. It was his weapon of choice and he had used blades many a time in his line of work.

He was introduced to knives by one of his mum's many boyfriends. Roth's dad had disappeared long before he was born, so he never knew him, but he was introduced to many 'Uncle' Terrys or Jimmys and fuck knows who else.

Mum Sheila had been a good-looking and popular girl with the men. She worked two jobs to keep a roof over their heads and food on the table, but sometimes it was not enough, so she used her good looks and shapely body to earn some extra money.

It was one of those 'Uncles', a black dude named Wallace, who sparked his interest in blades. Wallace was some sort of Martial Arts nut who had a vast array of exotic weapons which he trained with. He had dozens of knives in his collection that he let a young and impressionable Roth look at.

Roth recalled the very first time that he used a knife and that had been way back at St. Martin's Secondary School in Gateshead when he was twelve years old. He was suffering constant bullying by a big ginger-haired lad named Gordon Grimes. He made Roth's life a misery every day.

It all came to a head one day in the school canteen at dinner time. Roth was minding his own business eating his food when Grimes walked past his table and lifted a sausage from his plate and ate it in front of him, whilst his cronies all laughed. He then spat on Roth's food and swaggered off to get his own meal.

Andy Roth sat in silence and then something snapped inside him. He picked up his dinner knife and walked over to Grimes' table. Gordon Grimes looked up from his food when he saw Roth stood by him. Through a mouthful of potatoes, he snarled.

"What the fuck do you want, arsehole?"

Roth remained silent. As Grimes went to speak again, Roth moved with incredible speed and drove the dinner knife he had hidden in his hand down into Grimes' back. It buried itself up to the handle.

Grimes clutched at his back frantically with pain and fear in his eyes. Roth liked that.

"Not so fucking tough now are you, Grimes, you wanker."

Everybody was in total shock. The headmaster called the police and Andy Roth was taken away. It was the talk of the school for weeks.

Grimes survived but never came back to St. Martin's. Roth was sent for a psychiatric evaluation and then ended up in Juvenile Detention.

This started his journey in and out of the prison system over many years where he met his future boss Kenny Robbins.

He spent ten years in Belmarsh prison for knifing three guys in Tesco for pushing in front of him at the checkout. He waited until they were in the car park, then set about them like a fucking ninja, slashing and stabbing them all with a pair of Filipino butterfly knives which were all the rage in the '80s. He often joked the offer of the day in Tesco was stab one, stab two free.

When he was finally released from the prison system, he sought out Robbins and was welcomed into his criminal empire. He became one of Robbins' loyal and trusty enforcers.

Robbins knew Roth was unstable and unpredictable, but he could keep him in line and only used him when there were no other options.

Roth idolised Robbins and would do anything he was asked without hesitation. Many others on the inside of Robbins' business did not like Roth or having him around, but they kept their opinions to themselves.

The death of Robbins had been a shock to Roth and that was why he was now here. Sure, this Crane character was the man who actually killed Robbins, but his boss would not have been in the coffee shop if he had not come looking for Slade who was trying to make off with his Missus. Tony Slade was responsible in his book and in that case, he had to pay. Pay with his life.

Teresa went back to her work. She was covering Nurse O'Neill's shift today as she had a day off. She was surprised Rosie O'Neill took the day off, since she was always being chased by her superiors about overdue holidays.

Before leaving yesterday, she had reeled off a list of things for Teresa to do, including keeping an eye on Tony Slade. Teresa thought that Rosie had developed a soft spot for him.

Well, Tony was going to be over the moon that his one and only brother had flown in all the way from New York to visit him. That was going to be a massive surprise.

Tony came back into A block and headed for the lifts. Stubborn as he was, he had to admit, it had been a tougher trek back here than he imagined.

He decided to sit down a moment on the sofa in the reception area. It was then that he heard his name being announced over the hospital's speaker system to come to reception.

Tony headed over there and introduced himself and was immediately handed a phone. He was surprised to hear Hettie Brown's voice on the other end. It was full of concern.

Andy Roth heard the call go out. Something was not right. He could sense it. He went to the door and looked down the corridor. He saw the young nurse speaking on the phone and now glancing in his direction. Shit, he had somehow been rumbled.

He had got this close. He was torn between waiting for that bastard Slade or making his getaway and coming back another day.

Fuck it. Slade was not coming back to his room. The plan had gone pear-shaped. He now needed to get out and away before being apprehended. He began to walk down the corridor. He heard footsteps hurrying behind him and the young nurse calling his name. He just kept walking towards the lifts.

Just then the doors opened, and three security guards spilled out and looked in his direction. The largest of the three that looked like he spent most of his spare time eating through the *Greggs* menu shouted out.

"Oi you, stop right there!"

Roth turned back the way he came and spied the young nurse. He ran and grabbed her by the hair and at the same time, produced the combat knife and held it across her throat.

The security men came to a halt in front of him.

"Get the fuck out of my way or she dies. I am not fucking joking."

The big security guard looked first at the terrified nurse's face and then at the determined features of the man. He sensed this guy meant business. He held up his hands in a calming gesture.

"Okay, mate. I hear you. Look, the police are on the way. Why don't you just drop the knife? You are only making things worse."

Time seemed to stand still. The rest of the people in the ward had backed away in fear.

Roth and the nurse, Teresa Wicks faced off against the three security men.

Andy Roth could sense fear in their eyes. They were out of their depth having probably only dealt with showing a few drunks the exit on a Saturday night. They had now entered another league. He started moving forward.

"Right, fatso. You and your cronies fuck off out the way and let me get to the lifts now."

The big man held his ground. His voice had a tremor in it when he announced.

"I can't let you do that."

Roth's face broke into an evil grin.

"This is your last chance. Get the fuck out of the way or I slit this bitch's throat."

Teresa's pleading eyes looked towards the security guy that she knew as Barry Meyers.

"Please, Barry. Let him go. Please."

Tears rolled down her cheeks. Barry regarded the young woman. He had a daughter around the same age. Slowly, he stepped back and gestured for his colleagues to do the same.

Roth nodded.

"That's more like it. That was a smart decision."

The three men watched Roth back up to the lift and press the button. Never taking his eyes off the security guards, he told them.

"Now, nobody try and be a hero and the girl will be just fine."

The lift made a tinging sound as it arrived and the doors slid open. It was empty. Roth smiled and backed in with Teresa. The doors closed and he was gone.

Immediately, the security guards headed for the other lift and the stairwell. They had to try to contain him in the hospital until the police arrived. Barry Meyers produced his mobile phone and now informed the police that the suspect was armed. They confirmed that a firearms unit was being deployed. Meyers prayed that they would get there soon.

The lift door opened on the ground floor and Roth stepped out with the nurse. Security was there to greet him.

"Back off. Fucking back off now," Roth shouted.

They did what they were told, but stayed just on the perimeter. Roth heard sirens in the distance.

He headed to the main doors. He needed to get to his car.

Just then he saw Slade in the crowd gathered. Roth's face broke into a sneer.

"Well, if it isn't the Judas himself. You must have more lives than a fucking cat, Slade."

"Just let the girl go. The police are on their way."

Slade moved forward from the crowd.

He knew he was in no fit state to tackle Roth, but he hoped that he might distract him. Roth knew that getting to Slade was now out of the question. He had to get away.

"Fucking stay where you are you. Don't come any closer."

Tony raised his hands.

"Okay. Just go. Leave the girl and get out while you can."

"You are a lucky fucker, Slade, but I will be back for you. Wherever you go, I will find you."

"Yeah, whatever you say, Roth, you pussy. I will be waiting for you."

In that few seconds of exchange, Roth's concentration was momentarily distracted by Slade's words. He wanted to kill him so bad that he could taste it. His grip relaxed slightly on Teresa. She sensed an opportunity and more out of luck than judgement, she drove her elbow back sharply into his stomach.

Two months ago, many of the nursing staff had undergone some basic self-defence training from a renowned local Bristol Jujutsu instructor because of the rising violence in the NHS. Teresa had remembered this simple move and it now had just saved her life.

Roth let his grip on her go completely in pain and surprise and Teresa ran to freedom. That was the opportunity that Barry Meyers had been waiting for and he lunged forward.

Tony saw what was going to happen.

"Wait!" he shouted to the big man.

With his adrenaline on full charge, Barry Meyers did not hear him.

Roth had gained his composure quickly and as the big man bore down on him, he plunged the Mohican combat knife deep into his belly. Meyers came to a sudden halt with a look of surprise on his face. Roth ripped the blade upwards and downwards before pulling it free.

Time seemed to freeze in the hospital reception as the bystanders could not comprehend what had just happened. This allowed Roth to sprint out of the main doors and head towards the car park.

Barry Meyers dropped to his knees frantically trying to hold his internal organs in place as they spilled out of his body. Blood began to pool around him.

The place was stunned to silence.

Meyer's colleagues ran forward to help him, but there was nothing they could do. They shouted for medical help.

The big man's frantic movements slowly ceased, and he collapsed to his knees before dropping on his side in a foetal position. His hands were still clutching hold of his bloody entrails.

Tony stood helpless as medical staff came to his aid. Then, police cars and vans came to a skidding holt outside the hospital's main doors.

The violence had started again, and it was all Tony's doing.

He hung his head in disbelief. Would it never end?

Just as he thought it could not get any worse, he saw Detective Chief Inspector Wyatt and Sergeant Richmond walk through the door.

They surveyed the carnage and then spotted Tony.

By the time the police swarmed all over the hospital, Andy Roth was back in his Mercedes and heading out the gates. He needed to get away fast before the police took up pursuit.

Slade had got away from him for now, but he would return.

Chapter Nine

It was chaotic in the hospital reception with armed response police and then doctors and nurses milling around.

Hospital staff and patients were in shock over what had just transpired. The word was that the killer had escaped. The eyewitness identification of the man was a little sketchy.

At this moment in time, the police did not have much to go on and were now attempting to get hold of CCTV footage from the hospital to see if they could get a positive ID on him.

The body of Barry Meyers had been transported to the hospital morgue.

As the aftermath of the incident unfolded, Tony Slade found himself back in his room along with Detective Chief Inspector Wyatt and Sergeant Richmond.

"Well, Tony. Trouble seems to follow you around. Do you mind telling me what happened here?"

Wyatt stood expectantly with pen and notebook poised. Tony was sat down in his bedside chair. He suddenly felt very weary.

Roth the crazy bastard had come looking for him as Tony had expected all along. The death of the security guard had been an unfortunate occurrence.

Tony felt sorry for the man. He had been in the wrong place at the wrong time. On any other day, he would probably still be alive.

The death of Robbins had obviously caused shock waves through his firm and vengeance seemed high on the priority. Roth was not a man to give up easily. Slade knew he would be back.

Tony sighed as he slumped back in his chair and ran his hands through his hair.

"I was on my way back from my treatment when I got a call to go to the reception. When I did this, I took a phone call from my physiotherapist Hettie Brown.

She informed me not to go back to my room. She asked me had she got it right that I told her earlier that I didn't have any family alive. I confirmed this to be true. She then said that I had a visitor in my room telling nursing staff that he was my brother from New York. Alarm bells had sounded.

So, I stayed put in reception. The next thing I know, the lift doors opened and this lunatic with a knife got out with a nurse as hostage."

Richmond broke into the conversation.

"Have you ever seen the man before? Was he familiar to you?"

Tony regarded him, his face never betraying a flicker of a lie.

"No. I have never seen him before."

Richmond rolled his eyes.

"Come on, Slade. Enough of your lies and tell us the truth."

Tony spread his hands.

"I don't know what I can tell you."

Richmond leaned in close to Tony.

"You can start by cutting your bullshit and telling us what this man wanted. An innocent man is dead because of this."

Tony remained impassive.

"I am truly sorry for what happened to the security guard, but that was not my fault. Like I said, I don't know why he was here."

The sergeant's voice raised an octave.

"Whatever this lunatic wanted, he wanted it bad enough to kill for it. For Christ's sake, Slade, he was here to see you. Early evidence from the CCTV in reception suggests you approached the killer like you knew him."

"That's bullshit. I was just trying to help the girl. I felt responsible in some way for the situation."

"I bet you fucking did, Slade."

Tony remained silent.

Richmond turned to his superior in frustration.

"Gov, he is fucking lying. Let's arrest the prick for obstruction. Slade, you just admitted yourself that alarm bells sounded when you were told about this man waiting for you. Now why was that if you are innocent?"

"I have been hounded by the press earlier trying to get to me under false pretences. I thought it was one of them again," Slade replied.

Richmond threw his arms up in the air with frustration.

"Bollocks, Slade. That is a fairy tale and you know it. You think you are so fucking smart."

Wyatt held up a hand.

"Okay, Sergeant. Let's calm down, shall we? You need a breather. I suggest you go back down to reception and see if you can get a few more witness statements from anybody else who saw the incident while I finish interviewing Mr Slade. Also try and rustle up some tea or coffee while you are there. I will join you shortly."

"But Sir..." Richmond went to protest, but Wyatt cut him off. "Sergeant, just do it now please."

Richmond sighed in resignation and moved towards the door.

"An Americano for me please, Richmond. No sugar." Tony called.

Glancing back to give Tony the evil eye, Richmond replied.

"Fuck you, Slade."

He disappeared out of the room.

Detective Chief Inspector Wyatt sat down next to Tony on the edge of the bed.

"Tony, I suggest you tell me whatever you know right now or as soon as you are well enough, I will arrest you for obstruction."

Tony turned to the D.C.I.

"Like I told Richmond there..."

Wyatt now cut Tony off in mid-sentence.

"Don't treat me like a muppet. I have been in this game too long to be fucked around. I am not buying your story and I am not leaving here until I have the truth out of you."

Tony knew he had to buy himself some time here or Wyatt would be breathing down his neck every second of the day and there would be no hope of a getaway.

"Look, Inspector. I can only guess what that lunatic wanted me for. I am the only witness of the coffee shop massacre. Now whether he had a connection with this Crane bloke, I don't know, but I suspect he wanted to ask me some questions just like yourself about what happened in the *Alpha* that morning."

Wyatt digested this observation.

"I suggest he wanted to do more than talk to you armed with a knife, don't you?"

Tony nodded in agreement.

"Yeah, I would agree with you on that."

Wyatt continued.

"The question is why he might want you dead."

"Like I said, maybe he is a pissed off friend of Crane's looking for justice and thinks that me being the only survivor has something to answer for."

"I don't buy that. Crane was a loner. He did what he did on his own. I don't see anybody else looking for vengeance for his acts. I think this guy has something to do with Robbins."

Slade tried to look surprised as if he had not considered this option.

"You think so? Why would any of this Robbins' boys hold me responsible for his death? It makes no sense."

Wyatt raised his eyebrows.

"I think it makes perfect sense, Tony, because I believe that you knew Robbins and that you were in that coffee shop to meet with him. How am I doing?"

Tony allowed a small smile to play on his lips.

"It's a theory, I give you that. But it doesn't carry any substance. Like I told you, I don't personally know Robbins."

"Yes, alright, I have heard it before. It is all a coincidence. Two men who live in Newcastle upon Tyne both separately go into a coffee shop in Bristol at the same time. Give me a fucking break."

Tony remained silent.

"I must admit, Tony, for a man who has had one person shoot him and another come looking for him with a knife in the short space of a few weeks, you seemed pretty unperturbed."

Tony regarded Wyatt.

"Army training. Lived with death in one shape or form all my life. That's all."

The D.C.I smiled wryly.

"Maybe but my theory is that you were expecting trouble to be coming your way."

The D.C.I suddenly rose from the bed.

"Our investigations are ongoing with our colleagues in the police force in the North East and if I find any sort of connection between you and Robbins, I can promise you that I will be down on you like a ton of bricks.

You see, young Richmond is still a bit Gung Ho. Rushes in too much for my liking. He likes to get things sown up as quickly as possible.

Now me. You could say that I am a plodder. I keep going and won't give up no matter how long it takes. I have a good track record of arrests.

I am on the rundown to retirement and I am looking to go out with a bang, not a whimper."

Tony nodded.

"A very admirable quality. I admire that in a person."

Wyatt smiled.

"Think you have all the answers, do you, Tony? Well, we will see. I know it's an old cliché, but don't go anywhere without telling us first. You can guarantee one thing, I will be back soon, and I will get to the bottom of this."

With that, Wyatt strode out of the door. He then suddenly stopped.

"Oh, by the way. You have now become an extra special witness to two major incidents, plus a suspected attempt has been made on your life, so as a precaution, I am going to station an officer on your door for your own safety."

"No need to go to all that trouble for me, Detective Chief Inspector."

Wyatt smiled.

"No trouble, Slade. I need to keep you safe for further questioning."

With that, he was gone, and Tony was now panicking.

Fucking Wyatt. He was like a bloodhound. Tony believed what the policeman had said. He was in no doubt that he would be back. So too would that psycho Roth.

A copper on the door was going to make getting out of there even trickier, but also maybe keep Roth at bay for a while.

He reached for his phone and dialled Doug Jacobs' number. He answered on the first ring.

"Tony, my old mate, I was just about to ring you. It's all set up. We are on."

Tony felt the knot of tension that had appeared and stayed in his stomach since Wyatt had been here loosen a little.

"Thank Christ. The police have been all over the place here. I need to get out."

Doug's voice showed concern.

"Okay, my friend. It is in hand. Now tell me what has been going on."

Tony relayed to Doug the incident with Roth and then his conversation with Wyatt. When he had finished, his friend let out a low whistle.

"Fuck me, my old mate. Things have got a little lively. Don't worry. I will be in tomorrow afternoon at visiting time. I will get you in a wheelchair and tell the staff I am taking you out for a little ride in the hospital grounds.

I will have a vehicle ready and I will drive you to Cardiff and there at the dockside, we will meet a friend of mine who has a ferry boat. He will get you over to Graig o Mor."

"What about the fucking copper on the door?" asked Tony, "Wyatt will want to know who is visiting me. If your name flags up, he will be all over it."

"Let me worry about that. I will think of something and ring you back. Now I hate to ask this, my friend, but about this money?"

Tony thought of the money in the boot of the Audi. He prayed the car was still there.

"It will be fine. I have it. But I need you to do me another couple of favours, Doug."

"Shoot. What are they?"

'Firstly, clear my stuff out of your flat. I have a large suitcase under the bed. Just put my clothes and other belongings in there. I have an unopened bottle of Bushmills sixteen-year-old single malt in the wardrobe. It is yours. Now secondly and more importantly...

A couple of streets away from the *Alpha Coffee House* I have parked a car. It is a silver Audi. It is a 64 plate. The street name is Clover Close. I am parked halfway up on the left heading from the coffee shop. Can you confirm it is still there and that it hasn't got any tickets or notices on it? I have your money in the boot."

"No worries. I will do that and drop you a text once I have looked, okay?"

"Nice one, Doug. I can't thank you enough for what you are doing for me."

Doug laughed down the phone.

"I can never let a fellow soldier down. Anyway, you would do the same for me."

His voice then became serious again.

"Tony, I have to ask. I know you need to get out, but are you well enough?"

"I will fucking have to be Doug. I have run out of choices."

"Okay. Hang tight, buddy, and I will be in 2.00pm sharp for visiting time tomorrow. Be ready."

Tony ended the call.

He felt a little better. Tomorrow he would be out of it. Away from Wyatt and Richmond and, more importantly, away from Roth.

He wondered what this island was going to be like. No picnic, he suspected. Hell, he survived the Falklands. It could not be any worse.

His thoughts turned to Annette. He still felt hollow inside. He wondered if that feeling would ever go. He missed her so much.

Life certainly had a knack of throwing unexpected shit at you. Tony had had his fair share and then some.

A short while ago, he had been heading to sunnier climates with a beautiful woman that he loved. Now he was going to be hiding out on some barren godforsaken island in the British Channel.

D.C.I. John Wyatt sipped a cup of coffee as he stared at his computer screen. He was alone in his office at Bridewell Police Station. It was gone midnight, but he couldn't think about sleep.

Going home did not appeal to him. The house was too big and empty since his wife Helen had passed away. It was two years ago now that breast cancer finally claimed her. He missed her every day. She had been the childhood sweetheart that he married nearly forty years ago.

Helen had died before they had celebrated their ruby wedding anniversary where they planned to finally take that Mediterranean cruise that Wyatt had been promising for so long, but his work had kept getting in the way.

His work. It had always taken priority, even over his own marriage. Helen said on many occasions that he was married to the job and not her. She had been right. Policing had been in his blood since joining the force as a young man.

He had given his best years to the job, but the price he paid was taking his wife for granted. When that fact had finally dawned on him, it was too late. She was gone.

Their marriage had produced a son, William. He lived in Australia with his family. Wyatt could not remember the last time he had seen him. He even struggled to remember his age now that Helen was no longer here. She had dealt with birthdays, Christmas and special occasions. He was hopeless at that stuff.

William and him had not been close. Yes, the job again had been responsible for that. He had let his son down far too often to forge a bond between them.

He had missed too many parent nights, sports days, presentations and even William's graduation. He had lived for the job and now that was all he had.

Wyatt leant back in his chair and sighed, then turned his thoughts to the case. At present, it was bugging him. The hospital CCTV footage had produced very little.

The killer had cleverly concealed most of his face with the baseball cap he had been wearing. The car park CCTV had caught images of the man getting into a black Mercedes, but when they ran the license plate, it had come up as false.

This led Wyatt to believe that the man was a professional, which tied up with his theory that it was one of Kenny Robbins' men looking for Slade.

What the fuck had Slade done to piss off Robbins and why was there an obvious contract out on him?

He knew Slade was withholding evidence and part of him wanted to go along with Sergeant Richmond's suggestion of arresting him for obstruction, but another part of him thought if Slade was still out there in circulation, they may get more answers that way.

Wyatt felt that Robbins had met Slade in the coffee shop. What for he did not know. But it must have been important for Robbins to venture out of Newcastle and come to Bristol in person.

Then, this lunatic Crane had burst in totally unexpected and they all got caught in the crossfire. Somehow Slade had survived.

When a well-known gangster like Robbins and a couple of his henchmen wind up dead on his patch, he needed answers and he knew Slade had them.

The dead woman was a bit of a puzzle. It was Annette Rossi. She had been Robbins' long-time girlfriend.

What puzzled Wyatt was why she was there. If Robbins and Slade were up to some shady deal, why would Robbins bring his women all that way with him when the situation might be dangerous?

Tony Slade had the answer. He was sure of that.

Now with another dead body on his patch because of this stranger looking for Slade, he was under pressure from the top brass to get to the bottom of it all sooner rather than later.

Any survivors of the coffee shop massacre that had come forward to volunteer information had not really give him anything worthwhile to go on. They remembered Crane, but not much else.

He had briefly spoken to the manager Kim Walters not long after the incident, but she had been in shock and could not remember much. She did suggest that Crane had come into the *Alpha* to extract some warped revenge on her for dismissing him from her job. She also confirmed that Slade had been using the coffee shop regularly in recent times.

Beyond that she had not said much. Maybe she was worth another visit now the dust had settled.

Also, they had briefly spoke to the nurse, Teresa Wicks, but she was still in shock and had not said much since the incident. He would speak with her again. Wyatt decided he would do that tomorrow. Shit, it was tomorrow.

At 11.30am, he had to speak at a press conference to let the media know about any progress in this big newsworthy case.

Earlier in the day, he had been summoned to Chief Superintendent Timothy Hardwick's office for an update on the case.

Hardwick, or *Hard Dick* as he was known out of earshot, was not impressed that Wyatt had nothing more concrete about the case. He stressed in no uncertain terms that at the press conference tomorrow, Wyatt better find something to pacify the circling vultures.

A mass shooting in his own city was bad enough news, but in amongst the victims was a well- known Geordie gangster. This intrigued him, but also sounded alarm bells.

The hospital knifing only compounded the problem.

Hardwick stressed it was essential that Wyatt gave the press something to pacify them.

As usual, Hardwick would not be in the firing line and Wyatt would be the man on the spot. Great.

Wyatt now made his mind up to interview Nurse Wicks and Kim Walters before the press conference and see if he could get any positive leads to give to the circling media.

The missing gun was a mystery. Where had it gone? Too many loose ends. He did not like loose ends.

He took another swig from his cup and turned off the computer. He reached for his jacket hanging on the back of his chair.

His body felt weary. It had been a long day. He felt in his pocket for his car keys. Time to head home and see if he could catch some sleep.

Chapter Ten

Susie Rawlings sat at her desk in the offices of the *West Country Press*. It was 8.00am and the place was reasonably quiet.

News yesterday had leaked about the stabbing at the hospital and this just reinforced the fact that Slade was hiding something. She had gone to the scene of the crime and picked up any information she could, but was told that Slade was off bounds. She knew that she was onto something big and it frustrated her that she could not get any more information.

Across the way, her colleague, Matt Sloan, was sat at an untidy desk, working his way through his second bacon and egg McMuffin. Susie thought he resembled a large water buffalo chomping noisily on some grass. He was oblivious to her stare as he fiddled with his mobile phone, totally wrapped up in his own little world. Sloan was a good photographer, but some of his personal habits left a lot to be desired.

She sipped her coffee and looked at her computer screen. She had managed to get a bit more background on Tony Slade. Through a contact, she had succeeded in pulling up his army record. It was mighty impressive. But she needed his personal story before the other tabloids got their foot in the door.

The *West Country Press* couldn't afford the money that the big boys would be offering Slade for an exclusive. Tony Slade may be reluctant to speak to her, but once these guys came knocking and waving their cheque books, things would be different. Everybody had their price.

"I need to somehow get back in that hospital and have another crack at Slade," she said.

Matt Sloan looked up from his phone.

"How? He is off limits. You said so yourself."

"I know, but I am doing no good sat here. I need to do something positive."

"Do you want me to come with you?" asked Sloan.

Susie smiled and shook her head.

"No thanks, Matt. No disrespect to you, but I can see you being a red rag to a bull where Slade is concerned. I don't even know if I will even get near him, but I must give it another go. I can't let the chance of an exclusive slip through my fingers. We are a Bristol paper and we should have the story. Slade's refusal to talk to any of the press is the only reason why they haven't already grabbed the exclusive. Jameson won't be happy if the story goes to *The Sun* or *Mirror*."

Her ears were still burning from the roasting he had given them the previous evening.

Carl Jameson was the newspaper's editor and was not known for his patience when it came to a worthy piece of news. The Bristol shootings had been the biggest news they had received in a few years since the capture of serial rapist John Mulholland. He wanted the story and Susie Rawlings was a keen up and coming reporter and he felt that she could get Slade to talk.

First thing on her agenda before going to the hospital, however, was to attend a press conference later that morning. Detective Chief Inspector John Wyatt was due to give an update on the shootings plus the hospital stabbing.

Wyatt was a good policeman. She had reported on the Mulholland rape case when Wyatt ran the investigation. She had found him a very thorough and down to earth detective. It would be interesting to see what he had on this case.

Sloan went back to the remains of his muffin.

"Okay, but I am here if you need me."

Susie nodded and finished off her coffee.

Hopefully, come visiting hours, she would be back at the hospital with a new angle to work on Slade.

The media room at Bridewell station was packed with journalists. There was a buzz around the place. Everybody waited in anticipation for Detective Chief Inspector Wyatt to enter the room. Susie Rawlings had got there early and managed to get a decent seat near the front of the room.

She looked around the group of assembled journalists. She knew many of the faces. All experienced and world-weary individuals jostling for a tasty titbit. She felt a tingle of anticipation in her stomach. That was why she loved the job. It made her feel alive.

Susie noticed some of the big tabloids were there poised to pounce given the opportunity.

She checked her watch. It was 11.25pm. Nearly time.

Behind the scenes, Wyatt was getting a last-minute briefing from the police corporate communications press officer, Bernadette Coleman. She was making clear to him what he could and could not answer.

Wyatt was old school and did not welcome the advice. But this was the latest policing protocol. The press officer was a mediating bridge between the press and police to improve their image. In recent times, the press had complained that the police had been too secretive and reserved about the information given out to the media.

Wyatt checked his tie in the mirror. In the reflection, he could see Chief Superintendent Hardwick and Bernadette Coleman in close conversation. Both glanced towards Wyatt.

Typical of Hardwick. Worried about what he might say but did not have the balls to put himself in the firing line. Fuck him.

Wyatt was going to go with what he had, which was not a lot.

Earlier, Wyatt called in at the hospital, but was told that Nurse Wicks was under sedation and asleep. She had been admitted into hospital for shock due to collapsing after the incident of the previous day. Instead, he had gone to Kim Walters' flat. Once inside, he noticed that she was packing up and planning on moving out.

Over a cup of coffee, he asked Kim once again whether she was sure that Colin Crane had just randomly targeted people in the coffee shop or had he focused on Robbins and the people with him.

She assured him that it was random and that he had returned with some sort of sadistic revenge on his mind and she had been the main target.

He then asked if Tony Slade had been in the coffee shop before Robbins came in or had they all come in together.

Kim told Wyatt that Tony had been coming into the *Alpha Coffee House* regularly for a week or more, always on his own.

Wyatt asked if she had spoken to Slade.

She told him that they had passed the time of day and he had given the indication that he was down in Bristol for a job.

Wyatt digested this information. It tied up with what Slade had said and what Doug Jacobs had confirmed when he had visited him at his business premises. He knew that Jacobs was an old army buddy of Slade's and could well be covering for him, but Kim Walters had no reason to. Did she? It all seemed to neat.

Finally, he had asked Kim if she had witnessed the killings of Robbins or any of the others with him and she replied that she had not seen anything, as she was cowering behind the counter. It was only after it had all gone quiet that she had come out of her hiding place and surveyed the scene.

He asked if she had touched anything or gone near the bodies. She told him that she had walked amongst the carnage to see if she could help anybody, but she had not touched anything.

He then asked if she looked at Tony Slade. Kim told him that she had. Wyatt asked if she had seen a gun in his hand or near him. She answered not that she recalled, but the whole thing was rather blurry.

Wyatt seemed to be satisfied with this and asked Kim for a forwarding address in case he needed to contact her again.

He left her flat none the wiser than when he entered it.

"Are we ready, Detective Chief Inspector?"

It was Coleman's voice asking the question.

Wyatt turned from the mirror.

"As I will ever be."

Hardwick raised an eyebrow. Wyatt saw this.

"Don't worry, Sir. You can be reassured. It will be fine."

"I hope so, Chief Inspector. We need to convince the public we are doing all we can to get to the bottom of this accident."

This rankled Wyatt.

"We are doing all we can, Sir. Maybe you would like to join me and show a united front?"

Hardwick coughed awkwardly.

"As you said, I am sure you will be fine."

Bernadette Coleman sensed the tension and stepped forward.

"Shall we go, Chief Inspector?"

Wyatt nodded and they headed out into the glare of bright lights and flashing cameras.

As expected, the questions came thick and fast from the four corners of the room.

Firstly, the topic was the hospital killing. Can you identify the killer? Was he there to kill Tony Slade? Did they have any solid leads? The questions were deflected as Wyatt told them it was too early to speculate.

The questions then turned to the coffee shop murders. Was Crane politically motivated? Was he working alone? Do you know where the firearm came from? Was it true that North East gangster Kenny Robbins was amongst the dead? Why was he in Bristol? Had this Slade character shed any light on what went down in the coffee shop?

Coleman orchestrated who was getting an opportunity to ask questions and fielded away any awkward moments for Wyatt. He had to admit that he was now glad she was here.

He could confidently answer some questions, but others, he did not have a clue about, but his experience kept him pretty much unruffled.

He had been in this position many times before with some big profile cases. He was used to the pressure, but sometimes, the whole thing could get overwhelming, even for the most case-hardened policeman.

In general, Wyatt felt that he had done a satisfactory job and was now looking towards Coleman to begin to wrap things up.

"Okay, everybody. One more question."

Coleman pointed at Susie Rawlings.

Susie Rawlings had been waiting for her chance and now eventually she had it and she was determined to grab it with both hands.

"Chief Inspector Wyatt. Can you confirm whether the murder at Southmead Hospital the other day is linked to the shootings at the *Alpha*?"

Wyatt knew this question would come up and was not surprised that Susie Rawlings had asked it. She was a smart lady and a good reporter.

"Good morning Miss Rawlings. In answer to your question, as far as we know, there is no apparent link to the two incidents."

Susie looked confused.

"Are you sure about this, Sir?"

Wyatt sensed that Rawlings had more to say and so did Bernadette Coleman.

She moved in quickly.

"I think the Chief Inspector has answered that clearly. Shall we move on?"

Rawlings was not going to miss her opportunity.

"With respect, Sir. Isn't it a big coincidence that the only surviving person from the coffee shop massacre, a Mr Tony Slade, was in that hospital as a patient? Was the killer looking for him?"

A buzz went around the room and a sea of faces waited expectantly for Wyatt to answer.

There it was. The question Wyatt had been dreading. He did not want a media frenzy about the possibility of faceless psychotic killers roaming the streets of Bristol randomly killing people.

In the same token, he wanted the connection to Slade to stay out of the newspapers' hands until he got some concrete evidence. He could not afford to have the press come to their own conclusions and cause public panic.

He chose his words carefully. He knew Hardwick would be listening somewhere.

"I will not deny that Mr Slade was in the hospital at the time of the unfortunate murder of a security guard, but at this moment in time, we have nothing solid in the way of evidence to connect the two incidents. I don't want to speculate. That is all I have to say on the matter at present."

Coleman sensed the mood in the room.

"Okay, ladies and gentlemen. That is all for today. Thank you for coming."

Susie Rawlings could not resist one last probe.

"So, in that case, in the last few weeks, we have experienced two separate incidents of violent and random murder on our streets. This isn't the Middle East or South America. Are our streets being policed effectively? The public have a right to know."

Wyatt picked up his paperwork.

"I can assure you, Miss Rawlings The streets are being policed correctly and these two incidents, as you well know, are not the norm on the streets of Bristol."

"Can I ask, Sir? Have you got any solid evidence on this case, as it doesn't appear so?"

She knew that she was not getting an answer, as Wyatt was heading for the door, but she knew he had heard her words and so did the rest of the room. She was sure that Slade was the common denominator in all of this and she was determined to find out what he was hiding.

Wyatt came into the back room followed by Coleman. She shut the door. Wyatt loosened his tie and let out a sigh. Hardwick stood there regarding him.

"That Rawlings woman was pushing hard. Is she going to be a problem to this investigation?"

Wyatt poured himself a glass of water from a jug on a nearby table. He really fancied a scotch. He swallowed a large mouthful before answering. It was ice cold and tasted good.

"No, Sir. She won't be a problem. I know her. We have an understanding between us. I can handle her."

"Well, I hope so, Chief Inspector. We need some hard evidence to move this case along."

Wyatt finished his water.

"Well, if I can get back out on the streets instead of fannying around here, I just might be able to get that evidence... Sir."

Both men glared at each other. Coleman coughed awkwardly.

"Well, we are all finished here, Chief Inspector. I think it went okay."

She looked at both men. Hardwick reached for his cap.

"Okay, Chief Inspector. I hear you. Go on about your business."

"Thank you, Sir."

Wyatt turned to go and heard Hardwick add.

"I want to be kept up to speed with any new evidence, understood? You are a good policeman, but if I think it is all getting to much for you, I have DCI Horner waiting in the wings."

Wyatt headed for the door.

"Well, it's nice to know I have your backing, Sir."

He slammed the door shut before Hardwick could reply.

Outside the back of the police station, Wyatt found a quiet spot and lit up a cigarette. He had tried to give them up on numerous occasions knowing all the health warnings, but he could not. He blamed the pressure of the job. He also blamed the job for drinking too much whisky as well.

Fucking Hardwick threatening him with DCI 'Little Jack Horner'.

He was the new golden boy in the force. New breed. Right up Hardwick's ass. Sucking up to him looking for approval. Well, fuck him. There was no way he was getting this case.

Rawlings had been right, though. He did not have a fucking scrap of evidence on this case beyond knowing that Colin Crane had been a looney tune.

It was the Robbins/Slade connection that intrigued him. He had not lied to Rawlings in the fact that they had no evidence that connected the two killings. He was 100% sure that Tony Slade was the connection. The hospital killer had come looking for him, but why? His thoughts were suddenly interrupted as Sergeant Steve Richmond approached him.

"Sir, we might have a break. A witness has come forward from the *Alpha* shootings. They saw a car outside the coffee shop pulling away just after the shootings. The driver looked nervous."

Wyatt took a long drag on his cigarette.

"And?"

Richmond smiled.

"It was a black Mercedes C class."

Wyatt's eyes grew wide with surprise. He dropped the remains of his smoke and crushed it into the ground with the heel of his shoe.

"Just like the car that the killer at the hospital drove off in. Another coincidence I don't think. Excellent work, Steve. Let's go talk to this witness."

The witness was a seventy-five-year-old pensioner named Harry Pope. He was waiting in one of the side rooms of the station reserved for interviews. He had come in at his own accord.

Wyatt noticed that the man looked sprightly for his age and when he started talking, he seemed on the ball, which was all good for a possible key witness.

Pope told Wyatt and Richmond that he was standing across the road from the *Alpha* on the day of the incident. He was waiting for his wife to come out of the chemist where she was picking up her prescription for blood pressure tablets. They were then planning on going to get a cup of coffee in the *Alpha*.

He carried on saying that he noticed a slick looking black Mercedes pull up outside the coffee shop and a group of men and a lone woman got out and went into the *Alpha*. The car and its driver waited outside. As it was only fifteen minutes reserved parking, he guessed whoever had got out of the car was popping in for a takeaway.

Wyatt asked if he had taken a good look at the people who got out of the vehicle, but Pope told him no as he had been answering a text on his phone from his grandson.

After five minutes had passed, nobody had returned. The driver looked edgy as he sat in the driver's seat smoking and glancing towards the shop door.

At one stage, he got out of the car and walked to the coffee shop's window and glanced inside and then returned to the vehicle.

Wyatt asked if he could describe the man. Pope told him he thought the man was in his mid-fifties, around 5ft 10ins. He had gelled-back black hair and a small goatee beard. He was wearing a heavy dark coloured leather jacket. From where Pope stood, he could see no further details.

Just as he was going to check on his wife, he heard what sounded like gun shots from inside the coffee shop and then all hell broke loose, as people spilled out onto the pavement. He saw the driver of the Mercedes make to get out of the car, but then he seemed to change his mind and drove quickly away. Then, the police arrived and soon, the road was shut off both ways.

Harry Pope did not really make a connection between the shootings and the car straight away. He had gone off for a fortnight's holiday in Bournemouth with his wife Edith. He had kept up to speed with the case in the newspaper and it was no until he came home again that he remembered the car and thought it might be of importance.

Richmond asked him if he was sure that the car was a Mercedes C class. The older man said that he was 100% sure, as he used to be a car salesman and had worked for Mercedes for a spell. That was why it had drawn his attention in the first place.

Richmond took all the details down and told Pope if he would be happy to look at some mugshots and see if he could identify the mystery man in the Mercedes.

Pope said yes, so a young W.P.C. escorted him to Wyatt's office. Wyatt told him he would join him in a moment.

Richmond spoke.

"Well, Sir, this could be a breakthrough. That description of the driver has similarities to the killer at the hospital."

Wyatt felt like another smoke.

"Maybe, but the clever fucker at the hospital was wearing a baseball cap to hide his features."

He paused in thought.

"Steve, have the lads at the hospital turned up anything new on the footage in the reception?"

Richmond shook his head.

"Nothing yet, Sir."

Wyatt continued.

"I have a gut feeling this is the same man. If so, that means he worked for Robbins and that means he came back to Bristol to hunt down Slade. We need to ID this man. I also need to find out why he wanted Slade dead. If they were all here in Bristol to do a job, I want to know what.

You go back to the hospital and speak to Nurse Teresa Wicks. She is the only person that saw this guy up close and personal.

Also, ring D.I. Burton again up in Newcastle. Give him the description of the Mercedes and see if he can link it to anybody that worked for Robbins."

Richmond grinned.

"Let's nail this bastard, Sir."

As they walked towards their car, Wyatt's mobile phone started ringing. He fished it out of his jacket pocket and pressed the receive button.

"D.C.I. Wyatt."

Wyatt listened and nodded. A small smile crossed his face as he hung up.

"Well, Steve, the Gods seem to be shining on us today. That was W.P.C. Gillian Thomas who has been keeping an eye on our young nurse Teresa Wicks. She is awake and talking. She has just told Thomas that she thinks she can give a positive ID of the killer and she also said she thought the killer and Slade knew each other from some dialogue they had between them before the stabbing."

Richmond punched the air.

"I am on my way, Gov."

Chapter Eleven

Tony sat on the bedside chair waiting for Doug to arrive. Every now and then, he glanced at the door because this morning everybody and his dog seemed to be coming in to see him. Doctors, nurses, medication to take, breakfast, more pills, lunch.

He was due for physiotherapy this afternoon, but he did not plan to be around for that.

P.C. Ben Jordan was stationed outside, as Wyatt promised. He seemed a nice kid, but a bit green. Still, he was a thorn in Tony's side. He was like his shadow.

The young policeman had been given a list of people he should expect to visit Slade. D.C.I. Wyatt had added Doug Jacobs' name to the list, giving P.C. Jordan strict instructions if he visited Slade to inform him immediately.

He was keen to impress his superior and wanted to do a good job.

Tony checked his watch. It was 1.30pm. Visiting started in half an hour and Doug said he would be first there.

He had spoken to Doug earlier on the phone and he confirmed, much to Tony's relief, that his car was still parked safely. He had got all his belongings in the suitcase in the back of his own vehicle and everything was set to roll. He had also given Tony a name to add to his visitors' list. It was fake and one he was going to use.

Doug then explained exactly the plan he had in mind to get Tony out and deflect any suspicion from himself. It seemed workable if everybody played their part.

Tony was now anxious to go. He half expected Wyatt and Richmond to come bursting in any minute to arrest him or that female reporter to come snooping around again. Worst of all, he feared Roth would make another attempt on his life.

It was cool in the room, but Tony began to feel uncomfortably warm. The lunch of chicken soup, a ham sandwich and a strawberry yoghurt sat uneasily in his stomach.

Nurse Rosie O'Neill suddenly breezed into the room.

"I will just get rid of your dishes, Tony. Visiting time nearly. Anybody coming to see you?"

Tony smiled.

"Oh, you know, the usual people. Kim Kardashian, Donald Trump, Lionel Messi…"

Rosie did not even react. She was getting used to Tony's sense of humour.

"Yes, very funny, Tony."

Tony laughed.

"Actually, an old friend. It's a lovely day, so I think he plans to take me around the grounds in my wheelchair. I am really looking forward to getting some fresh air and a bit of sun on my face."

Nurse O'Neill nodded.

"That's nice. It will do you good. Things are going well. I expect you to be out of here soon."

Sooner than you think, thought Tony.

When Rosie returned from her day off, she had been shocked to hear what had happened and he knew that she suspected there was something that Tony was hiding. He knew this made her warier of him, but ever the professional, she carried on with her care and said nothing.

He liked Rosie and would miss her. Part of him did feel bad about just going and not telling her, but he did not want her to cause him any hassle. Plus, he did not want to get her involved.

"Right, I am off. Don't forget your session with Hettie at 3.30pm," she said.

Tony threw up a mock salute.

"Aye, aye, Captain."

Doug Jacobs parked his Range Rover outside the main hospital gates.

In the passenger seat next to him was a girl named Daisy Jones. She was the daughter of an army buddy of Doug's, Barry Jones.

She had run away from her home in Birmingham at the age of fourteen. Her stepfather had been abusing her since she was twelve. She had finally told her mother, but she chose to turn a blind eye telling her not to make up stories. The abuse got worse as she got older and with nobody to help her, she decided to run away. She had come to Bristol because it was the first coach waiting to pull out of the bus station.

Barry Jones was divorced from Daisy's mother and he had been serving time in prison with no idea his daughter had run away until he got out. He had found out from his ex-wife Sue when he had phoned to ask to visit Daisy. She had told him that Daisy had phoned her a week after running away, telling her that she was in Bristol and not to come looking for her.

Barry had asked her why Daisy had run away and Sue blamed it on a broken marriage and home. Barry was guilt ridden and blamed himself, knowing nothing about the abuse claims. He told Sue he would find her. He knew immediately who to call to track her down. Doug Jacobs.

Doug eventually did find her. Daisy had been living on the streets of Bristol as a prostitute since sixteen. She also had a heroin habit.

Doug had helped her get off the streets and to get clean and into one of his accommodations. She chose to carry on living in Bristol. That had been five years ago.

Some ex-military buddies had seen to it that the low street pimp who had got her hooked on drugs was never going to do that again to another young girl.

Later, after Barry had talked to his daughter and found out the truth, her scumbag stepfather had also received a visit in the small hours of the morning. His card was well and truly marked.

She was basically a good kid that had just got herself into an unpleasant situation with the wrong people and lost her way. The mental scars would never really heal and Doug likened her to a stray cat. She could never be fully tamed.

These days, she was doing okay and attending open college and also working occasionally for Doug. Today, Doug was now going to cash in a favour from her. He finished his call and pocketed his phone.

"Right, Daisy, you know the plan. Just stick with me until you do your stuff. Okay?"

Daisy ran her hand through her short dirty blonde hair and chewed on her gum. She now looked up from fiddling on her phone.

"Okay, Doug. I have got it. No sweat."

Doug nodded.

He regarded Daisy. She was an attractive and bright twenty-one-year-old but with far too many piercings for his liking and more front than Blackpool.

"Right, let's do this."

They both got out of the vehicle and walked towards the hospital.

"Slow down a bit, will you, Daisy. I am still getting used to this Bionic leg, remember," said Doug

Daisy rolled her eyes.

"Yeah alright, Grandad."

Once inside, they made their way to the lifts and headed up to Tony's ward, but not before they called in to the hospital shop.

P.C. Ben Jordan checked his clipboard. On it was the list of Tony Slade's visitors. They would need to produce ID before he allowed them into the room. To be honest, the list was sparse.

He had been on the assignment a few days and already he was bored. In his mind, the likelihood of the killer coming back was minimal, but Wyatt was insistent that he stayed on the job until further notice. At least it was better than giving out speeding fines.

He now noticed a middle-aged man and a young girl walking up the corridor towards him. The man walked with a limp. He wore a blue baseball cap with the New York Yankees logo on it in white lettering. He sported an impressive beard and was carrying a large bottle of what looked like Lucozade. The girl was carrying a bunch of flowers so big that it almost obscured her face.

She was a looker and Jordan estimated that she could be no more than twenty or so. He could not help but notice that she wore an impossibly short denim mini skirt that showed off her long-tanned legs. She wore an impressive pair of bright yellow Dr Marten boots on her feet.

The fake name Doug was using was Brian Eccles. This was one of the names Tony had fed the young P.C. whist compiling the list.

P.C. Jordan approached them.

"Are you hear to visit Tony Slade?"

'Indeed I am, Officer. My name is Brian Eccles. I should be on the list and this is my niece Daisy Archer."

P.C Jordan checked his list.

"Ah yes, there you are Mr Eccles. May I see some ID, please?"

Doug produced a fake driver's license and handed it to the policeman. Jordan studied it and gave it back without question.

"What was the young lady's name again?"

Daisy pushed forward a little closer and smiled her sweetest smile. Then, she stared Jordan straight in the eye

"Daisy Archer."

Jordan could now see that the girl was a stunner. He coughed awkwardly as he broke from her gaze and looked at his clipboard. He then frowned.

"Something wrong, Officer?" asked Doug.

"Yes. No Daisy Archer on here."

"Is that a problem?"

"Well, yes, Sir. Only visitors whose names are on the list can visit, I am afraid. It is strict police policy due to the recent incident here."

Daisy lowered the flowers.

"Uncle Brian, I told you I wouldn't be able to get in. I have come all this way for nothing. What a waste of time."

Doug raised a hand.

"Now hold it a minute, Daisy. Maybe the officer can make an exception here."

He looked at P.C. Jordan.

"Come on, Officer. This is my niece. Does this young lady look like an assassin to you?"

Daisy gave P.C. Jordan yet another engaging smile when he glanced at her.

"I understand what you are saying, Sir, but I have to go by procedure."

Doug made to plead his case again, but Daisy interrupted.

"It's okay, Uncle. This handsome dude is right. I will wait out here with him. He is only doing his job and I do like a man in uniform."

P.C. Jordan felt himself blush slightly. Suddenly, Tony appeared in the doorway.

"Brian! Daisy! It's great to see you both. Thanks for coming. Give me a moment, will you."

He looked in the direction of P.C. Jordan.

"Sorry, Ben. I need the toilet urgently,"

He then started walking off down the corridor.

P.C. Ben Jordan was getting flustered.

"Hang on a moment, Tony. I need to…"

He was interrupted by Doug and Daisy now in a heated debate.

"Uncle Brian, I will be fine here. I haven't wasted my day. I will grab a coffee down the corridor and sit out here."

She pushed the flowers at him and made to walk off.

"Wait, Daisy. Just a moment."

Doug turned towards P.C. Jordan and pressed the flowers into his arms.

"Hold these a minute, will you?"

The young officer found himself with an armful of flowers.

"Oh, and this please."

Now P.C. Jordan had a bottle of Lucozade to contend with.

"Daisy, hold up one second, will you? Let me buy you the coffee."

Daisy stopped. Doug caught up with her.

"Look, I will be twenty minutes and then I will take you to lunch as a way of an apology, okay?"

Daisy's featured gradually broke into a coy smile.

"Alright, Uncle. You got a deal."

Meanwhile, P.C. Jordan shouted to Tony.

"Wait up. I need to accompany you."

Doug cut in.

"Look, I can do that. It won't take a second really."

Doug began to walk after Tony.

"No, I have to do that. Stop."

P.C. Jordan looked at his arms full of things that were not even his. He offered them back to Daisy as the situation got worse.

"Please take these now."

Daisy grabbed them and let the bottle of Lucozade slip from her fingers. It smashed all over the floor soaking the young policeman's boots and trousers.

"Oh shit," he exclaimed in frustration.

Daisy dropped to her knees in front of him blocking his passage to Doug and Tony who were disappearing down the corridor.

"I am sorry. It was an accident. Oh God, I am so clumsy."

She took out a handkerchief and began wiping the policeman's boots. But now Tony and Doug had disappeared around the corner and P.C. Jordan had lost control of the whole situation.

Around the corner, Tony sat into a waiting wheelchair and Doug sped as fast as he could to the lifts. The doors opened on the first press of the button and they were inside and heading for the ground floor. Both men regarded each other and burst into laughter.

"Fucking hell, Doug. That was some performance back there. The girl was great," said Tony.

Doug smiled.

"Yep. She will keep that young copper tied up for another little while. That will be enough time to get you away from here. Not bad for a man in a wheelchair and his one-legged friend."

Both men started laughing again.

When the lift opened, Doug wheeled Tony out and headed for the exit. As they went past the reception, Tony saw Nurse Rosie O'Neill talking to a doctor. She looked around and their eyes met. Something passed between them at that moment.

"Everything okay, Tony?"

Tony nodded to her and smiled. She turned back to carry on talking to the doctor. When she instinctively turned around again, Tony was gone through the exit doors.

Tony guessed Rosie knew that he was not coming back. He also knew her well enough not to say anything. He would always be eternally grateful for all she had done for him, but it had to be this way.

Outside Doug's Range Rover, the wheelchair was ditched and both men got in. As Doug started the engine, they saw Daisy running towards them. She opened the back door and jumped in. Doug spun the wheels and the Range Rover took off out of the hospital car park and down the road.

"How is P.C. Jordan?" asked Doug.

Daisy smiled.

"The last I saw of him, he was going into the toilets calling Tony's name."

Tony turned around and offered his hand to Daisy who shook it.

"Nice to meet you, Daisy, and thank you for the help."

"No problem, I enjoyed it."

Doug dropped Daisy off further down the road.

"I will speak to you soon, Daisy. Thanks again, love."

Daisy got into a red Kia and waved goodbye before pulling away.

"Right," said Doug as he pulled the false beard he had been sporting from his face.

"Let's go get this car of yours. Time is now very important. That young copper will have called this in already. I know you aren't exactly on the FBI's most wanted list, but I suspect that D.C.I. Wyatt character will be straight on your ass trying to find you."

Tony nodded in agreement.

Chapter Twelve

Susie Rawlings had watched Tony Slade get into the passenger seat of the Range Rover and followed it as it sped out of the hospital's exit and head up the road. She had been waiting for visiting hours to see if she could get in to see Slade. Now here he was.

Susie knew she was on to something. She did not know who the driver or the young girl were, but she was certain they were part of a plan to get Slade away from the hospital. She started her blue Ford Fiesta and followed the vehicle out of the gate.

Susie could not identify the registration of the vehicle, as the plate was splattered with mud. In fact, the whole Range Rover looked like it had done some recent off-road driving.

The Range Rover made its way from Southmead to Westbury on Trym before getting to the Clifton area of Bristol.

For a moment, Susie thought they were going to stop at the *Alpha Coffee House*, which was now a forlorn boarded up building. Nothing had been decided on what to do with the building since the shootings.

There were numerous bunches of flowers and cards propped up outside its doors and it had become a place of pilgrimage for those who had lost loved ones, but also a place for the morbid and macabre vultures who seemed to be fascinated with death to congregate.

The vehicle slowed but did not stop. It turned into a side street and then began making a series of turns into other cluttered streets in a residential area where double parking seemed to be the norm.

Suddenly, the Range Rover pulled over and Tony Slade eased out with a suitcase in his hand. He seemed to be in pain and finding it difficult to walk. He glanced around the street. Susie sat low in her seat.

Tony walked slowly to a parked silver Audi and she heard the click of locks opening as he pointed a key fob towards it. Tony opened the boot and dropped in the suitcase and then spent a few moments checking something else in there. From where she was positioned, Susie could not see what he was doing.

Suddenly, he slammed the boot shut and gave the thumbs up to the man in the Range Rover. Slade got awkwardly into the driver's seat of the Audi and started it up and pulled away. The Range Rover followed. After a few moments, Susie pulled away in pursuit.

Doug had spotted the Focus following them back in Clifton Village and had alerted Tony to the fact. Tony had watched from the side mirrors and recognised the features of Susie Rawlings. He had let Doug know who she was.

When he had got out to go to the Audi, the thumbs up signal was not just to confirm the bag of money was safe in the boot, but also to confirm that it was Susie Rawlings.

They now watched her behind them driving at a seemingly safe distance. She was no expert at this. But Tony and Doug, with their army training and bodyguard work, were.

Doug spoke into his vehicle's radio system, which was connected to his phone by Bluetooth.

"Okay, Tony. We take her to the motorway and then we crank up the pace and lose her. When we get out on the main road, let me overtake you and then you follow me."

Tony confirmed that he understood.

They headed back the way they had come from Westbury on Trym to Southmead Road onto Muller Road. At the bottom at the large roundabout, they took the second exit onto the M32 motorway. They then joined the M4 for Cardiff and headed to the Severn Bridge.

As Susie joined the M4, she called Matt Sloan and informed him that she was in pursuit of Slade and heading towards Cardiff. He told her to be careful and not to do anything silly. He also told her to keep in regular phone contact. Susie asked him to let Carl Jameson know that she was on to a lead.

"You lost them. Is that what you are telling me, Jordan? Did they just vanish into thin fucking air?"

Sergeant Richmond was at the hospital reading the riot act to a rather red-faced P.C.

"It wasn't like that. They must have planned it all. The man, the girl. It was a set up to get Slade away from here."

"Too right it was a set up and you fell for it like a fucking muppet. This was an important job and you balls it up. The boss will have you directing traffic by tomorrow. If it was me…"

"Alright, Sergeant. That's enough."

D.C.I. Wyatt walked up behind Richmond.

"I think you have made your point. I will handle it from here. Go and see if anybody saw them leave the hospital or car park."

Richmond wandered off mumbling to himself.

P.C. Jordan stood waiting for another dressing down. But it never came.

Wyatt had underestimated Slade. Knowing he was ex-military, he should have realised that Slade would be cunning enough to pull this stunt. In retrospect, he should have put a more experienced officer on the job. What was done was done.

"Anything you can tell me about the couple that visited Slade? Anything that could help?"

The young policeman found it hard to look into his superior's eye. He was still smarting from the rollicking he had received.

"I think I told Sergeant Richmond all I know, Sir."

"Alright, lad. Go get a cuppa and then back to the station, okay?"

P.C. Jordan nodded and walked off dejectedly. Wyatt called after him.

"Son, we all make mistakes. It's how we bounce back from them that counts. Understand?"

Ben Jordan afforded himself a small smile.

"Thank you, Sir."

He made to walk off, but suddenly stopped.

"Sir, there was something. I don't know whether it is important or not."

Wyatt's ears pricked up.

"Let me be the judge of that, P.C. Jordan. What is it?"

"The man who got Slade out. He walked with a pronounced limp. I didn't think of it to now."

Wyatt chewed the bit of information over.

"Thank you, P.C. Jordan."

When Jordan had gone, Wyatt wandered into Slade's room. He checked around. There were no personal items left behind. His street clothes were gone, and the bedside locker was clean. No surprise.

Wyatt absently picked a couple of grapes off a bunch in a plastic punnet on the table. He was lost in his thoughts. That bastard Slade had been hiding something as suspected. The local airport and other transport stations had to been contacted. He could not afford Slade to slip out of the country.

No doubt, he was involved some way in the killings of Robbins and his goons, plus the killing of poor Barry Meyers.

They were in the process of checking CCTV footage to see if they could shed more light on Slade's visitors. They were checking out the names that they had given to P.C. Jordan.

What a fucking mess. They had no idea at this moment in time where Slade was. He had played them like fools.

Suddenly, Wyatt became aware of somebody entering the room. It was Nurse O'Neill.

"Oh, Detective Chief Inspector. I didn't realise you were in here. I can come back."

"No need, Nurse. I am just going. By the way, did you speak to Slade before he disappeared?"

Nurse O'Neill thought carefully about her answer.

"Yes, I did. He told me that at visiting time a friend of his was going to take him out for some fresh air in the grounds. I thought nothing of it. Mr Slade was well on the mend, so it was quite normal."

"Did you see this friend? Had he visited before?"

"I caught a glimpse of him, but he didn't seem familiar."

Wyatt nodded.

"Did you actually see them leave the building?"

Nurse O'Neill paused in thought for a moment.

"I did see them come out of the lift, but I was busy on reception. When I next looked, they were gone."

"Did you not think it strange that they were heading for the car park instead of the gardens around the back of the hospital?" Wyatt queried.

As she busied herself stripping the bedding, Nurse O'Neill replied.

"Not really. You can cut through the car park. It's a longer route to come around to the gardens. A lot of patients do it. Some sadly go that way to have a crafty smoke."

Wyatt walked towards the door and then stopped.

"This friend of his. You are positive you never saw him visit Slade before today? He walked with a limp."

Nurse O'Neill didn't look up from her task.

"No, Inspector. I've never seen him before, but to tell you the truth, I didn't take a lot of notice. As I mentioned, I was busy at the time."

Wyatt thought this over.

"You must have got to know Slade quite well. Did he ever mention a friend? Somebody he could trust? Did he have any regular visitors since he was in here?"

"I was his nurse, not his confidant, Inspector. He struck me as a loner."

Wyatt nodded.

"Thank you, Nurse. You have been most helpful. Goodbye."

As he came out the room, he saw Richmond walking up the corridor.

"Anything?" asked Wyatt.

"A couple of patients outside said they saw two men and then a girl climbing into a dark green Range Rover after ditching a wheelchair."

"Registration number?"

Richmond shook his head.

"Afraid not."

Wyatt cursed under his breath.

"Tell traffic to be sure to let us know if they think they spot it."

"Will do, Sir. But there is a lot of green Range Rovers out on the roads."

Wyatt regarded his Sergeant.

"True. But there is only one with Tony Slade in it. Make sure they are on it, okay?"

Richmond nodded and headed off back down the corridor. Wyatt's phone suddenly rang. He pulled it out of his pocket and looked at the screen. He saw that it was Superintendent Hardwick calling. He put the phone back in his pocket.

Bollocks. He would have to wait. He was not about to tell him just yet that Slade had done a runner and that they did not know where he was.

Susie Rawlings had managed to keep pace with both vehicles over the Severn Bridge. She had been over it many times and never failed to marvel at this incredible 1.6km long, 136m tall structure. But today, her mind was elsewhere. It was on a front-page scoop that would have her editor Carl Jameson drooling.

At the toll booths, Susie Rawlings saw both men pay and come off the bridge into South Wales. She was four cars behind. She knew that she had to be quick getting through. Otherwise, the vehicles could now come off at any of the slip grounds coming up soon.

The cars moved through slowly. The woman in the car in front was searching in her handbag for her purse. *Why the fuck did people like that not have the change ready if they were paying with cash*, thought Rawlings.

The toll booths were to be removed soon all together.

About fucking time, she mused. They had existed since the bridges opened in 1966 and the price had steadily increased over the years. Originally, a toll was charged coming into Wales and out, but in 1999, it was changed to just entering. It had always been a source of controversy and debate.

At this moment in time, Susie did not care either way as long as she got through them.

Eventually, the woman in front paid and drove off.

Armed with her credit card, Rawlings was soon through behind her. She floored the pedal and started scanning the road ahead for any sign of the Audi or the Range Rover.

Tony followed Doug as they now headed towards Newport. This was a busy stretch of road that was not helped by speed restriction signs that seemed to suddenly pop up out of nowhere, but Doug assured him it would be fine.

As they approached the Brynglas Tunnels that carries the M4 motorway under Brynglas Hill in Newport, they spotted Susie Rawlings' Focus a dozen or so cars behind.

"Tony, when we get through this tunnel, get into the outside lane as soon as possible and put your foot down. We will lose this woman before she gets out. Look for junction 29 signposted The Bay as we hit Cardiff and we come off there. Okay?"

"Yeah, I got it, Doug. Let's do it."

It was a slow drag through the tunnel, but once out the other side, both men gunned their vehicles forward. Susie Rawlings saw this, but was powerless to do anything, as she was still stuck in the slow-moving traffic of the tunnel. She cursed and hit the heel of her hand on the steering wheel. The bastards had spotted her.

When she finally got out of the tunnel, she also picked up her speed weaving in and out of traffic.

She glanced frantically around her looking for a glimpse of the two vehicles. As she passed Junction 29, she glanced across at the slip road going onto the A48 and there was the Green Range Rover and the Audi.

"Shit," she exclaimed. Susie looked back helplessly as the two cars disappeared.

She would have to drive on to the next exit and hope and pray she might find them in Cardiff city centre. Susie could not afford to lose this lead. It was too important. Slade was up to something and she was determined to find out exactly what it was.

An hour later, she was dejectedly heading back over the bridge, the trail cold. It had been like looking for a needle in a haystack. She cursed herself for not being more aware and letting Slade get the better of her.

Once she was back in the office, she told Matt Sloan what had happened. He got her a coffee and told her not to be too hard on herself, as both Slade and Jacobs had been highly trained military personnel. He also told her to relax, as Jameson was out of his office at present.

It did not really pacify her, as she knew she had let a potentially big news story slip through her fingers. As soon as Jameson found out, he would have her back covering local fetes and the opening of supermarkets.

She was determined to keep digging into the background of Tony Slade to see if she could find a clue to where he might have gone.

Andy Roth pulled the baseball cap tight down on his head and walked up the steps to a Victorian style house just of Gloucester Road. This part of Bristol was a vibrant gathering of local businesses, shops and cafes. Many students inhabited the area.

Earlier, he had seen the girl jump out of the green Range Rover that Slade had been in and get into a red Kia. Previous to this, he too had been in the hospital grounds disguised as a postal worker. A friend of his who worked in the postal service had managed to smuggle out a uniform and bag for him.

Roth had thought it would be the perfect cover to get back inside the hospital without suspicion and get to Slade again. But he had been taken off guard, as he had suddenly seen Slade with another man heading across the hospital grounds and out to the car park and get into a green Range Rover.

As part of his cover, he had parked his car a few streets away and had rode in on a bicycle, also courtesy of his friend.

As the Range Rover pulled away, Roth had jumped on the bicycle and pursued it. When it stopped to let the girl out, he decided it was a better plan to follow her, as once the Range rover got out onto the main roads, he would have no chance of keeping up with it. Maybe the girl would know where it was heading, as she seemed to be in on the plan.

He watched her go through a gateway that led to a large Victorian house. She fished out her key and entered the house. Roth waited five minutes, then headed through the gateway and across the large secluded garden and up the path. He had great natural cover. Just what he needed.

He dumped the bike in the bushes out of sight.

As he walked up the steps to the front door, he reached into his coat pocket and felt the knife he was carrying. It was a karambit. Another blade from his extensive collection. This type of knife originated in West Sumatra in Indonesia, where it is believed that the Minangkabau people modelled the first karambit after a tiger's claw.

He smiled. If the bitch knew anything, he would get it out of her.

He rang the doorbell and he heard a female voice speak through the initial crackly static of the intercom on the wall.

"Yes. What is it?"

She sounded a bit flustered.

"Postman, love. I have a letter for you that needs signing."

"Really?"

"Yes, really. Do you want it or not?" replied Roth.

There was a moment's silence and then the female voice answered.

"Okay. Keep your hair on. Give me one minute and I will be there."

Roth smiled. He reached into his pocket for a pair of surgical gloves and slipped them on and then snapped open the knife. The curled wicked looking blade glinted in the watery afternoon sunshine.

A lamb to the fucking slaughter.

Forty minutes later, Roth reappeared from the flat. He checked that the coast was clear. He then got onto the bike he had left concealed in the front garden and pedalled away out of the gateway.

He was still in a state of arousal from killing the girl.

She had tried to put up a fight, but she had been no match for him.

Once he had pushed her into the flat and she realised why he was there, she had tried to run to the kitchen and escape through the back door, but Roth had caught her by the hair and dragged her to the floor.

She was feisty enough initially to try and kick out at him, but a couple of well executed punches to her face and body had taken the wind out of her sails. He had produced some cord from his pocket and tightly secured her wrists and stuffed a dishcloth in her mouth. Once this was done, he moved to the living room and removed all his clothes.

He returned to the kitchen completely naked. He did not want any blood or DNA on his clothes.

When he had straddled her body and pressed the knife to her throat, he could see the terror in her eyes. He then removed the gag after warning her not to scream and asked her where Slade was heading. She stupidly denied knowing anything.

Roth then clamped a hand over her mouth as he proceeded to sever through her left ear. During this vicious maiming, her muffled screams soon turned to pleading for him to stop and then she spilled the beans about where Slade and the other man were heading.

She had told him that they were heading for Cardiff Bay and the man driving was named Doug Jacobs, but she did not know any more than that.

The knife cutting around both her nipples did not change her story, so Roth guessed that she was telling the truth.

Roth had thanked her. She was a sexy young thing and it had turned him on when she pleaded for him not to hurt her.

She swore that she would not tell anybody about what had happened, but unfortunately, he knew she was lying to save her life. She would be straight on the phone as soon as he left. He could not afford that.

He had helped her to her feet with soothing and reassuring words of comfort and had then spun her around quickly and moved behind her.

The knife had been brutally efficient in slitting her soft white throat open. The huge arterial blood spray had completely missed him and covered the kitchen wall.

He noticed most of the blood had shot over a large film poster of Jason Vorhees, the masked killer of the Friday 13th films. How fucking ironic, he mused.

Roth then let her limp body drop to the floor and he stayed long enough to watch transfixed as the light went out of her eyes. He always enjoyed that moment.

He had been careful. He was clean apart from the gloves which he had stuffed in his empty letter sack. He would dispose of them in due course.

Roth went upstairs and showered thoroughly and dressed before leaving the flat.

Roth now had to return to the hospital and retrieve his car. It was pointless heading to the Severn Bridge and into Wales. The trail was cold for now. He would wait and track down this Doug Jacobs. He would lead him to Slade.

Doug and Tony pulled their vehicles into an underground car park just off Cardiff Bay. The rest of the journey into Cardiff had been without incident. They had lost the reporter.

Doug now informed Tony to take everything out of his car, as he was going to have to leave it here.

When this was done, Doug took the keys and told Tony a contact would come to pick it up later and he would store it somewhere for him for now.

Tony opened the holdall that contained somewhere near £250,000 pounds and counted out some money for Doug. In his other hand was a suitcase with all his worldly possessions now in it.

The men walked to Mermaid Quay, the busiest and most vibrant part of the Bay.

Doug knew Cardiff well and had been there many times. As they walked along, he pointed out well known landmarks amongst all the cafes, restaurants and bars.

The imposing Millennium Centre. A key cultural and physical landmark, first opened in 2004. It hosted a wide range of performances from ballet to comedy and musicals.

They walked along the Roald Dahl Plas. The former oval basin dock was now a 10,000-capacity outdoor public entertainment area.

As they walked along the waterside of the docks, Tony spied a large impressive red brick building. He asked Doug what it was.

Doug informed him that it was the Pierhead, a historic Grade One listed building that was built in 1897. Its large clock on the front was unofficially known as the Welsh Big Ben. The Pierhead was once the focal point of commerce in Wales, but now it was a museum and venue for live discussion and debate.

Tony smiled.

"How the fuck do you know all this shit, Doug?"

Doug laughed.

"I had a lot of time on my hands when I was recuperating from losing my damn leg."

"So, where are we heading?" enquired Tony.

Doug pointed.

"We are here. That boat over there is going to take you to your new home. Let me introduce you to the skipper and ex-para Joe Williams. He is a sound guy and knows not to ask any questions. He lives on Graig o Mor. He runs a commercial boat touring business and a corporate fishing boat.

That is his fishing boat. The beam trawler over there. *Gipsy of the Waves*. It will sail you over to the island. It will take approximately an hour to get there.

Use your cover identity that we sorted. From now on, you are Tony Swan. Your passport, credit cards all say the same.

If your story has reached the island through the papers or fucking carrier pigeon, nobody will suspect you.

This is where I say goodbye for now, my friend. I have organised a cosy little Fisherman's cottage for you to stay in. Basic but functional. Itis stocked with food and drink. Plus, a bottle of Jack Daniels to keep the chill out. You rest up and recuperate.

Joe will fill you in on island life and anything else you need. He doesn't know your story, but he is a trusted and loyal friend to me. He will help you in any way he can."

Tony embraced his friend.

"I can't thank you enough, Doug. I don't know how I will ever be able to repay your kindness."

"You just get well for now and keep your head down. I am sure I will think of some way you can repay me in the future. Maybe we both get a holiday on a tropical island paradise sometime."

Tony nodded.

He felt a slight tugging on his emotions as he thought of Annette and their plans to disappear to foreign parts. He pushed the memory away.

"Will you be okay if the police come sniffing? You know they will."

Doug clapped his hand down onto his friend's shoulder.

"Don't you worry. I can handle them. No problem. Remember, Tony. Don't go back to Cardiff. Stay on the island for now. I am pretty sure you will be safe, but best not to take any chances. Now take this."

Jacobs handed Tony a pay as you go phone.

"I have one also. It's a burner. If you don't use it regularly, it will be almost impossible to trace. My number is already in yours. We can keep in contact safely with these."

Tony nodded.

"I understand."

"Here. Take this as well. You may need it."

Doug passed Tony a plastic bag.

"I have another contact in a pharmacy. In the bag is medication, painkillers and fresh dressings to help you in the short term."

It felt heavy.

Tony stole a glimpse inside and amongst the medication, he saw a Sig Sauer p226 automatic handgun with three ammo clicks.

"I don't know if I should take this, Doug. The last handgun I fired nearly cost me my life and then my liberty."

"I understand, my friend, but if this Roth character finds you, he won't be coming with a fucking pea shooter, so keep it for insurance. If you don't use it in the end, dump it in the sea."

"Okay. Thanks, Doug."

Tony stored the bag into his holdall. Doug nodded in satisfaction.

"Right then, let me introduce you to Joe. The sooner you are on the high seas, the better I will feel."

"Okay, let's do it."

Both men headed towards the boat.

The trip took around fifty-five minutes. Tony had found Joe easy to get on with. Their army back ground was a common link.

The island suddenly appeared out of nowhere. It looked grey and foreboding. Tony felt the first drops of rain on his head.

"Fucking great. That is really going to lighten my mood," he muttered to himself.

The boat eased its way to a harbour at the bottom of the rugged cliffs. Joe threw out a rope towards the dockside.

"Welcome to Graig o Mor, Tony."

Tony surveyed the bleak surroundings that were to be his home for a while. He didn't feel infused by what he saw.

PART TWO

Chapter Thirteen

Present Day (six months since Tony Slade's disappearance)

D.C.I. John Wyatt looked up from his computer screen. He took off his reading glasses and placed them on the desk. He then rubbed the palms of his hands into his eyes. He was tired.

He had an ever-increasing case load to deal with. Increasing knife crime. Moped riding muggers and the still unsolved murder of a young woman, a Daisy Archer, which was high on his agenda. The murder was still another tangible link to Mr Tony Slade. The case still haunted him.

This deceased girl had turned out to be the girl that had helped Tony Slade with an unknown man to leave the hospital and transport the bastard away somewhere. He was still frustrated that the trail of Tony Slade had gone stone cold.

After Slade had disappeared from the hospital, he had gone to his one and only lead, Doug Jacobs. The man Slade had told him he had originally come to Bristol to see on a promise of a job.

He had suspected Jacobs was the mystery man Brian Eccles at the hospital, as the real Mr Eccles had died ten years ago. He had also found out Jacobs had a prosthetic leg and definitely walked with a limp, just like the mysterious Mr Eccles.

He had tried to find a link between the dead girl and Jacobs, but with no success. He could not match a green Range Rover to him and the hospital CCTV had been inconclusive.

Jacobs was a slippery bastard.

They had asked him into the station twice for questioning and both times, he came in voluntarily. He had answered all their questions and denied knowing anything about where Slade was. He had gone on to say that he and Slade had been army buddies and he liked to help men that had left the forces with work if he could, but apart from that, he and Slade had not been that close.

Jacobs had told him that he had gone to visit Tony once in hospital, as up to then, he thought he was dead. But apart from the previous job offer, he did not really know Slade that well.

He also stated, just as Nurse O'Neill had observed, that Slade was a loner and liked to play his cards close to his chest.

They had to let Jacobs go. They just did not have any evidence to arrest him or any concrete links to Jacobs and Slade being more than casual friends.

As Jacobs had told them, he was well known for helping many ex-army comrades down on their luck. In some circles, people thought Jacobs was a fucking saint.

Any major transfer links out of the country had no recent reports of Slade or anybody like him. The D.C.I. felt that Slade was still in the country.

One positive bit of news was that they had come up trumps with an ID on the man who had murdered the security guard in the hospital. It had come from Teresa Wicks.

The name they came up with was an Andrew Roth. He had a string of offences that made interesting reading. He was one dangerous fucker. The icing on the cake had been when they passed his ID on to D.C.I. Burton in Newcastle. He confirmed that he was a known associate of the late decreased Kenny Robbins. Bingo, they had the connection.

But like Slade, this Roth character had seemed to have vanished off the radar.

Wyatt was now convinced that Roth was the man who had also murdered this Daisy Archer. Roth had somehow tracked her down in the hope that she would tell him the whereabouts of Slade.

He had gone to Jacobs with this evidence to see his reaction, but he had not flinched. He still maintained that he knew nothing.

Wyatt's final word to Jacobs was that if he did have a connection to this murder, then he should be a worried man. As Wyatt pointed out, he presumed Roth would also be coming for him. He thought he had seen a flicker of emotion in Jacobs' eyes, but it had quickly passed.

Wyatt had his sergeant keep an eye on Jacobs. They watched the premises of his import/export business by Avonmouth Docks and his home address at Stoke Bishop. But up to now, he had not done anything out of the ordinary and Roth had not come looking for him either.

The Police knew that Slade had driven over the Severn Bridge and towards Cardiff, but then they had lost his trail.

Wyatt realised the key to solving Slade's whereabouts was in Cardiff, but he needed Jacobs to lead him to Slade.

But after all this promising progress, things had again ground to a halt and hopes petered out.

There was no sign of Slade or Roth and no movement from Jacobs. It was frustrating.

Superintendent Hardwick had not been happy with the whole mess and had read Wyatt the riot act.

After months of fruitless searching for both men, Hardwick told Wyatt in no uncertain terms that two unsolved murders in the city was not good enough and he was taking increasing pressure from above. If they did not get a break in the case soon, heads would roll and Wyatt's was first on the block.

Hardwick told him that he could not guarantee any spare manpower to watch Jacobs around the clock, as they did not have any evidence that he was involved with hiding Slade.

That was it in Hardwick's book. He was getting pressure to clamp down on the increasing spate of muggings from youngsters on mopeds and solve two teenage gang-related stabbings. Plus, Bristol was soon due a visit from Prince Harry and he could not afford money for wild goose chases.

Reluctantly, Wyatt had to let the search go for now, but he and Sergeant Richmond were still determined to find Slade and learn what really happened in the *Alpha Coffee House* and his link to the deceased Kenny Robbins.

Since Slade had landed in Bristol, it had been one bloodbath after another and Wyatt would not rest until he got answers, even if it meant doing it on his own time.

The case remained open, but it was in danger of being swallowed up and forgotten. And new crimes were being committed every day, which meant that Wyatt's case load was getting huge. He needed to get results and his obsession with the Slade case was not going to help his cause.

Hardwick was breathing down his neck to get a result on recent cases and using veiled threats that the files on Slade would become a cold case and assigned to another division as he had seemed to come to a dead end.

Susie Rawlings sipped her cappuccino and looked at her laptop screen. She was sat in a branch of *Costa* in the city centre.

She had needed to get out of the office and away from Matt Sloan and his lunchtime habits. He was the only person that made eating a pulled pork and salad wrap an x-rated experience.

She decided to work from the coffee shop for a few hours.

Susie was working on a breaking story about a sex scandal in a local school between a fifteen-year-old pupil and his thirty something French teacher. It was a juicy enough piece to be involved in, but she was still frustrated that she had not got that one big front-page scoop that would have had the London tabloids clambering for her services.

The Tony Slade case still haunted her.

After she lost the Range Rover that day just over the Severn Bridge, she had drove on into Cardiff on more than one occasion and roamed the city centre in the hope that she might see Slade. But it had been like looking for a needle in a haystack and she knew it. He seemed to have disappeared off the face of the earth.

She had then contacted D.C.I. Wyatt and put him in the picture that she thought Slade was somewhere in Wales. Wyatt had been grateful for the lead and promised to keep her in the loop if anything came of it.

Not long after this, she was called to help on a story of the murder of a girl named Daisy Archer. She recognised the girl from somewhere and it was not long until she realised it was the girl from the hospital that had helped Tony Slade get out of the place. Her brutal murder just could not be a coincidence. It had to be linked.

She mentioned this to her colleague writing the piece, Gerry Smart, but he did not seem to be concerned about her observations and was more interested in getting his name on the front page.

Susie went to her editor Carl Jameson. He asked her if she was sure that it was the same girl and she told him that she was. Jameson asked her to dig into some background on the girl, which she did. She was then instructed to give it over to Gerry Smart, so he could write up a follow-up piece.

Susie had argued with Jameson that she should write it because it was her initial observation and then her follow-up work, but he would not listen, spouting something about Smart being more experienced and not prone to fuck ups.

Jameson still seemed to harbour a grudge towards her after losing the trail on Slade months ago and she knew she had been fortunate not to be back writing gardening tips and recipes.

It was common knowledge in the office that Jameson and Smart were also sleeping together. She could not compete with that. Nor did she want to.

Susie now looked out of the window. It was a grey Thursday. Light splashes of rain marked the window. She was in a rut. Her life had seemed to have stalled. Whilst Jameson was editor at the *West Country Express*, she was not going anywhere and there has not been any better offers.

Her private life was no better. There was no man in her life since Adam two years previously. She really thought he was the one until she came home early from a weekend seminar and found him in bed with her flatmate Holly. They were both sent packing.

After that, Susie could not be bothered with another relationship, so a bottle of Chardonnay each evening and the company of her cat Oscar was all she had to look forward to going home to.

She was twenty-seven years old and had nothing concrete to show for it. Except for an ever- increasing credit card bill and waistline.

Her mother and father were disappointed in her. She had left the family home in Worcester at seventeen years of age with such high hopes.

Now look at your brother Graham. Her parents would remind her on a regular basis about what a successful businessman he was, owning three of his own health food stores.

Well, fuck Graham and his wheatgerm, raspberry ketones and fucking turmeric tablets.

Suddenly, her mobile rang and brought her back to reality. She saw the name on the screen. It was D.C.I. John Wyatt calling.

Puzzled, she pressed answer.

"Hello."

"Miss Rawlings. This is D.C.I. Wyatt. I would like to meet you and have a little chat, if possible."

"Detective Chief Inspector. It's been a while. May I ask what about? This is all a little unexpected."

"Yes, it is a bit, I suppose. It's about Tony Slade."

An hour later, she sat in a corner booth in a wine bar named Ziggy's just off Whiteladies Road in Clifton. She sipped a glass of Australian chardonnay. Opposite her sat D.C.I. Wyatt nursing a single malt scotch.

"Well, Inspector. How can I help you? I haven't heard the name Tony Slade for a while. Are you still interested in him?"

"Are you, Miss Rawlings?" answered Wyatt.

Susie smiled.

"Let's say he is still on my mind."

It was now Wyatt's turn to smile.

"Mine to."

Wyatt leant forward.

"What I am going to tell you now is strictly off the record and if you breathe a word of it to anybody or print a word of it, I will have your ass locked up in a jiffy. Understand?"

Susie Rawlings nodded. She was intrigued and she felt a tingle of excitement in her stomach. Wyatt continued.

"My superior told me to ease off the Slade case as there were more pressing issues to deal with. The prick is even threatening to assign it as a cold case. But I can't rest until I find that bastard Slade. I need to know the truth about what really happened in the *Alpha Coffee House*.

I also believe the murder of Daisy Jones is connected in some way. She was the girl in the Range Rover that got Slade out of the hospital. My theory is that her killer was the same man who came to the hospital looking for Slade and ended up murdering the security guard. I will get on to that matter in a minute."

Susie Rawlings listened intently to what Wyatt told her.

"I am inclined to agree with you, Detective Chief Inspector. I wanted to pursue the story, but it has been taken away from me by my dick of an editor. I feel as frustrated as you. So, how can I help?"

Wyatt took a sip of his whisky.

"Well, it looks like we are both in the same boat, doesn't it? I feel if we join forces, so to speak ,then we can keep this thing alive and pick up the trail again. On our own, I don't think we are going to get the time or opportunity."

"So, what are you proposing?"

Wyatt put his empty glass down on the table.

"I want you to keep a watch on my only lead to Slade and that is Doug Jacobs. He is an old army buddy of Slade's and I believe he was the driver of the Range Rover. I have got nothing on him, and he is a clever fucker, but I think he can eventually lead us to Slade's whereabouts.

It has been nearly six months since Slade went to ground, but I believe he is still in this country and if I am right, I would imagine the dust has settled enough for him to maybe come out of hiding and contact Jacobs or the other way around."

He slid a card across the table to Susie.

"His home and business addresses are on there. When you think that you can keep an eye on him, let me know. I will do the same for you. My sergeant is also in on this. I think between the three of us we can catch Jacobs out."

Susie finished off her wine.

"Okay, we have a deal. But if you unearth anything from this, I want an exclusive from you, okay?"

"Deal."

They both got up from the table and shook hands.

"By the way," said Wyatt, "We are not the only people after Slade. There is a man called Andy Roth. He was one of Kenny Robbins' enforcers. He has a long history of violent crime. Word from the North says he has gone rogue and is out for vengeance. I believe he is the killer of the security guard and the girl Daisy Jones."

Wyatt reached in his inside coat pocket and took out a photograph which he handed to Rawlings. She regarded it.

"He looks a right charmer."

"No, Miss Rawlings. He is a killer and fucking dangerous. If you come across his path whilst watching Jacobs, stay well clear and contact me. Do you understand? There has been enough death around here recently."

Susie Rawlings put the photo into her handbag.

"'I understand, Inspector."

Just then, Wyatt's phone went off.

He took it out of his pocket and looked at the screen.

"I must take this, Miss Rawlings. We will keep in touch, okay?"

Susie nodded and left the wine bar.

Wyatt sat back down. The call coming in was from D.I. Tom Burton up in Newcastle.

"Tom, how are you? What have you got for me?"

Tom Burton's rough Geordie voice sounded excited.

"Well, John. I have been doing a bit more digging and I have come up with some interesting stuff."

Wyatt also felt a tingle of excitement.

"Okay, Tom. Let's have it."

"Right. Firstly, I found out that Robbins' business empire was just about to be taken over by a Dutchman named Bergkemp. But when Robbins was murdered, he got cold feet and headed back to Holland double quick. He's clean.

At present, two of Robbins' old hands, Danny Ewan and Joe Walsh, are keeping things running. Everybody up here involved in Robbins' business interests are keeping quiet, but I have a contact on the street that knows the word out there. I couldn't locate him earlier as he has been in hospital with pneumonia, but he is out now and on the mend."

Wyatt coughed impatiently.

"So, what did he tell you, Tom?"

Burton sensed the impatience in his colleague's voice.

"Apparently, both are not happy that Roth has gone rogue. They warned him not to go looking for Slade, but he ignored it. They have put a couple of right lunatics onto finding him. The McQueen brothers. If they catch up with Roth, there is going to be a fucking bloodbath. But at present, Roth now seems to have disappeared himself.

This all confirms your theory that Slade knew Roth, which points to your suspicions that Slade was working for Robbins all along and he knows what happened in that coffee house."

"Any idea where this Roth character is now?" asked Wyatt.

"No, John. It's a mystery. Something must have interrupted his plans."

"The McQueen brothers catch up with him?"

Burton thought for a moment.

"It's a possibility, but I think we would have heard. But my guess is that he not going to give up his search and will probably appear back down your way soon. If he murdered that young girl Daisy whatshername you told me about, then I reckon she would have told him where Slade was heading before dying."

Wyatt thought this over.

"You just might be right. Thanks, Tom. Keep in touch if you find out anything more. You have been most helpful. Next time I am up in Newcastle, I owe you a drink."

"Oh right. Cheers, John. Are you planning to come up anytime soon?"

D.C.I Wyatt smiled to himself before answering.

"No."

He hung up before he could hear Burton's response.

Wyatt suddenly was in a better mood. At last something had shifted in his favour. He felt new optimism in this case. A young female member of the bar staff passed his table.

"Would you like another, Sir?"

She pointed to his empty glass.

Wyatt handed it to her.

"You know what? I think I will. Single malt whisky please."

146

Andy Roth sat in a motorway service station just outside Birmingham. It was late evening. In front of him was a cold cup of tea. He watched the two men sat across the cafeteria area from him. They pretended not to be interested in him, but Roth knew better.

In recent times, wherever he had been, he had saw a black Range Rover with these two clowns in it. They had been trailing him since he had first visited Bristol some months ago when he came looking for Tony Slade.

He was sure that Danny Ewan and Joe Walsh had put them onto him. Surveillance to make sure he did not do anything crazy.

They must think he was a right Muppet. Fuck them all. Andy Roth answered to nobody. His place was already guaranteed in hell.

After killing the girl in her flat, he was all set to hunt down this Doug Jacobs, but he had received a phone call from Ewan. Roth expected it to be a message for him to get his ass back up to Newcastle as he needed a serious word with him, but instead it was unexpected news.

In Roth's life, he did give a fuck about anyone. Robbins had been an exception and the only other person being his dear old mum, Sheila.

Growing up, his mum was the only person to try and help him. She had always been there for him, even when he habitually got in trouble. At school, the kids would bully Roth, calling his mum a tart and a whore. This made Roth mad and he would fight everybody and anybody who said anything wrong about her. This resulted in him being expelled from more than one school and eventually leaving altogether after the dining hall stabbing. Gradually, he then drifted into a life of crime.

His mum was now eighty-five years old and had been in a nursing home for the last five years. Roth visited when he could and helped pay her bills. He owed her a lot.

The phone call had told him to come home as she was dying. Immediately, Roth shelved his plans for Slade and went back to Newcastle. His mum had hung on for four weeks and passed away in her sleep with Roth sat at her bedside.

The funeral was a cheap burial with a handful of mourners. Roth knew none of them and left immediately after. He then had to stay in Newcastle to tie up some legal paperwork, which had stalled his plans for Slade.

Joe Walsh and Danny Ewan had asked to see him. They offered him their condolences, but Roth knew why they really wanted to speak to him.

Walsh had told him once again to ease off looking for Slade. The firm was now ready to act and find him. They added that when Slade was found, Roth could be in on it when the time came, but they could not and would not allow some one-man revenge mission to go on. They let Roth know if he continued his lone search that they would not be responsible for the consequences. Roth thanked them for their candour and left.

As soon as he had gone, Walsh got on the phone to Eddie McQueen and his brother Billy. When Roth had decided to go back up North, their services were no longer needed. But now Walsh told them to come back to the UK and resume the tail on Roth. If they suspected for one minute that he was back on the trail of Tony Slade, they were advised to do away with him discreetly.

Roth was a fucking liability and always had been. He had only stayed connected to the firm because Robbins liked him. Nobody else did, especially not Joe Walsh. In his opinion, Roth was a complete headbanger and a law onto himself. He crossed swords with Roth a few years back when he started showing an unhealthy interest in his sixteen-year-old daughter.

It could have got nasty, except that Kenny Robbins had stepped in and smoothed it over, sending Roth to Cumbria to look after a few of his business interests up there. When Roth returned to Newcastle, the incident seemed to be forgotten. But Walsh had stored it away for a rainy day. Now, that day was coming fast.

The McQueen brothers were not much better than Roth, but he could not afford anything coming back to him. In the wake of Robbins' death, the firm were receiving too much interest from all quarters. He needed to smooth a pathway and take the heat off before tracking down Slade.

If Roth was a problem, that needed to be sorted. He did not want to be within a hundred miles of it. The McQueens would do a good job and disappear back to Spain. Nothing could be traced back to him or the firm.

Roth got up from the table and headed for the exit. As soon as he went out into the car park, the McQueen brothers got up and followed him.

Roth had booked into the Travelodge opposite the motorway services. It had been a long drive down and now he needed sleep. He would pay this Doug Jacobs character a visit tomorrow. He had found his business online. *Jacobs' Enterprises*. He looked forward to calling on him.

Roth carried a brown leather holdall. In it was a change of clothes, wash kit and some tools of his trade, which he would be introducing to Jacobs very soon. It would not be long before he found out where that bastard Slade was hiding.

In the meantime, he had to deal with the two pricks that were following him.

The McQueen brothers watched Roth go into the hotel.

"Let him book in and then we will get a room too," said Eddie.

Eddie was two years older than his brother. He was a big man. He stood 6ft 4ins and weighed around 110kg of steroid-induced muscle. He had short blonde hair and was ruggedly handsome.

Billy nodded in acknowledgement.

He was shorter than Eddie and built like a pitbull. His 96kg were also the product of long hours humping iron in the gym. His head was shaven, but he sported a large, bushy trademark beard.

Roth looked out of the window of his room. It overlooked the car park. He saw the two men walking across it heading for the entrance. He smiled to himself. If these boys wanted trouble, they had come to the right place.

He studied them. They were both big fuckers, but Roth's blade would cut them down to size.

He noticed that they both wore long heavy overcoats, no doubt concealing hardware of their own.

Roth moved to the bed and unzipped his bag that sat on it.

The McQueen brothers wondered into the reception of the hotel. In a loud enough voice so that the young girl behind the desk could hear, Billy said, "Where the hell has he gone? Typical. Leaving us with the luggage. I bet he has booked in already, lazy bugger."

Both men walked up to the counter. The girl at reception was no older than eighteen and was more than intimidated by these two big men.

"Excuse me, love. Has our mate booked in already? Dark hair, goatee?"

The girl, whose name was Penny, became a bit flustered by the abruptness of the man with the thick Glaswegian tone.

"You mean the guy who came in five minutes ago?"

She looked at the card that the man had signed when he had paid cash.

"Mr Smith?"

"That's him, love. What room is he in? We have some of his belongings here."

Penny looked at the card again.

"He is in room 120."

Eddie smiled.

"Have you a room nearby?"

Penny now checked her computer screen.

"We have 115 free. Is that suitable?"

"Spot on, sweetheart. We will take it. How much?" asked Billy.

"£85."

Billy drew out a roll of notes and peeled off the right amount. Penny took the money and asked Billy to fill in a card. He signed them in as Mr Cannon and Mr Ball. Penny did not seem to notice. Probably too young to make the connection with two comedians from the '80s. She was just glad when they took the room card and moved to the lifts.

The McQueen brothers stood outside room 120. They looked up and down the corridor. It was empty both ways. Eddie pulled a machete out from under his coat. Billy did the same.

"Right, how do you want to play this?" asked Eddie.

"Straight forward element of surprise, I think. Kick the fucking door in, do the bastard and leave."

Eddie chuckled.

"Sounds like a plan. Just be careful. This Roth character is meant to be a bit tasty."

"Fuck him. He is no match for us."

Out of instinct, Eddie tried the door handle and to his surprise, he found the door on the latch. He exchanged looks with his brother.

"Right, nice and steady," he whispered, "This could be a set up."

He pushed the door wide open and scanned the room. The curtains were pulled, and the lights were not on. This made the interior of the room dark and shadowy. The lighting was operated by the room key card and it was not in the electricity slot. The men heard the shower running and the bathroom door was shut.

They moved into the room cautiously. It appeared empty.

Eddie and Billy now nodded at the bathroom door and moved in front of it. Billy again nodded and Eddie kicked the door in. They both moved into the bathroom like a pair of marauding lions.

Billy ripped back the shower curtains and raised his machete in readiness to strike. He found the shower cubicle was empty. For a moment, both men were confused. That was long enough for Roth to spring out of the wardrobe.

He was completely naked. In his right hand, he brandished a jet-black Fairbairn-Sykes World War Two commando dagger, which he drove with pinpoint accuracy into Eddie's left kidney, sinking the blade up to the hilt. The big man howled in pain and fell into the shower.

Billy tried to react, but Roth was too fast for him. He plunged his blade into the man's jugular vein and carotid artery.

Billy dropped to his knees clawing at his neck. Blood fountained towards the ceiling. He was seconds from death, but it did not stop Roth from driving the blade again, this time through his right eye, penetrating his brain.

Billy dropped face first to the tiled floor, which was now awash with blood.

Eddie gamely tried to pull himself out of the shower, but it was slippery with blood. Roth was on him in a flash and viciously pulled back the big man's blonde hair.

"You pair of sad wankers. Did you think you could take me? Not a fucking chance. You are both amateurs," he snarled in his ear.

Roth then drove his blade through one side of Eddie's neck and out the other before pulling the blade forward to sever his windpipe. It was pure execution style, just like a commando. Roth liked that.

It was over. Both men were dead.

Roth washed his hands and the blade in the wash basin. Then, he calmly repacked his bag and rummaged through both men's coat pockets until he found their room key. He also found a Browning automatic which he threw into his bag.

Guns were not his thing, but he felt that he might just need it when he caught up with Slade.

He glanced at the two bodies and then left shutting the door behind the carnage and hanging up the Do Not Disturb sign.

Roth slipped into room 115 and enjoyed a long hot shower, using up all the free shower gel. He put on clean clothes and shoes. He had no bloody clothes to get rid of. Once done, he left.

Walking through reception, Penny called out to him.

"Excuse me, Mr Smith. Did your friends catch up with you?"

Roth carried on walking, not breaking his stride.

"Yes, pet. They certainly did."

He walked across to his car, dumped the luggage in the boot and drove out of the car park, gunning the car towards the South West. This was it now. His final chance to find the elusive Tony Slade.

Chapter Fourteen

Doug Jacobs left his business premises around 6.00pm.
He glanced across the road and saw the blue Fiesta
parked exactly where it had been parked yesterday and
the day before that. He knew it belonged to the news
reporter Susie Rawlings. She had been watching him on
and off now for weeks. If it was not her watching, it
was the two coppers that had pulled him in several
times for questioning.

They were all wasting their time. There was no way
he would lead them to Tony, and he was not planning
on a trip out to Graig o Mor any time soon. Doug was
too smart for that.

It was several months since he had helped Tony
escape.

Tony was nearly back to full fitness and his days on
the island were numbered. Once he was well enough to
get on a long-haul flight, then that would be it over.

Doug was then planning to sell up his own
business and head to the States. Over the last few
years, he had made some good contacts out there
and was ready for a new life in the land of the free
with his wife Sarah. They had married earlier in
the year and honeymooned in New York and it was
there that they had fallen in love with the American
way of life.

Sarah was his rock and he knew she had put up with his wheeling and dealing ways. It was time to now give her a better life.

Their romance had first blossomed when she was his physiotherapist after he lost his leg in a landmine accident in Northern Ireland. Many friends of Doug told him how dreadful the landmine incident was, but Doug assured them that he got out the luckiest. The other three men with him were killed.

Sarah had helped his recovery. Without her, he may not have made it. They had been inseparable ever since.

He smiled as he thought of her. Maybe he would ring her and take her out for a meal tonight. As he opened his car door, he waved towards Susie Rawlings and then slid into the driver's seat.

Susie Rawlings watched Jacobs drive off in the red BMW. She cursed him under her breath. *Cocky bastard.* She had been watching him now on and off for weeks and he had not put a foot out of place. Susie smiled wryly at her little pun.

It was now getting tiring and frustrating watching him. It looked like Slade had well and truly disappeared. Every time she was ready to give up, D.C.I. Wyatt would persuade her to go on a few more weeks.

There had been a time when she had been desperate for this story, but now her enthusiasm was waning. The long hours of surveillance were beginning to affect her work and the surveillance did not pay her bills; her job at the *West Country Express* did and she was clinging onto her job by her fingernails. Furthermore, her boss,

Carl Jameson, was after her blood for some below par journalistic writing.

She watched the taillights of Jacobs' car disappear. She took out her mobile and rang D.C.I. Wyatt. He answered after two rings.

"Well, anything, Susie? Tell me you have something for me."

Susie sighed.

"Sorry, John. Nothing. He just isn't doing anything out of the ordinary. Plus, he still knows he is being watched."

"Shit," exclaimed Wyatt, "All these weeks and we have fucking nothing. It's like Slade has disappeared in a puff of smoke. I have worked some hard cases in my time but this one is a bitch.

I am running out of ideas myself. I was sure Jacobs would make a mistake and lead us to Slade. He could be anywhere by now. My contacts around the UK have come up with nobody matching his description and there hasn't been any credit card trail."

"I know, John. Maybe we should just accept this and call it a day. What do you say?"

There was silence at the other end of the phone.

Wyatt and Susie were now on first name terms and had been for a while due to a drunken and desperate night a week ago, which saw them end up in bed together. It was a mistake and they knew it. After all, Wyatt was old enough to be her dad.

But on that lonely night, they had both succumbed to the need to be with another and just hold each other for a few hours and forget about the job and the shit that went with it. Anything had been better than returning home to their empty houses.

Wyatt suddenly broke the silence.

"I can't, Susie. I am near to retirement and if I don't crack this case, it will haunt me to my grave. If you wish to pull out, I understand and there will be no hard feelings, but I am going to keep going."

Susie felt a flutter of emotion once again for the policeman.

"Maybe I can also spare another few weeks then."

"Good girl. Now go home and get some sleep."

"Goodnight, John."

She hung up.

Susie sat for a long time in the darkness of her car thinking about her life and her waning ambition to be that big newspaper reporter covering the major stories. Somewhere, her career had stalled and now she was a little lost. But she did have to admit that the Slade case did still intrigue her and she would hate it if in a few months' time, somebody else broke the case and grabbed the story. She decided to give it another while and pray they got a break.

Finally, she started her car engine and begun driving for home.

Doug had rung Sarah three times without success. He was not overly worried as she may be in the shower or nipped out to the local shops. He had decided to go out for dinner after all. He was guilty of working long hours and it had been a while since they had dined out together.

Sarah understood his need to work. He was the exception to the rule when it came to success in business after leaving the forces.

He had done remarkably well over the years and that was why he started up his unofficial 'help the ex-army' side-line. Doug wanted to give something back and help men that now felt surplus to requirement and worthless gain some pride and purpose once more. Some of his methods were not exactly by the book, but his intentions were good.

As he battled the rush hour traffic, he thought of Tony Slade. They spoke regularly on their burner phones and he knew he was doing alright.

He was coping with the sea air and the laid-back life on the island, but as Doug well knew, Tony was a military man at heart and one of life's travellers. He could not stay in one place for long and he was beginning to get itchy feet.

Both men knew it was only a matter of time. If the police and press kept digging, it would dawn on them to check the islands off the coast of Wales.

They had been lucky up to now. Tony had done well keeping a low profile, but as they say, all good things come to an end.

Doug was thinking of asking his old friend if he fancied going to the States with him.

He turned on the radio and the sound of Bruce Springsteen's *Born to Run* filled the car. He grinned to himself. Very appropriate.

As he neared his street, he tried phoning Sarah again but still with no luck. As Doug pulled up in front of his home, he saw Sarah's white Volkswagen Golf in the drive, but there were no lights on in the house.

He found that unsettling and suddenly, he had a bad feeling wash over him. He rang her phone again and once more, it went to answerphone. He spoke on the beep.

"Hi, love. If you are there, pick up, will you? I just want to know if you are okay."

He parked his car next to the Golf and got out. He surveyed the front of his house. All seemed as it should, but the lack of lights on inside bothered him.

His old army training kicked in. He may have an artificial leg, but he was still a fucking handful for anybody. He went to the boot of the car and pulled out an aluminium baseball bat that he kept wrapped up in an old coat. It was there for emergencies.

Doug opened the front door of his house and entered the hallway.

"Sarah, are you home?" he called.

His voice seemed overly loud in the silence of the house. All he heard in reply was the ticking of the grandfather clock. A present for his sixtieth birthday from Sarah. He had always wanted one.

Doug went through to the lounge, then the kitchen and out to the utility room, but there was no sign of Sarah. He came back into the hall and that was when he heard a floorboard creak over head from their bedroom. He went to the foot of the stairs and called Sarah's name again, but was only greeted by silence once more.

He began to feel increasingly uneasy. He gripped the bat tightly and went up the stairs. On the landing, he looked down the hallway to the master bedroom and saw a dim light shining from under the door.

Maybe Sarah had taken a nap. She did suffer from migraines and sometimes when she slept, it was heavy, especially if she took any painkillers.

As he walked along the landing, he tried to convince himself that there would be a perfectly simple explanation for this. Doug listened outside the bedroom door. He heard nothing. He turned the door knob and eased the door open.

The bedside light was on and he immediately saw Sarah lying on the bed.

She was not asleep. Her eyes were wide open, a look of desperation and fear were in them. He quickly registered the gag around her mouth and her wrists bound.

"Sarah, what the fuck is going on?"

Doug entered the room and that was when a fist exploded out of nowhere onto his jaw. The last thing he remembered was his wife's scream before he hit the carpet and things went black.

When Doug came to, he was still lying face down on the bedroom floor. He could taste the coppery tang of blood in his mouth. He rolled over to his back and groaned as the pain in his jaw hit his senses. He was now aware that his prosthetic leg had been removed, making him virtually helpless.

Doug shuffled backwards and propped himself up against the wardrobe door. He could now see the bed and Sarah was still lying there in a state of shock.

Sat next to her was a man that he had not seen before, but his instincts told him that this was Andy Roth. The guy Tony had mentioned was coming for him. Fear gripped his belly.

The man was levelling a gun at him. His face suddenly broke into a sickly grin.

"Welcome back to the land of the living, 'Long John'. Sarah and I have missed you, haven't we, pet?"

Roth glanced at Sarah and put his arm around her. She tried to pull away, but his grip tightened on her.

"No worries, Douglas. I have kept her good company."

Doug grimaced through bloodied teeth that felt loose.

"Take your hands off her. Who are you and what do you want?"

Roth stood up and walked around the bed towards Doug, the gun still pointed towards him.

"Ah, straight to the point. I like that. My name is Roth and I am here for you to tell me were that bastard Tony Slade is hiding. Before you answer, think very carefully about what you say."

Roth reached out to the bed and picked up the baseball bat that Doug had been carrying earlier. Doug watched Roth get closer.

"Nice weight. I like a bat. Not as much as a blade though. But I don't want to get messy with blood today."

Doug's stomach tightened. He knew he was in trouble.

"So, Long John, where have you hidden him?"

"Can't help you. I haven't seen him for months. I dropped him in Cardiff and he went on his merry way. I should think he is in the Bahamas by now."

Roth smiled once more.

"Oh, Doug, I thought this was going to be a friendly discussion."

He tucked the gun into the waistband of his trousers and gripped the bat with both hands. Without warning, he brought it down sharply across Doug's collarbone. The bone broke on contact. Doug cried out in agony.

"Well, I am going to let you reconsider that answer while I go back to Sarah. If you don't come up with the right response, I am going to start using the fucking bat on her."

Sarah screamed behind her gag and tried to get up, but it was a futile attempt.

"Leave her be, you bastard. She has done nothing wrong," shouted Doug.

"You are right, my friend, . More the reason to come clean. Surely Slade doesn't mean more to you than your wife?"

Doug was desperately trying to buy time, but he knew he was in a no-win situation.

"I am telling you the truth. I don't know where he went. I haven't heard from him."

Roth moved back to the bed. He raised the bat high.

"I fucking warned you. I am not playing games. I did in that little bimbo friend of yours who drove the red Kia, so this isn't going to be a problem to me."

Doug felt a pang of sorrow and regret.

The news of Daisy had hit him hard. He had read about it in the newspapers and he had wanted to attend the funeral, but he could not expose a connection with her as he knew the police would be in attendance. He felt responsible for her death. He should not have got her involved.

Doug felt the bile rise in his throat as he looked at the scum who had brutally took her young life.

"I am going to ask you one more time. Where is Slade?"

Doug was now overwhelmed with anger.

"Fuck you, Roth," he spat.

Before Doug could finish his words, the bat dropped with a sickening thud onto his wife's left wrist. The gag on Sarah could not quite contain the blood curling scream.

Doug closed his eyes and suppressed a groan. He was helpless. He could not move. Roth raised the bat again.

"Okay. Okay. Fucking stop. I will tell you where he is. Just leave her alone, please."

Roth lowered the bat. Sarah slumped back on the bed whimpering in pain and fear. Roth moved around the bed once again to Doug. He bent down close to him. Doug could see the malevolence in his eyes.

"Well, where is he?"

Doug mumbled something incoherently, spitting blood onto the mat.

"What was that you said? I didn't catch it. Speak the fuck up."

Roth leaned in closer and that was close enough for Doug to drive the car keys he had taken unseen out of his trouser pocket into Roth's cheek.

Roth roared in pain and staggered backwards falling to the floor. The bat slipped from his hands.

"Run, Sarah! Get out of the house to a neighbour now and get the police. Go!"

Sarah staggered off the bed on unsteady legs and moved towards the door. As she passed Roth, he made a grab for her ankle, but she kicked him squarely in the face sending him sprawling backwards once more. Sarah ripped the gag from her mouth.

"What about you, Doug? Let me help you."

"No time, sweetheart. Go now. Get help."

Their eyes met and something passed between them silently. Roth was now getting to his knees. He held out the bat once more and brought it down on Doug's shin. Doug shouted out in pain.

"Run, Sarah. Fucking go or he will kill us both."

This broke the freeze that she had gone into. Sarah ran out the bedroom door and down the stairs. Before she ran to the stairs, she heard another scream and her husband shout through his obvious pain.

"Fuck you, Roth. You aren't going to find out anything from me."

She ran from the house with her hands over her ears trying to block out the screams of pain from her husband. She knew that she would never see him alive again.

D.C.I. Wyatt was sat at his desk nursing a cup of coffee deep in thought. He had just come on morning duty. He had not slept well again the previous night. The conversation with Susie Rawlings had played on his mind. Maybe he had become obsessed with the Slade case. But there were too many loose ends that needed tying up.

There was a knock on the door. This shook him out of his reverie.

"Come," he shouted.

The door opened and in came Sergeant Richmond grinning like a Cheshire cat.

"What's up with you, Steve? Got your leg over last night, did you?" quipped Wyatt.

"Yes, I did actually, but I have better news than that for you."

Wyatt sat back in his chair and clasped his hands behind his head.

"Let's have it then, son. Spit it out. I could do with some good news."

Richmond gestured to the chair in front of Wyatt's desk.

"Knock yourself out," said Wyatt.

Richmond sat down and leaned forward.

"I just passed Gary Ellis, the night duty desk sergeant. He was just knocking off. He was told the emergency services received a call last night from a frantic woman around 9.00pm who claimed that her and her husband were being attacked in their house in Stoke Bishop. Some fucking lunatic broke in.

The woman was injured in a skirmish and is in deep shock, but her husband fared worse. He was smashed up badly. A baseball bat, I think. They are both in Southmead Hospital."

Wyatt had sat forward.

"So, what is the significance? Go on, Steve. What is it you haven't told me?"

"The woman's name is Sarah Jacobs."

Wyatt was blank for a moment. Richmond added.

"Her husband is fucking Doug Jacobs."

Wyatt's heart pounded.

"Jesus Christ, why wasn't I told about this earlier?"

"Well, the detective on the scene, D.I. Marsh wasn't familiar with the Slade case and didn't make a connection. It was Gary Ellis who did when he finally got the information through."

"Did the wife say who the attacker was?"

Richmond grinned again.

"Yes, she did, Sir. It was Andy Roth."

Wyatt grabbed his coat off the back of his chair.

"At last we have got a fucking break. Let's get to the hospital. Roth tracked down Jacobs for the same reason as we have been doing. He is looking for Slade and by now, he may well know where he is and is going after him again. If we don't stop him, we are going to have another bloodbath on our hands."

PART THREE

Chapter Fifteen

Present Day (six months since Tony Slade's disappearance)

Tony walked along the cliff path. He was heading towards the island's small harbour. The watery sunshine filtered out over the sea. There was still a chill in the air although it was now 10.00am.

He looked around at the rugged scenery of sparse grass and granite. This place had become home. It was barren and desolate. The last place Tony had been that resembled this had been the Falklands in the 1980's conflict as part of the parachute regiment.

He had initially struggled with the isolation having become used to the hustle and bustle of the cosmopolitan North East city of Newcastle upon Tyne in recent times. Gradually, it had got more bearable.

A while back, he had been planning an escape to sunnier climates, but his plans had drastically and tragically changed. The loss of people near and dear to him had changed his mind. Suddenly, it did not seem as appealing on his own.

At this moment in time, Tony was drifting. He had no idea what to do with his life now that he had lost Annette. Her death still haunted him six months down the line. So did the death of his old friend and mentor Ray Steele.

Ray Steele had been like a father figure to him. He taught him how to fight when he was a young man using the discipline of Jujutsu and had watched his back many a time working on the doors of clubland back in the day.

Both Ray and Annette had been callously murdered. Doug had also informed him of the brutal killing of Daisy. It had Roth's signature all over it.

He felt guilt and responsibility for everything. If he had not done what he had done, they would all be alive. He had put them all in grave danger and they had paid the ultimate price, yet he had survived. There was not a day that went by without him brooding on that fact.

Tony found himself here on Graig o Mor more out of necessity rather than choice. He had wanted to become invisible for a while and this seemed to be the ideal place to do it.

The small island was sixty kilometres squared or, as Tony preferred twenty-three, square miles. It was eleven miles long and six miles wide. Its population was 925. That was until he had arrived to make it 926.

Graig o Mor translates as *Rock of the Sea*. It lies in the Bristol Channel between the southern tip of Wales and the west coast of Somerset, England. The Vale of Glamorgan was its nearest neighbour on the mainland. This made the island officially Welsh.

Being a remote place, it is not easy to reach. A ferry service can get you across from Cardiff, but that depends on the season and the weather. Most people that inhabited the island were born and bred there. The joke was that nobody would come and live here willingly unless, of course, they wanted to keep a low profile.

In the winter, it could be a godforsaken place. The summer months brought the tourist trade. The island did have some interesting wildlife and nature, however.

Birdwatching was popular with many species visiting, including the rare Storm Petrel and Manx Shearwater. Butterflies such as the Adonis Blue and Large Skipper have been spotted and wildflowers like the Ghost Orchid and Spider Orchid were known to grow there.

Although small and relatively unknown to most of the public, it had a rich and chequered history. It boasted very early inhabitants. In 1970, a prehistoric vertebra of a red deer was found in a sea cave. A Bronze Age axe head was also unearthed in the '80s dating back to 700BC. Roman remains of some sort of tower had also been excavated along with cooking utensils, and as late as 1999, a sword of Viking origins was unearthed on the pebble beach.

There was also an active lighthouse on the island and a long disused fort with army batteries and barracks going back to the 1860s.

Since being here, Tony had passed many a lonely evening reading. He had read lots about the local history of the island and the surrounding areas and picked up a fair amount of knowledge.

His life certainly was not as action packed as it used to be, but he was okay with that. Keeping a low profile and out of trouble was his priority for the moment.

He watched Skipper running around up ahead. The dog had been a present from Doug. Tony had him as a puppy. He had never owned a dog before and had had reservations about it, but gradually, the Jack Russell had become good company and a loyal companion.

So far, apart from Doug, nobody else knew where he was. To the islanders, he was Tony Swan working on the boats for Joe Williams.

He had heard nothing from the police or the media. Most importantly, he had heard nothing of Roth either. But every day, he lived with the anticipation that one or all of them would soon find him.

The newspapers still carried the odd story about him even after all this time, which told him that they still had interest in his whereabouts.

His body was healing nicely, and he was feeling much fitter and healthier. It must be all the sea air he was getting and the amount of fish he was eating.

Doug phoned him whenever he could, but it had been a while now as he the last time they spoke he had told Tony that he sensed that he was being watched.

Tony had phoned Doug half a dozen times in the last couple of days, but with no success. This gave him a feeling of unease. This only convinced Tony that now he was back to good health that he should get his act together and consider leaving the UK. But he had not wanted to travel whilst he had been healing. When he left, he was planning on a long-haul journey and he needed to be up for it. He knew deep down that he had been dragging his heels on this matter.

As you would imagine, Graig o Mor did not hold much in the way of entertainment. Occasionally, he would venture out to the one and only pub on the island, *The Smugglers Haunt*.

Internet was amazingly available but ran very slowly and not many islanders bothered with it. His cheap laptop allowed him to stay in touch with what was going on in the world.

He did not watch much television. Although receiving a signal to be able to watch it was sometimes sketchy, the same could be said for a mobile phone.

When the television did work, there were too many soap operas and reality shows for his liking. Apart from reading he still enjoyed his music. Not the modern stuff though. He listened to the classic cuts. Led Zeppelin, Elton John, The Stones, Bruce Springsteen and Tom Petty were some of the many artists from the '60s, '70s and '80s that he played. For Tony, after the '80s, music had gone gradually down the pan.

Some people would say that Tony Slade liked living in the past. Maybe he did? But what did the UK have these days but not its past? The present did not hold much for him. Not without Annette.

Six months on since her death, it still hurt when he thought about her. He wondered if the pain would ever leave him.

In his lengthy career as a soldier, bodyguard, doorman and fighter, he had experienced just about every type of physical pain you could imagine and survived it, even the recent shootings, but the pain of the emptiness and loss he felt was totally different.

It was not a wound you could stitch or dress. You could not see or touch it. You just felt a dreadful aching down inside.

He breathed in the salt air and walked on. He spied the old lighthouse out to the west. Standing proud above the cliffs like a sentinel. It stood 98ft high. The first lighthouse on the island had been built way back in 1735 after a tragic boat accident claimed the lives of a dozen sailors.

The present lighthouse was not the original. That one had got damaged in a terrible storm in 1891.The lighthouse keeper, a Thomas Evans, was nearly killed by being swept into the raging seas from the cliffs. After the storm, it was rebuilt and fortified to survive the battering that it took from time to time with Britain's unpredictable weather.

1988 saw the lighthouse become fully automated and keepers were withdrawn. In 1997, the light was modernised and converted to solar power. The foghorn was fully restored and could again be heard when the mists rolled in.

Tony felt a sense of peace around the lighthouse and regularly walked up to it and, in recent times, jogged. It was a pity the public could no longer climb its steps to the top.

Graig o Mor certainly had its history and his mysteries.

At first, the locals had viewed Tony himself as a bit of a mystery. His past was unknown to them. They wondered why any man who had lived outside of this island would suddenly make his home here.

It was intriguing for the islanders and obviously, made big news around there. Everybody knew everybody else's business here, even if they did not want it to be known.

It was not like the large cities where you could walk around anonymously. Hell, in a big city, you could live next door to somebody for years and not even know their name. But not on this island. Tony thought if you broke wind, it would make the chapel's noticeboard on Sunday.

A stranger around here was newsworthy.

The couple who ran *The Smugglers Haunt*, Gareth and Jenny Edwards, loved it when he came in for a drink. They tried every approach to get information out of him without much success.

The Smugglers Haunt was built on the foundations of an ancient inn which was constructed in 1840. The island had then been leased to a Colonel Brunswick. He opened the inn for sailors. The inn was run on the rum and tobacco bought from the ships that docked there.

A so-called secret tunnel on the north of the island supposedly connected natural tunnels to a concealed exit to the sea. Contraband had been smuggled onto the island that way.

Back in the day, the customs and authorities were powerless to act, as they had no boat to take them to the island. Even if they had, the tides and the rocks were extremely dangerous around that inhabited part of the island.

The pub along with the chapel of Saint Brendan were the island's hub.

The first chapel on the island was a 12th century one. St. Jude's. It only measured 70ft by 15ft. It gradually fell into ruin through disuse depending on whether the island was inhabited or not. In the 18th century, the stone from the ruined church was used to make a handful of fisherman's cottages like the one Tony lived in.

Another church was built in 1850. St. Brendan's which still stands today.

Tony did find the situation of him being there amusing and kept cleverly dodging the questions. Initially, the rumours circulated like wildfire but without any substance. Tony had kept himself pretty much to himself and been courteous and polite when encountering the locals. That had been largely down to Joe Williams.

His old friend Doug Jacobs had been right about Joe. Joe was an ex-paratrooper like him but a little younger. Once people knew that he was an ex-soldier and friend of Joe's, they seemed to be satisfied about him and the questions became less.

Joe and Tony often laughed about the tight knit islanders. Joe joked that when he first returned to the island many years ago, one night he answered a knock to his front door and when he opened it, it was a neighbour, Alwyn Rees. He introduced himself and then said, "I would like you to meet my wife and sister" and there was only one woman stood next to him!

Tony and Joe had hit it off straight away. Ex-army seemed to do that. There is a bond and an unwritten code between them.

Joe had seen plenty of active soldiering just like Tony. Following the 1982 Falklands War, 5 Airborne Brigade was established as a light, rapid reaction force for similar requirements. The brigade was made up of the Parachute Regiment and support units. The Brigade identified a requirement for an independent intelligence collection capability, deployable into a hostile or non-permissive environment ahead of the main force, so in 1985, the Pathfinder Platoon was established with personnel drawn initially from the patrol's platoon of each of the three Parachute Battalions.

For many years, it was not an officially established unit, being financed from other parts of the Brigade's budget. But in 1999, 5 Airborne Brigade merged with 24 Airmobile Brigade to form the present day 16 Air Assault Brigade with the platoon remaining attached to the Brigade headquarters. Joe had been a big part of this and had seen action in the Balkans War in Kosovo in

1999, Sierra Leone in 2000 and Iraq in 2003. He left the forces before Afghanistan and returned home.

Joe had been an islander born and breed. His family history went way back on the island. His father, grandfather and great grandfather had all been fishermen here. They say there had been a Williams on the island since time immemorial.

On returning to Graig o Mor, Joe took over his father's fishing business due to his ailing health. But it was struggling and near bankruptcy. Fishing had become a tough and uncompromising business.

When the old man died of lung and stomach cancer, which the doctor attributed to his habit of smoking forty untipped senior service cigarettes and drinking a bottle of Lambs Navy rum daily, Joe decided a change of direction was needed, especially to keep the bank off his back.

He sold one of the two remaining fishing vessels and bought a 20-feet Jata-sloop, *Mermaid*. He got licensed to use it as a pleasure boat that took people from the island over to mainland Wales and back on day trips and to explore some of the other small islands out in the channel. The sloop could accommodate a dozen people. That had been a good little earner in the summer months.

He could not compete with the big boys on the mainland using their commercial rigid inflatable boats from the marina, but he managed to keep the business afloat, so to speak.

The commercial boats did not like the fact that Joe was taking a piece of the action, but as an islander, it was all legal and above board.

He kept the other fishing boat *Gipsy of the Waves*. It was a 30-feet 1989 Cygnus GM28.

In Joe's opinion, the Cygnus was the best multi-purpose coastal vessel. It had a proven classic design and was recognised as the standard model for a coastal fisherman. He now captained it as a corporate fishing charter for businessmen to hire his boat and his services for a day's fishing in the Bristol Channel to catch a few bass, cod or whiting or if they were lucky, a thornback ray or maybe even a conger eel. Usually, though, the trip was a good excuse for the clients to have a piss up on the ocean waves.

The Caribbean or the Great Barrier Reef it was not, but the business could be a good little earner in the summer months.

Tony had asked Joe if he would like an extra pair of hands to help on the boats. Joe said he would welcome that, but could not afford to pay him. Tony had told Joe that he was not doing it for the money; it was to keep fit and stave off the boredom. Tony was no sailor or fisherman, but he was a willing grafter and could turn his hand to most things, so that suited Joe.

Doug Jacobs had helped Joe initially set up his business with a little loan. Doug was Mr Fixit and the man to go to for help if you were ex-military. Joe enjoyed Tony's company. Much of it down to their army experience and their shared love of rock music and a good whisky.

Joe lived alone in a fisherman's cottage not unlike Tony's, high up on the cliffs. A pathway from the cottage led down to the small harbour and long stone jetty that harboured his boats and his business.

He had got married some three years ago to a Cardiff girl named Marion, but the island isolation had put a strain on their already volatile relationship. She was a city girl at heart, but Joe would never consider leaving the island and the family business.

So, she had left him six months ago. She just got up and left. He had not heard from her since.

Of course, it made big news for a while, but eventually, it blew over as some other topic of gossip took precedence.

Joe had told his story to Tony one night in the pub over a few whiskys. Tony had sensed his grief. Joe seemed a haunted man at times and a man also with secrets. Tony had been tempted to share his story with Joe, but had refrained from doing so.

He had made too many mistakes of late and could not afford to make any more. He did not know Joe well enough. He did not want others getting drawn into his problems. When they did, they always seemed to end up hurt. For now, Joe knew him as Tony Swan, ex-army buddy of Doug Jacobs.

Even though he had been on the island a while now without incident, he could not shake off the feeling of impending doom. He found it unnerving. Maybe he was experiencing some sort of post-traumatic stress again, especially after the shootings and the loss of Annette. But his instincts told him there was more to it.

Maybe Joe would be a good man to have on his side if a time came when his prophecy became real. Down the line, he may have to tell him the truth.

To his credit, Joe never pushed Tony for information on why he had come to the island. He respected his friend's privacy, but Tony suspected that Joe knew he was keeping out of the way of something or somebody.

Tony walked on across the rugged landscape. He had hated it here when he had first arrived. He had craved to return to the big city life, but slowly, the place had won him around. He had begun to enjoy its sense of history and its easy pace of life.

He now spied the ruins of a fort. Joe had told him it was built in the early 1860's to fortify the islands defences against invasion from the French Navy on suggestion of Queen Victoria and Prince Albert when they visited some years previously.

The fort formed part of a line of defences known as Palmerston forts built across the channel to protect approaches to Bristol or Cardiff. They were named after the prime minster of the time, John Henry Temple, 3rd Viscount of Palmerston.

The forts were just for a show of bravado and many deemed them an unnecessary expense the country could not afford.

The fort was now a haven for wildlife or the occasional drunk or late-night courting couple.

Annie Yorath, who owned the only convenience store on the island and a source of all information useful and useless, swore it was haunted by the ghost of a white lady. The lady is meant to have been some lovestruck girl who waited by the fort for the return of her sailor love.

She spent night after night with a lantern scanning the seas for him, but he never returned. In a fit of anguish and grief, she supposedly flung herself from the top of the fort into the sea.

Annie tells anybody willing to listen that on stormy nights, if you look up to the fort, you can see the eerie glow of a lantern where the white lady is still grieving for her lost love. Many islanders staggering out of the pub at the end of the night also swear by the story.

Tony now walked the winding path past St. Brendan's chapel which would lead him on down towards a small rank of shops on the seafront including *Annie's* and *The Smugglers Haunt*.

Vicar Tom Gwynne was out the front of the chapel tending to his flowers, which he was passionate about. He was also in deep conversation with another boatman on the island named Jim Edwards.

Tom was a sprightly grey-haired man in his seventies. In his younger years, he had been an army chaplain and had spent time stationed in various parts of the world. In the early '70s, he was in Singapore for a short while before finishing his time in Northern Ireland from 1975 to 1978. Tony had done a few tours in Northern Ireland himself and both men often talked about their times there.

"Morning, gentlemen. How are you both today?" asked Tony.

Vicar Gwynne and Jim Edwards both looked around slightly startled.

"Tony. Good God, you startled me, man. Didn't see you there," said Tom

He straightened up from his job and grimaced as he rubbed his lower back.

"Damn back is playing up again, but apart from that, I am fine."

Jim tipped the peak of his battered fishing cap in acknowledgement to Tony.

"Well, must be on my way. We will speak soon, Tom."

Both men said their goodbyes to Jim.

"Time for a cuppa, Tony or something a little stronger, maybe?"

Tony laughed and shook his head.

"Not today, Tom. I have work to do on Joe's boat. Maybe tomorrow."

"Righto. No worries. I have a lovely double malt waiting to be sampled. A present from a grateful parishioner who probably thinks that, after a little of my spiritual guidance, I have guaranteed them a place in heaven."

Tony smiled.

"That's a date soon."

Tom Gwynne grinned widely.

"Have a good day, Tony."

As Tony walked off, he heard him add.

"Maybe I will see you at church this Sunday?"

Tony carried on walking and pretended he did not hear him.

Tom Gwynne had tried everything to persuade Tony to come to church since he met him, but for Tony, after what had happened to Annette, he could not even contemplate that there was a God that could be so cruel.

His past military service had also made him doubt God's existence after the horrors he had witnessed. Yet he admired that the Vicar, who had also seen his share of atrocities in wartime, still had his faith.

As Tony carried on down the hill, he tried to lighten his mood. He had lived most of his life on the dark side and he still hoped somewhere in his heart that he would somehow find peace. Maybe God was the answer? But Tony still believed that the devil owned his soul and was not going to give it up easily.

He now passed *Annie's*. A small throng of people where milling inside and out browsing the produce. Food had to be transported over to the island and must be brought over all at once. Nothing fresh. It all has to last the month. Packets and cans and a giant freezer for meat, fish, veg and bread. Annie Yorath saw him walking by and waved out to him.

She was a good-looking woman in her late forties. Divorced with two grown-up children. One living in London and the other in Paris. She had a dog named Punch, ironically, a boxer who got on well with Skipper, Tony's dog. He would leave the Jack Russell with Annie if he had particularly long days at sea. She loved animals.

She also had two cats. Ant and Dec were their names. She liked dancing, bingo and a good gin and tonic. Tony had learnt all this the first time he had met her in the pub.

He felt Annie had designs to have him in the running for her second husband. He tried his best to steer any conversation away from romance when they chatted.

Past *Annie's* were a few more businesses. A fishing tackle shop, a post office, a chemist and the pub. Beyond these lay a doctor's surgery, a few B&Bs and a small petrol station. A large tanker came to the island once a month with fuel.

There was also a tourist information office/museum where Tony had spent many an hour talking to the owner Graham Fox about the history of the island and the surrounding area.

McDonald's, Primark, Greggs and Carphone Warehouse had yet to make it to the island. In Tony's book, that could be a blessing.

The electricity here was generated by wind and solar, but that meant being very careful on an overcast day. If it ran out, huge diesel generators kicked in, which required refuelling. For hot water, wood burning stoves were loaded up and heated. In the summer, there was no need. The wood was shipped over and kept for the winter. Graig o Mor had few trees.

Tony now made his way down some ancient stone steps to the small wharf and the jetty where the boats docked. There were a few commercial ferries dropping tourists to the island or taking islanders over to Cardiff where many would shop or attend to their finances at a bank or building society. Many kept their vehicles on the mainland as there was not much need for them on Graig o Mor.

Tony spied Joe on board the *Gipsy of the Sea*. He had a fishing party to pick up from Cardiff and bring out into the Bristol Channel for a day out. Tony was going to help him out. Joe saw Tony walking along towards the boat.

"Morning, Tony, all ready to go?"

Tony nodded as he stepped aboard.

"Alright, Joe. Yes, I'm all set. Let's get to it."

Soon, the boat was cutting across the waters towards the mainland.

"So, what have we got today, Joe?"

Tony had to shout above the noise of the engine and the strong breeze which sped them along. Joe stood at the helm steering the boat, guiding it with an expert hand.

"We have a group of local rugby lads to pick up. An afternoon of fishing and no doubt boozing on the menu.

It could be a bit lively, but they are paying top dollar for the experience, so we will have to cut them a bit of slack. I could do with this little earner this month."

"Business is alright, isn't it, Joe?"

Joe kept his gaze straight ahead.

"Yeah. It's fine. No problem."

Tony nodded and took a sip of his coffee being careful not to spill it because of the boat's erratic movements over the waves.

"So, what you are really saying to me about these rugby boys is for me not to choke the fuck out of one of them."

Joe laughed.

"Yeah, that's about the top and bottom of it, my friend. None of that Jujutsu shit you told me about, okay?"

Tony regarded Joe as he negotiated the boat through the choppy sea. His face was craggy and tanned from the sea air. His hair and beard were neatly trimmed short. Under the heavy woollen jumper that he was wearing was a muscular body honed by rigors of a busy boating job that required a lot of manual work.

Joe played the gentle seafaring captain to the tee by being courteous and polite to his customers, but from some of the stories he had told Tony from his past, he knew he could handle himself if a situation turned nasty. Between them both, they made a good team.

For the rest of the journey, Tony busied himself getting the fishing gear ready for the party. As they pulled into the dockside, he saw a group of six men between twenty and forty years old. From their size and the few cauliflower ears on display, Tony guessed this was their charter.

The men seemed like they had already sunk a few beers and were loud and animated. Tony felt that familiar tingle of adrenaline seep into his blood stream. He pushed it down. It was his body's way of telling him to keep his wits about him.

As the men piled onto the boat, between them all they carried three boxes of Stella Artois. They were certainly looking for an entertaining trip.

The leader of the group was a big man named Nathan. He looked the oldest member of the party and he appeared to be their spokesman and organiser. Joe chatted with him about where they were going and the type of catch out in the waters of the channel. He seemed satisfied with what he had been told and the group settled into the seats available on deck and cracked open their beers.

Once the boat reached its designated spot, Joe switched off the engine and let it drift. All the men grabbed a fishing rod and casted out their lines. They were still a little rowdy but, in general, it was all good. Every now and then, they would ask Joe and Tony questions about the surrounding islands or fishing.

There was banter when they found out Tony was a Geordie and had a go at him about Newcastle United. Tony gave as good as he got pointing out that Cardiff City had not exactly set the Premiership alight either. The men said that rugby was their first passion as it was played by real men, not like the pampered pussies in football. It was all good-natured stuff.

There was some success in the group with their catch. Bass, cod and whiting were caught. Nathan nearly caught a conger eel, but he lost it at the last minute.

The afternoon moved on and the beers got lower. Things would have been fine until a couple of the younger lads who were referred to as 'B.J' and 'Topper' started throwing their empty beer cans into the water. Joe asked them not to do this, but they were too drunk to listen or care. As the guy called 'B.J.' went to throw another can, Joe caught his arm and held it tightly.

"Hey, fella. That's enough. Put the can down."

B.J. ripped his arm free.

"Or fucking what pal?"

He squared up to Joe. His arms splayed, chest puffed out. A classic show of threat display. 'Topper' lurked behind him. Joe calmly stared the lads down and firmly said.

"This is my boat and while you are on it, you will abide by the rules. So, put the fucking can down. There is enough shit in our oceans as it is."

Things had gone quiet on the boat as the others saw what was developing. Tony appeared up from the galley. He had a large filleting knife in his hand. His eyes were scanning the rest of the group. The tension hung heavily in the air.

"Alright, guys. Anybody fancy some of that fish from the catch for an early dinner? I am going to prepare some now."

Not a word was spoken by the men. Tony moved closer.

"Are we alright here?"

He knew the men had saw the knife in his hand. There was a standoff between Joe and the lad named B.J. Joe stare's was unwavering.

"Don't make the biggest mistake of your life, son."

Suddenly, Nathan walked forward.

"Do as the man says, B.J. Put the can down. You have had too much to drink."

The lad broke his stare with Joe and regarded the older man. Nathan nodded.

"Put it down. We have had a good day. No need to spoil it now over nothing."

B.J. hesitated a second more and then dropped the can into a plastic dustbin. The tension instantly eased. Tony seized the opportunity.

"So, who is up for some grilled fish then?"

The men nodded in agreement.

The remainder of the trip went without incident, although B.J. sulked in the corner like a naughty schoolboy.

Once the boat docked back in Cardiff, the men cordially trooped off. Nathan shook Joe and Tony's hands.

"Thanks for an enjoyable day, gentleman. And apologies for our young friend. He was out of order and stupid."

"No problem. Its forgotten," replied Joe.

Nathan smiled.

"I am glad I persuaded him to put the can down. Something about you guys tells me he might not have fared to well if he didn't. Am I right?"

Tony smiled.

"Just as well we didn't have to find out."

Nathan nodded and climbed off the boat. The men walked away. Joe breathed a sigh of relief and clapped Tony on the back.

"Well, partner, that could have been interesting."

"It sure could have, my friend. But we handled it like professionals"

Joe's craggy features broke into a wide grin.

"I am glad of that. I didn't fancy cleaning all the blood up off the deck if you decided to go all John Wick with that filleting knife. Preparing fish for dinner, my ass."

It was Tony's turn to smile now.

"I don't know what you are on about. Come on. Let's get back home and I will buy you a pint."

As autumn sun began to set, Joe sailed the boat back home to Graig o Mor.

Chapter Sixteen

Sat at a table by the roaring log burner in *The Smuggler's Haunt*, Tony and Joe supped on their pints and tucked into their steak and kidney pies. It was a nice way to end a busy day.

The pub was reasonably crowded and Gareth and Jenny worked tirelessly behind the bar, always with a smile on their faces and time for a word with every customer.

Tony felt mellow and embraced the warmth of not only the fire but the atmosphere. Joe finished his pie and sat back in his seat with a contented sigh.

"Best steak and kidney pie by miles."

Tony raised his glass.

"I will drink to that, my friend."

Joe returned the salute and took a huge gulp of his beer.

"Look, Tony. I know you like to play your cards close to your chest, and I respect that, but I have got to ask, now you are on the mend, do you plan to move on soon?"

Tony regarded his friend.

"Maybe, is that a problem?"

"No. Not a problem, but I kind of got used to you working for me. It's made the job a damn sight easier and more interesting."

Joe's words hung in the air.

"I sense a but coming here, Joe."

Joe smiled ruefully.

"I must admit that going back to working on my own won't be the same."

"There must be others you could employ?"

"The truth is, Tony, I am struggling with paying bills at present. Things are a bit tight and I am not sure I have the spare money to pay anybody. I hope to get things straightened out soon."

Tony leaned forward.

"I thought your business was doing okay. How bad is it, Joe?"

"Like I said, Tony. It will sort itself out. Just struggling against the competitors. Next month will be better."

"Don't bullshit me, Joe. I can see it in your eyes. What is it you aren't telling me? Come on. Spit it out. Are you in trouble? Maybe I can help?"

Joe suddenly got agitated.

"Don't take this the wrong way, but it is not your problem. When you are gone, it will still be here and I will have to deal with it."

Tony was taken back by Joe's attitude.

"Hold on, partner. I was just trying to help."

Joe was still angry.

"Well, I don't need your help. I did okay before you came here, and I will do alright again."

Tony held up his hands.

"Hey, It looks like I stepped out of line. I best go."

He made to stand up, but Joe grabbed his wrist.

"Wait, Tony. I am sorry for flying off the handle. I was out of order. Long day. That's all. I am being a dick."

Tony stared into Joe's eyes.

"Apology accepted. And yeah, you are being a dick."

Tony nodded and drained his glass.

"Let me get you another," he gestured to Joe's glass.

"Sure thing."

Tony made his way towards the bar. Joe was certainly uptight about something, but he did not want to push it any more tonight. If his business was in trouble, he just might be able to help him out, but Joe needed to be honest with him.

Tony then found himself half smiling. *Be honest.* He was a fine one to say that when he had told Joe nothing about why he was here on the island. It was Joe's business and if he wanted to talk to him, then he would do it in his own time. Standing at the bar, he caught Jenny's eye. She came over to him.

"Same again is it, Tony?"

"Sure is," he replied.

He watched as she brushed a strand of her flaming red hair from her face and began to pull the first pint of rocket fuel or, as the islanders preferred to call it, Smuggler's tipple. A 6% by volume local real ale.

Jenny was a good-looking woman. Gareth, her husband, was a lucky man to have her in his life.

Suddenly, Tony felt a moment of melancholy touch him as he thought of Annette. He then became aware of Jenny speaking to him.

"Here, Tony. Got the television visiting Friday."

"Television. What's that all about?"

"It's that Channel 5 programme *Where the Land Meets the Sea.* You must have heard of it?"

"Can't say I have," replied Tony as he accepted the first flowing pint. Jenny continued.

"You must have seen it. It's been around a few years now. They visit coastal towns and islands looking at their history and collecting stories from the locals. The host is that good-looking guy, Alistair Henry."

Tony still stared blankly.

"No, I still haven't heard of it."

Jenny rolled her eyes.

"Anyway, the programme is coming live from here on Friday and they are coming to the pub to interview me and Gareth. Its ever so exciting. Make sure you are around if you can."

Tony paid for the pints.

"Yeah. I will see what I am up to."

Tony walked back from the bar deep in thought.

He needed to be right out of the way come Friday. He did not want anything to do with being caught on film. Hopefully, Joe might have a job to take them out of the way for the day. Otherwise, he was going to have to lock himself away in this cottage and say he was ill.

Both men left the warmth of the pub around 11.00pm. They walked along the quay front. The night was certainly chilly and dark clouds covered the sky threatening rain after such a lovely day.

"We all good then, Tony?" asked Joe.

"Yeah, of course."

Joe shook Tony's hand.

"So..." asked Tony, "What's the schedule for the rest of the week, Joe?"

"Well, tomorrow we have another fishing party. But hopefully, it will be without incident. It is a bunch of

OAPs from Penarth. They are part of the Royal British Legion. They book every year. They are sound guys."

Tony nodded.

"Ok and Friday?"

"Friday, we have a few trips to the Bay to ferry customers out there. That's it."

"Great. I am on board for the company and exercise. Nothing else, okay?" replied Tony.

Joe grinned.

"Okay."

"Walking my way?" asked Tony.

"I have to collect a few bits and pieces from the boat. You carry on and I will see you for 10.00am in the morning," replied Joe.

Joe's phone buzzed and he looked at the scene. He cursed under his breath.

"I have to take this Tony. Sorry."

"Okay, see you tomorrow. Good night."

Tony walked around the corner of the pub but stopped. He stayed close to the wall out of sight as he eavesdropped on Joe's conversation. He saw him put the phone to his ear and begin to speak.

"Mr Coates, what can I do for you? Bit late to be calling, isn't it?"

The man on the other end of the phone was Ronald Coates. He worked for Ingram and Marshall Finances.

"That is because you have ignored my calls all day. Believe me, I have better things to do at this hour than to be speaking to you, so I will make it brief. As you probably know, this is now four payments you have missed on your loan with us. Mr Marshall and Mr Ingram are very concerned about your outstanding debts."

"Hey, Ron. Business was a bit slower than anticipated this summer due to the crap weather, but I think I am turning the corner. I am sure next month I will have the money…"

Coates cut him down in mid-sentence.

"Words, Joe. Just words. So, I tell you what, you have until the end of the month to settle the debts or we will collect them in whatever assets you have. Understand?"

"Ron, just listen…"

"No, you fucking listen, Joe. The time for games is up. Pay up or you are out of business. Goodnight."

The phone went dead.

Joe walked over to a bench on the waterfront and slumped down.

Fuck, fuck, fuck. What a mess. It was ironic. When he inherited the business from his dad, he thought that the old man could not run it properly. Right now, he was no better.

He had been okay initially, but gradually, the bigger boats increased their presence and Joe could only compete by undercutting them. But by doing that, he struggled to pay his bills.

Unless business improved drastically, he was going to be in big trouble. When Marion had been with him, they had been a team and he drew strength from her, but once she had left him, he slowly began to unravel.

Just like his old man, he had gradually tried to find solace in a bottle. He then thought he could recoup some money with online gamble, but dug himself a bigger hole.

He had thought of going to see Doug Jacobs, but it was Doug who had helped him set up the business in the first place and his pride just could not admit to Doug that he had fucked up.

Then, Doug had called him looking for a favour and asked if he would take Tony into his care for a while. How could he refuse? Doug had paid him a good retainer for his services, but in an effort to score big and get his business back on track, he had gambled the money and lost big. The picture he had painted Tony was far from the truth. He was going down if he did not find a solution fast.

Maybe when Tony left the island, Doug might show his gratitude with a few more quid? At this moment, anything would do. He was getting desperate.

In the shadows, Tony listened to snatches of the conversation. It sounded as if somebody was putting the squeeze on his friend. He could not work out how hard though, but Joe did not look a happy man.

Chapter Seventeen

Sergeant Steve Richmond drove the Ford Mondeo over the Severn Bridge towards Cardiff. In the passenger seat was D.C.I Wyatt. In the backseat was Susie Rawlings and Matt Sloan.

Yesterday, he had visited the hospital to see Doug Jacobs. He was in intensive care and wrapped up like an Egyptian mummy.

The doctor told them it would be touch and go over the next few days, as he had considerable head trauma and multiple broken bones.

They were not going to get anything out of him. Roth had done a proper job on him and probably left him for dead. They could only presume Roth had got the information he needed out of Jacobs.

It was his wife Sarah that had finally given them a vital piece of information. She had recovered enough from her ordeal to speak with them while she kept vigil at her husband's bedside.

While going through the belongings he had been wearing when he had been rushed into hospital, she had found a pay as you go phone in a hidden pocket inside his jacket. She told them that she had never seen it before. On examination, Wyatt found only one number in the directory. He deduced that it had to be Slade's.

He had rung it and somebody answered almost immediately. He recognised the voice and the Geordie accent. It was Slade's.

Wyatt had not said anything, as Slade repeated Jacob's name over and over and asked if everything was okay. Then suddenly, the phone had gone dead.

Although this was a major breakthrough, it did not tell Wyatt where Slade was as a burner phone was notorious for being hard to track. Obviously, therefore, the criminal fraternity liked to use them.

Sarah had also said that she had travelled to Cardiff Bay on a few occasions and Doug had met a man there in a coffee shop. She went shopping while this happened and never heard their conversations, but by the man's dress and appearance, he looked like a fisherman or a ferryman. She added that she thought his name might be Jim, Jack or maybe Joe.

Wyatt asked her if she had suspected anything untoward was going on, but Sarah had replied that her husband had dozens of business contacts and she was used to meeting them or seeing them coming and going from their home regularly. It was not anything unusual.

Richmond confirmed with her that she had not heard the name Tony Slade until the other night and that she had also never seen Roth before.

They thanked her and gave their best wishes for her husband.

As they walked back across the car park to their vehicle, Richmond asked.

"Well, Gov. What are you thinking?"

Wyatt slipped a chewing gum into his mouth.

"I think Slade is close to Cardiff Bay. This guy with the boat was a mate of Jacobs and he has sailed Slade off somewhere. We have just got to find out where and we have got him."

Richmond nodded.

"So, what now?"

"Let's get back to the station and dig out a fucking map of the British Isles and let's see what is beyond the English Channel."

Back at the station, they folded out a large Ordnance Survey map onto Richmond's desk and pegged the edges down with an object that would do the job in arms' reach. They tried to narrow it down by rejecting the idea that he had gone as far as places such as the Isle of Man, the Orkneys or Skye.

Wyatt theorised that it had to be a rush job. Somewhere out of harm's way but close enough for Jacobs if he needed to get there. Also, this boatman had to take local trips.

They came down to maybe the Anglesey Islands, Gwynedd Isles, Pembrokeshire islands or smaller places such as Graig o Mor, Herring Island or Great Stack.

They decided first thing in the morning that they would set out for Cardiff and loiter around the Bay area and see what boats came in and out and find this mystery boatman.

Later that evening, Wyatt phoned Susie Rawlings and put her in the picture and told her he would pick her up in the morning. He also told her to bring her best notebook and a good photographer. They were planning on going fishing and Tony Slade was the main catch of the day along with Andy Roth hopefully.

If it went according to plan, this story and arrest were going to hog the headlines for weeks.

Wyatt had contemplated informing Chief Superintendent Hardwicke but then decided not to.

Hardwicke was more concerned with the impending visit of the Royal Highnesses, the Duke and Duchess of Sussex, to Bristol. He would not be happy if he thought Wyatt was off to Wales on what he would presume was a wild goose chase. Plus, Wyatt did not want his pompous superior getting any recognition for bring Slade in.

The four passengers were silent wrapped up in their own thoughts. It had been a long and frustrating time up to this point, but now, they could afford themselves a faint glimmer of hope. It was so good they could hardly bring themselves to believe it was happening. It was Richmond who broke the silence.

"Fucking great that you haven't got to pay that bridge toll anymore, robbing bastards. It's been long overdue. Why we had to pay to get into Wales in the first place is beyond me?"

Susie Rawlings piped up from the backseat.

"Maybe the Welsh wanted to keep people like you out. Ever thought of that?"

Richmond sneered.

"Why the fuck would they want to do that? Imagine what all those Welsh beauties would be missing out on."

Rawlings rolled her eyes.

"Hey, Richmond, I expect the sheep would have been gutted if you were banned from the Valleys."

Richmond looked in the rear-view mirror at her and mouthed *fuck you*.

Matt Sloan broke into the conversation through a mouthful of Mars bar.

"I think you will find the toll was for bridge maintenance."

"Bridge maintenance, my ass. If that is the case, what are they going to do now? Let it collapse into the sea?" replied Richmond.

Matt Sloan seemed to have no immediate response to this, so he went back to his chocolate bar.

As they headed into Wales, Wyatt spoke.

"Right then, enough of the banter. When we get to the Bay, we will split into two. Susie, you and Matt check out all the boat trips and their destinations. Steve and I will visit the Cardiff Harbour authority and see if we can track down this Jim or Joe character."

Everybody replied in the positive. Wyatt added.

"Also, keep your wits about you in case Roth is around. He is a complete psycho and will think nothing of hurting you if he feels you are getting in his way. You all have got a photo image of him on your phones, right?"

Everybody answered affirmative.

"The local plod has been informed that we are here on some routine questions, but they don't know the extent of it. So, don't expect any back up if needed."

Wyatt settled back in his seat and felt the reassuring weight of the police issue Glock 17 in a shoulder holster. He glanced across at Richmond. He knew he was armed too and a reliable partner in an emergency.

He felt alive and buzzing for the first time in months. Before this break, he had seriously thought about chucking things in and retiring early, but now, he had the bit between his teeth again. That old familiar feeling in his belly of the adrenaline rush felt good. He was shaken from his thoughts by his mobile ringing. He answered it.

The call was brief. Wyatt snapped his phone shut and addressed everybody.

"That was the hospital. Doug Jacobs passed away twenty minutes ago. We are now dealing with another murder."

A grim silence enveloped the car interior once more.

Andy Roth sat on the bed of his room in the Holiday Inn. He was still in Bristol. He was channel-hopping mindlessly with the television remote whilst he swigged Jack Daniels bourbon straight from the bottle.

He was frustrated and angry that he had got nothing out of that bastard Jacobs. He gave the old fucker his due. He had been a tough cookie. Even after inflicting untold damage to his body with the bat, he had told him nothing.

The half a dozen whacks to the head put him away for good. He was no longer of any use. Plus, that bitch of a wife had escaped and probably now had the police on his trail again.

Fuck it. Everybody and their dog seemed to be after Roth, but they had not caught him yet and he did not plan to be caught neither. He took another gulp of the amber fluid which burned a passage down to his stomach.

At this moment in time, he was out of leads to Slade's whereabouts and he knew it would only be a matter of time before Walsh and Ewan up North got the news of the untimely demise of the McQueen brothers and sent somebody else on his scent.

Through his drunken haze, he now watched a programme that had just started. He heard the presenter speaking.

"Hello and welcome to *Where the Land Meets the Shore*. My name is Alastair Henry and today we are coming live from Cardiff Bay where in a moment I will be taking a ferry boat trip to the little island of Graig o Mor to find out about the island's life and history. Why not join me?"

The words Cardiff Bay sparked Roth's attention. He now sat forward and regarded the screen as the camera panned around the Bay and the bustling harbourside. Television cameras were all around the dock area filming the boats coming in and out and the crowds gathered for the show hoping to get their face on the TV screen.

Then, out of the blue, Roth saw him. It was just like some sort of vision delivered from God Almighty. Tony Slade appeared as if by magic from nowhere. He was untying a rope from a ferry boat. Roth nearly choked on a mouthful of bourbon. He looked again to be sure before the camera panned away.

Shit. Even in his semi-drunken state, he knew it was Slade. Now where the fuck did that presenter say he was going?

An hour later, as the programme ended, Roth was 100% it had been Slade and had written down the name of the island Graig o Mor.

He now needed to sleep the booze off and then he was heading for Cardiff and the island. He was sure this was where Slade had been hiding. At last, his luck was changing. He dozed off with thoughts of finally extracting his long-awaited revenge on that bastard Slade.

He had never heard of this Graig o Mor, but he was certain of one thing: a storm was heading its way.

Chapter Eighteen

Tony cursed his luck. On the third trip over to the Bay to pick up passengers for the *Mermaid*, they ran into the television crew for *Where the Land Meets the Sea* on the dockside.

By the time he realised this, he knew the cameras might have picked him up. He moved to the far end of the boat out of view and hoped he was not spotted. Joe shouted out from the small galley.

"Undo the rope, Tony, will you?"

Tony cautiously made his way back to the other end of the boat and undid the rope. Suddenly, the show's host Alastair Henry was in his face with a microphone.

"Excuse me, Sir. Would you have a moment to have a quick chat as part of the programme?"

"No, sorry. I am busy right now."

Henry smiled his winning cheesy grin.

"Surely just a few minutes. You will get yourself on the television."

"No, thanks."

"Hey, you don't seem the camera-shy type," quipped Henry.

Tony's patience snapped. He pushed the microphone and Henry backwards.

"Get out of my face and fuck off."

Joe approached him.

"Hey, take it steady, mate. You alright, Tony?"

"Yeah. Fine, Joe. Just trying to stay out the way of these fucking cameras, that's all."

Joe clapped his hand on his friend's shoulder.

"Okay. We are going now. Cool down a little, okay?"

Alastair Henry had regained his composure and footing. He was not used to being treated like this. He confronted Joe.

"Is this your boat?"

Joe nodded.

"Yes, it is. Why?"

"You need to keep that caveman under control and teach him some basic manners."

Henry gestured towards Tony.

"Yeah, okay. Apologies. He is just having a bad day. No harm done, eh?"

Before Henry could answer, Joe moved away out of ear shot. Tony glanced up briefly to still see the television crew filming around the waterfront. As he walked back down the boat, he pulled his cap farther down on his head and sat at the bow. Joe came up close to him.

"Fuck, Tony. I didn't realise being spotted was that big a deal to you, but remember, I have a business and customers. I can't afford to lose any of them."

"Yeah. Sorry, Joe. It won't happen again."

Joe nodded and walked away. The *Mermaid* moved off and he began to relax a little. Joe began his spiel on the microphone welcoming people aboard and began talking about the history of Graig o Mor and what to look out for when they got there.

Tony looked out to sea. A watery sun reflected off the water. The afternoon temperature was pleasantly warm again for late September. He felt himself relax a little. He had come to a decision that at the end of this month, which was about a week away, he was going to leave. He could not afford to lose his rag like that again.

He was going to fly out to Lanzarote first to pay his respects to his old friend Ray Steele. Doug had told him a while back that Ray had wanted to be buried in Lanzarote next to his beloved wife Ellen. Tony felt he needed to go and make his peace. He still felt guilty that Ray had got caught up in the violence that seemed to follow him. It cost his friend his life.

It was the right thing to do. Plus, Tony could do with some warm sun on his back. The temperatures in the Canary Islands were still good this time of year.

Graig o Mor had been a sanctuary for him as he healed. He owed Doug so much and it did trouble him that he still had not been able to make contact with him.

The phone call he had received yesterday with no voice on the end of the line had unnerved him and had prompted his decision to get out of the UK.

Once he got back to the island, he would find the number for Doug's business and ring him there. He knew that it was against the rules they had set, but he was worried for his friend. He could not shake the bad feeling he felt in the pit of his stomach. He had felt it many times in his life, particularly in his army days. His instincts were normally right.

Up to this point, he had not really thought about what he was going to do with the rest of his life. He had just been focused on trying to get well again. He had now achieved this. It now seemed the natural process to move on.

Tony had learnt it did not help to dwell on the past. No matter how painful the memories, you had to move on and start again; otherwise, what did you have?

The time he had with his beautiful Annette was gone. Cruelly ripped away from him. But his mourning was done. The army had instilled in him never to give up and to keep going in the direst of circumstances, no matter how much discomfort you felt. That is what separated a paratrooper from the rest of the herd.

He was shaken from his thoughts as he heard Joe speak.

"Ladies and gentlemen, boys and girls, we will be docking in approximately five minutes. There is the island on the port side or your left."

Tony stood up and stretched. He began to walk towards the stern ready to work the rope again.

Later back at his cottage, he rang Doug's number and was surprised when he got an answer on the second ring. He did not recognise the voice on the end at first, but he knew it was not Doug's, which spelt trouble.

"Don't hang up, Tony. That is you, isn't it? This is D.C.I. Wyatt. Remember me?"

Tony said nothing.

"I suppose you are wondering how I got hold of this phone. I got it from your friend Doug Jacobs. Tony, I have some bad news for you. Roth caught up with him. He is dead. That is why you haven't been able to get hold of him."

This hit Tony like a bombshell.

"You are lying, Wyatt."

"Why would I, Tony? I am only concerned with catching you. I thought I would tell you out of courtesy. I don't care if you believe me or not. I will tell you, though, that I am coming for you. I have a lead to where you are and I am coming…"

Tony hung up. His mind was racing.

He rummaged in a bedside drawer and found a small battered notebook that he kept phone numbers in. He did not totally trust the modern technology of the mobile phone and preferred to keep a hard copy of his numbers in case his phone packed up. It did not take him long to find Doug's business number and ring it. A woman answered on the first ring.

"Jacob's Enterprises. Sally speaking. How may I help?"

"Yes, hello. May I speak with Doug, please?"

There was a brief silence and then the woman said.

"I am afraid that is not possible."

Tony got slightly irritated.

"It is urgent, and I am a close friend."

"In that case, Sir, I am afraid to inform you Mr Jacobs sadly passed away earlier today."

Her voice started to crack as she said this. Tony went cold. So, Wyatt had been telling the truth. After what seemed an age, he asked the woman what had happened. She informed him of the attack and the horrific injuries that had been inflicted on him which resulted in his death. Tony knew instantly that it had been Roth that caught up with him. His blood ran cold.

"Sir, can I take your name and number? If you would like details of the funeral, I can contact you when it is arranged."

Tony could hear her voice, but it seemed muffled and disjointed.

"Sir, are you still there?"

Tony hung up. He walked to the bed and slumped down on it. Doug was gone. Once more, another friend caught up in his shit.

Wyatt and Roth were now too close for comfort. They would soon find their way here. He did not know how long he lay on the bed going over and over all the events of the past year or more of his life, but the room was in darkness, except for the moon shining through a crack in the curtains, when he finally rose.

So many people he loved and cared for had gone. Yet he was still here. Why? What fucking good was that?

Suddenly, he was consumed by remorse. He reached under the mattress of the bed and his hand closed around what he was looking for. The Sig Sauer P226 that Doug had given him. He picked it up and felt its weight in his hand. He then then slid a clip into the handle and racked it.

He stared at the gun intently.

Maybe he should stick the barrel in his mouth and pull the trigger and end it all. After all, he only brought death and sadness to people's lives. He regarded the gun and brought it up close to his face. It could be done. It would be all over in seconds. All the pain gone in an instant. Tony Slade was a walking fucking liability. Who would miss him anyway?

Then, somewhere in his mind, an image of Andy Roth appeared smiling at him. Gloating at him. The bastard had murdered Doug. He could not leave that unpunished.

He knew in that instance that he had to kill Roth.

But now he also knew that he wanted Roth to come for him. The sooner the better. Tony was done running. If it was the last thing, he did in this world, he would kill the Roth and avenge his friend.

After that, he didn't give a fuck.

He got up and shook off the momentary dark thoughts. He had a job to do. A final mission.

Tony moved stealthy around the cottage making sure all the windows and doors were locked securely. He went back to the bedroom and peered through the crack in the curtains. The full moon lit up the outside and it all seemed quiet and as it should.

Tony then heard a noise at the bedroom door. It slowly pushed open and Skipper came padding in and jumped up on the bed. He remembered fondly the day Joe had delivered him to the island telling Tony it was a birthday present from Doug. Tony had never had a pet in his life, but had gradually grew fond of the little terrier.

Tony ruffled the dog's fur.

"It's just you and me now buddy."

He walked across the room and shut and locked the bedroom door. He had one final look out of the window and then lay down fully clothed on top of the bed, the gun close to his right hand. He felt the familiar feeling of adrenaline bubbling in his belly. It was some while before he eventually drifted off to sleep.

The weathered wood of the kitchen window did not put up much resistance. Once it was open, the man stealthy climbed through it and stepped into the kitchen. All he heard was the ticking of the clock on the wall above the stove. He crept across the room to what he presumed was the bedroom. He turned the handle of the bedroom door slowly and the door eased open silently.

Roth regarded the sleeping figure of Slade lying on the bed. At last, he had found him and what an easy kill this was going to be. He heard Slade's light snores, which told him he was sleeping soundly. He pulled the Bowie knife from its sheath. It was razor sharp. A piece of killing precision.

Roth crept silently towards the bed, the knife raised and ready.

He could see the rise and fall of Slade's chest as he slept. The chest was where he would plunge his first strike. As he stood at the edge of the bed and gripped the handle of the knife with both hands, he smiled sadistically.

Suddenly, a dog appeared from under the bed and barked loudly. It surprised Roth and in that instant, Slade's eyes opened.

He saw the knife and made a grab for it as it came downwards towards him with speed and power.

Tony awoke with a start and sat bolt upright in bed. It took him a few moments to realise that it had been a nightmare.

He was bathed in sweat. The clock at his bedside read 5.00am. His sleep had been restless. Not something particularly unusual. Tonight, it was dreams of his dead friend Doug to whom he never had a chance to say goodbye.

The final nightmare of Roth had been the most vivid. The evil bastard had to be stopped. He had murdered too many people.

He thought of the policeman. He wondered if he was also on Roth's trail. He seemed the determined type and so did his asshole sergeant. But if he was on Roth's trail, it meant it would also lead to him. He could up and go now, but he was staying around for Roth. He was not prepared to live the rest of his life looking over his shoulder. He had known deep down this day would come and now he had to prepare for it.

Tony got out of bed. He knew he would sleep no more.

He went into the kitchen and made himself a black coffee. He wrapped a blanket around himself and walked down to the beach to his usual spot. Skipper came and sat by his side. The sun was just rising. Everything seemed as it always did, but today, he felt uneasy. He knew change was coming and he had to be ready for it.

Half an hour later found Tony jogging up the hill towards the lighthouse. The sun warmed him. At the top of the hill, Tony could look out over the channel towards Cardiff.

Below, he could see a few fishing boats moving away from the quay. Tony carried on up to the lighthouse. Skipper ran ahead looking for rabbits in the undergrowth.

Tony ran past the lighthouse on towards the ruins of the military fort and battery, which still had three rusting remains of its guns in place. At one time, they were operational overlooking the sea ready for invasion if it came. Now, they were just lonely sentinels of a time gone by. Brave men had manned them ready to die for Queen and country. Tony could relate to that from his time in the Paras touring Northern Ireland and the Falklands.

There were many such ruins of batteries, forts and towers dotted around the coast now empty. They went back to a time where this country feared invasion from Germany which, thankfully, never came.

The fort had a melancholy feel to it. Once it had stood proud as a symbol of strength; now it was just another obsolete structure that no longer had any use except for cover from the weather for courting couples or teenagers seeking a hiding place to drink a few sly cans of lager.

Tony jogged on towards the north side of the island. He could feel a burning in his lungs as they fought to suck in oxygen. He was a long way off from peak fitness, but he was pleased with his progress. The bullet wounds seemed not to have impaired him too much.

The north side of the island was more barren and rugged. Boats rarely moored on the beaches there as the tide was unpredictable and the rocks deadly. Back in the day, many a ship perished there, and it was an idea spot for smugglers.

Smuggling was most prevalent in the 18th century in Britain. The government collected a great deal of its income from customs duties on tea, cloth, wine and spirits. This meant that the tax was high and made these items expensive. Smuggled goods were a lot cheaper.

Tony looked down onto a small pebble beach known as Buccaneer Cove. He was surprised to see Father Tom Gwynne and Jim Edwards pushing a small motorised dingy into the waves. They then loaded some fishing gear into it and hopped onboard.

Tom caught sight of Tony and waved. Tony returned it and shouted down to him

"You're up bright and early, Tom. I had no idea you were into fishing."

Tom smiled and called back.

"And I will make you fishers of men, Matthew 4:19. We can praise God in many ways Tony. Jim here is giving me a few lessons."

"Well, you go steady, Tom. Those waters can be treacherous."

"We will be fine. We aren't going out too far. I will see no harm comes to him," called Jim.

Jim was a bear of a man in his forties. He had ruddy features from a life battling the sea and winds. Tony did not know him that well, apart from the odd conversation on the docks when he was manning his ferry service like Joe.

Tony raised a hand in acknowledgement and resumed his run. He headed onto a small isolated stone mound which was where he would turn back for home.

It was a dolmen stone, a type of single-chamber megalithic tomb consisting of two or more vertical megaliths supporting a large flat horizontal capstone or 'table'. It dated from around 3000 BC. No one really knew whose tomb it was. It was part of the island's long and chequered history.

Tony stopped at the dolmen and dropped to the grass to go through a routine of push ups and stomach crunches. As he did this, he felt cold air blow on his face.

Intrigued, he stopped his exercise and moved some small rocks to reveal a rusted iron grill in the ground. He now put his ear to it and thought he could hear the sea. It looked like a drainage outlet.

This island was sure full of mysteries.

He rose to his feet and began to jog back down the hill. It was tough on his knees and he realised his body was getting older, but he was determined not to give in to the advancing years.

Your toughest enemy is old Father Time. You can run from him, but the bastard will get you in the end. He remembered those wise words from Ray Steele, one of the hardest men he ever met.

It suddenly made Tony think of those days so long ago as a young man training in Ray's Jujutsu classes, his boxing bouts under the watchful eye of Terry Norris and then working on the doors.

Great memories but now long gone. He realised that his circle of friends had drastically dwindled in recent times.

He picked up his pace and headed back home. It was now time for a hot shower and some breakfast before making some final plans.

Chapter Nineteen

Wyatt and the rest of the group all sat outside a café eating breakfast consisting of bacon rolls and coffee. They had all had an overnight stay in a local Travelodge. Basic but comfortable enough.

The weather was pleasantly sunny, but Wyatt's mood was dark.

Yesterday, Wyatt and Richmond had visited the Harbour authorities and after some digging had come up with three names that fitted the bill for their mystery boatman.

The first name was Jack Reynolds, a fisherman. They had excluded him right away, as he was a man in his seventies. Too old to match the description that Jacobs' wife had given them.

The other two were hard to separate as they were both in the right age bracket of their early forties. Jim Edwards operated the *Emperor* ferry boat and Joe Williams operated the *Mermaid*. They both made trips to the local islands.

They had decided to wait to the following morning and check out both boats when they came into dock.

Wyatt sipped his coffee thoughtfully and then addressed the group.

"Right, let's put together what we have observed. The fishing boats come and go regularly, but they are mainly going out to sea; they are not dropping anybody off, but the ferries certainly do."

Richmond swallowed a mouthful of bacon roll.

"The main place that these ferries seem to go to are three islands out in the channel."

He opened his notebook.

"They are Herring Island, Great Stack and Graig o Mor."

"Any thoughts on which one Slade might be on?" asked Susie Rawlings.

"Yes," replied Richmond, "None of them is exactly big or overpopulated."

"Herring Island is a bird sanctuary with a minimal staff working on it. It is not inhabited by humans, just birds, so I think we can tick that one off the list. Great Stack has a small population but nothing really of note on the island. I favour Graig o Mor. I am sure we will find the bastard. Once we see either of the boats we are looking for, we will question the owners."

"Do you think they are just going to give up any information willingly if one of them is hiding Slade?" asked Matt Sloan.

"Probably not," answered Richmond, "But we will get it out of them one way or another."

Wyatt finished his coffee and added.

"Remember, keep your eyes peeled for Roth. He may already be here."

He looked at Susie Rawlings and Matt Sloan.

"If you do happen to spot him, do not go wading in there without us. "We can't afford to lose anybody else.

They all nodded and got up from the table and made their way towards the ferry services.

From *McDonalds* across the road, Roth watched them go. He recognised the policemen from the hospital and the local news and tabloids. So, they had tracked Slade down as well.

He observed them as they walked along the dockside checking out the boats coming in and going.

He drained his coffee cup, paid his bill, slipped out the door and headed towards the dockside. He was also looking for a ferry to take him to Graig o Mor, but he needed to keep a low profile and not get spotted by the law. He wanted Tony Slade's blood, but he needed to be patient. He had made it this far. He could not afford to mess up now.

Joe started up the *Mermaid* and headed across the waters towards Cardiff. He was nursing an almighty hangover. Staying in bed would have been his first option today, but he needed to get more work in to pay off his debt and he thought it would be better on his own.

Yesterday, he had seen how edgy Tony had become when the television cameras had been on the docks. He had never seen him look so anxious. He could not afford any more incidents like that. It certainly was not good for business.

In recent days, he felt that Tony was a little edgy. He decided not to call him in for any work today.

In all the time he had known Tony, he had never asked him about his story and why he was on the island. Doug Jacobs had pay Joe well enough to shut his mouth and look after this man recovering from gunshot trauma. No questions asked. Up to now, Joe had been cool with that.

Island life kept you pretty much insulated from what was happening in the world. Many islanders did not even own a television. The world wide web was not exactly thriving here either. Although Joe did own a laptop computer, he rarely bothered to use it. Sometimes, no news was good news.

Last night when he got home, he had received another disturbing phone call, this time from a debt company calling in a loan he had taken out to pay for his boat rental charges. Stupidly, he had used the money to gamble and it had been a risk which saw him lose the lot. They told him in no uncertain terms what was going to happen to him if he did not settle his bill. They hinted that boats could be notorious fire hazards and he needed to be vigilant.

Joe knew only too well what they meant. The screw was being well and truly turned on him. He felt trapped.

After the call, he hit the whisky bottle and went online with the thoughts of signing up to another gambling site, but resisted the temptation. Instead, he read the latest world news. This was where he came across an image of a man who looked very much like Tony Swan.

The image was of a man then in his thirties wearing the parachute regiment purple beret. This man's name was Tony Slade. The news item was about his disappearance in connection with what they called the *Alpha Coffee House Massacre.*

Intrigued by what he read, he went on to pull up dozens of news reports on the coffee shop shootings and how Tony was the only survivor of the people shot. There were also stories speculating about his connections with a Northern gangster Kenny Robbins. The deeper he dug, the more he found. He realised the police were still looking for him in connection with the murder of Robbins and some of his cronies.

But the thing that really caught his eye was the reward from the homicide and major crime command who were offering £25,000 for information leading to his capture. That was a lot of money. Money that would dig him out of the deep hole he was in. Tony was on the radar of the National Crime Agency who list Britain's Most Wanted, and Joe knew exactly where he was.

Joe hated himself for even considering this thought, but he was in dire straits.

Fuck, he realised Tony was hiding something, but this was big. The police were desperate to find him, and Joe could provide that information. Nobody would know it was him who leaked Slade's whereabouts. He didn't owe him anything.

If his business folded, he would be ruined. His life was on the island. Apart from the army, this was the only other life he knew.

He could not start over again, not at his age. He loved his job. He liked being his own boss and being out on the waters. He could not lose all of that.

He downed the remainder of his glass and poured another.

He scanned the articles again and jotted down the names of the police involved and found the name of the man who had overseen the case. It was a D.C.I. Wyatt based in Bristol. There was an emergency number you could ring. He wrote it down.

Joe now eased the boat into the Bay. It was busy today. Weekends were always manic. All the big ferry boats had docked in the prime spots, so he was forced to find a mooring further down the dock than he would have liked. By the time any customers found him and his boat, the big boys would have taken most of the crowds with them.

He searched in his pocket for a mint and felt the scrap of paper with the police emergency number on. In the cold light of day this morning, things did not seem so clear cut and he did feel a pang of guilt.

His mobile phone suddenly sounded, and he took it from his pocket and regarded the screen. He sighed as he saw the name of the caller. It was Ronald Coates.

"Morning, Ron. What can I do for you?"

"The clock is ticking, Williams. Any news for me?"

"Look, Ron. I am out on the water now looking for business. I need a bit more time. That's all."

Coates chuckled.

"Don't we all, Joe. But you are beginning to sound like a fucking broken record. Make sure you are back on the island by 1.00pm. I have a couple of associates coming over to have a look at your business."

"Hey. Hold on a minute, Ron. There is no need for this."

"There is every need, Joe. Just some insurance against your debt. We need to know what assets you have because we will take whatever we need against the money you owe. Plus interest, of course.

Joe clenched his jaw.

"Fuck you, Coates. Send who you want. Yu won't get anything from me."

Coates laughed.

"We will see. Either way, it's happening, so be there."

The phone went dead.

Joe slammed his fist down on the steering column of the boat. Bollocks. Coates really meant it. The vultures were gathering faster than he had anticipated.

Wyatt and Richmond spotted the *Emperor* dock.

"Right, we will take this one. You two keep a look out for the *Mermaid*."

Susie Rawlings nodded.

"Keep in phone contact at all times," added Wyatt.

Both policeman walked towards the boat and produced their warrant cards to the owner.

"Mr Edwards. Jim Edwards?" asked Wyatt.

The man seemed surprised.

"Yes, that's me. How can I help you, gentlemen?"

"Mind if we come aboard a moment? We have a few questions to ask you."

Edwards tied off the rope of his boat.

"In connection with what?"

"I rather we did this in private, if you don't mind," said Wyatt.

Edwards seemed agitated.

"Well, as long as it isn't going to take too long. I have a business to run and Saturdays are busy. If people can't get onto my boat, they will use somebody's else's. Time is money."

"We will be as quick as we can then," answered Richmond.

Edwards looked around to a young girl on the boat who seemed in her late teens.

"Julie, collect the money from the customers, will you, love? And let me know when the boat is full. I won't be long."

The girl nodded.

"Okay, Dad."

Edwards looked back at the two policemen.

"Shall we?"

He gestured to the front of the boat.

Joe sat at the stern of his boat drinking a cup of takeaway coffee and cursing under his breath. Fucking Coates. He was turning the screw.

He reached into his pocket, took the scrap of paper out of his pocket and regarded the number and Wyatt's name. He now had no choice. It was every man for himself. He rang the number and told the woman on the other end of the phone that he had news in relation to Tony Slade and he would only speak to D.C.I. Wyatt. He was told that his message would be forwarded to him as he was out of the office at present.

Joe returned the phone to his pocket. His hand was shaking.

He was then surprised by a voice nearby. He had not seen a man walk up to the boat.

"Excuse me, pal? Are you going over to Graig o Mor?"

Joe regarded the man. He had gelled-back jet black hair and a small goatee beard. He also had piercing green eyes. He sensed something about this man, but could not quite put his finger on it.

"Yes, I am. Just need to fill the boat up before I sail."

The man smiled.

"Great, I will hop on then and wait."

"Sure, no problem. That will be £9.80, please," replied Joe.

The man produced a £10 note. Joe gave him a ticket. "I will just get you your change."

The man walked on up to the front of the boat.

"No sweat for 20p, pal. Just put it in the charity box."

Joe watched him go and could not shake the feeling of unease.

His attention was then distracted when he saw an attractive girl climbing on board his vessel. Her brunette hair was styled in a page boy haircut. She had cute elfin features. She was with an overweight guy carrying a couple of expensive looking cameras around his neck.

"Excuse me. What island are you heading for today?" asked the woman.

"Graig o Mor this morning. Is that where you want to go?"

"Spot on. Thank you."

The woman and man paid their fee and looked for a seat. Another half a dozen people now followed suit. Joe afforded himself a small grin. Ironic that he was going to have a boatful of passengers, but it was too little too late.

Chapter Twenty

Tony stood inside the doorway of Annie Yorath's store. He sipped on a cup of coffee and scanned the sea. Joe's boat had not been in the jetty when he had looked. He must have gone out early this morning. He wondered why he had not phoned him to accompany him out. Maybe he had private business to deal with in Cardiff.

He felt sorry for him. Tony had not had any idea that his business was in such trouble.

He thought momentarily of the holdall stashed away in his cottage that still contained around £240,000 of Kenny Robbins' money. He had hardly used any of it because it was his passage off the island and a fresh start. A start he had to now face without Annette.

Maybe he should ask Joe how much he owed. He might be able to help him and do something good before he left the island. He decided he would speak with him later. His thoughts returned to the sea.

Fishing boats and ferry boats dotted the ocean. He wondered who was on them and who was coming to the island. He touched the handle of the Sig in his coat pocket. It was reassuring to feel its weight.

He felt the ever-present tingle of the dripping tap of anticipatory adrenaline in his belly. He knew that sooner rather than later he would have to release it before the beast took control of him and not the other way around.

When he was a young soldier on patrol in Belfast, he lived with this anticipatory adrenaline every day. It was what kept him alive, but he knew it could be corrosive and tiring. It had been a while since he had felt it.

"No work today, Tony?"

It was Annie's voice. Tony turned his attention away from the sea.

"Not today, Annie. Day off, I guess."

Annie smiled.

"And you are spending it here. I thought a man like you would be heading for the mainland, looking for what they call a 'little action'."

Tony laughed.

"Annie, believe me, I have seen all the action I need to see in my life."

"Never, Tony. You are still a man in his prime."

"Never judge a book by its cover, pet. I might look in shape but under these clothes, my body is a wreck.'

Annie put on her best sensuous voice.

"That, darling, I have no evidence of, so to speak, unless, of course, you would like to show me."

Tony finished his coffee and threw the paper cup into a bin.

"I wouldn't inflict that on anybody, Annie."

As he said this, he gave her a wink and made for the door.

"Be seeing you, pet"

He heard her shout.

"You are nothing but a big tease, Tony Slade."

He walked along the front trying to enjoy the warm sun and the hustle and bustle of the simple island life. Most people were still buzzing about the visit of the television cameras and getting an opportunity to appear on the show *Where the Land Meets the Sea*. It made big news for them in their close-knit community.

He then heard his name being called. Tony turned to see Tom Gwynne walking towards him.

"Time for a cuppa today or something a little stronger, Tony? I have a spare hour."

Tony glanced towards the sea and thought about making his excuses, but decided this may be the last occasion he got to talk with Tom and he liked the old boy.

"Why not? Lead the way."

Once inside his cottage, Tom brewed some coffee and topped up the mugs with a generous splash of Jameson's whisky. They took their drinks to the cosy living room. Both men settled into armchairs that looked out through a feature glass window to the sea. It was idyllic.

"Catch anything this morning, Tom?" asked Tony.

For a moment, the old man looked confused.

"Catch?" he asked.

"Down at the cove earlier, remember?"

"Oh right. Sorry, the old grey matter isn't as sharp as it used to be. In answer to your question, no, I didn't. But to be honest, I am not much of a fisherman. I just enjoy the peace and solitude down there and Jim is good company."

Tom changed the subject.

"Well, Tony, what about you? What's new?"

"I am going to be leaving the island next week, Tom. It's time to move on."

The older man took a sip of his coffee and nodded. He did not seem surprised.

"I didn't have you down as a man who settles in one place long, especially here. The army can give you a wandering soul."

"So, how come you stayed here?"

The clergyman smiled.

"Ah. Well, I am seventy-five years old next month. My wandering days are well and truly behind me."

"No regrets?" asked Tony.

"Dear God, plenty, but you can't change the past."

Tony thought on this.

"No, I guess you are right. But what about your dreams? Have you lived them?"

The older man was silent for a moment. He then put his mug down.

"I had a few left, but unfortunately, my time has run out."

Tony was puzzled.

"What do you mean?"

"No one knows this, Tony, apart from Jim, who has been supporting me in recent times. But I am dying of cancer. Pancreatic. It's hard to detect early and very aggressive. 25% chance of surviving a year. It's not good."

Tony was genuinely shocked by this revelation.

"I am so sorry, Tom. I had no idea."

"Why would you? At present, I can still get about and perform my duties, so nobody would know, but that will all stop soon."

"How do you feel about that?"

"At first, I was frightened, then angry, but eventually, I accepted it. I have had a good life overall. I have made my peace with my maker."

"Have you any family, Tom?"

"I have a sister who is younger than me but lives in New Zealand. We lost touch many years ago. One of my regrets, I'm afraid. But recently, I tracked her down.

I had planned to find her and go out there to visit. The one last dream I cannot, unfortunately, now achieve."

Tom saw the concern on Tony's face.

"Don't worry. I will have care when the time comes, and I do not now fear death."

"How does your faith hold up when a thing like this happens? You have given your life to God and this is how he repays you. Why?" asked Tony.

"I have given my life to helping others, Tony, not just God. I did this through my religion. When I decided to do this, my own mortality never came into it."

"So, do you think God has bigger plans for you elsewhere?"

Tom laughed.

"Maybe he has. I will have to wait and see. For now, I will enjoy the time I have. I have the church and my congregation.

Most weeks I walk to the north side of the island a couple of times weather permitting and go down to Buccaneer Cove, as you now know, and meet Jim to fish and have a chat. I bought my own small motorised dingy to enjoy the sea. I keep it moored on the beach. It is safe. Nobody ever goes down there.

I do a bit of soul searching and, of course, I take a little hip flask with me for medicinal purposes, you understand. I don't need no more."

Tony raised his mug.

"Well, in that case, amen to that."

The two men become silent, both lost in their thoughts. It was Tom who broke the silence.

"Anyway, enough about me. Can I ask you something?"

"Sure," replied Tony.

"What or who are you running away from Tony?"

"What makes you think I am running away?"

The older man laughed.

"Tony, nobody comes to live on Graig o Mor unless they are trying to get away from their past. Am I right?"

Tony regarded Tom.

"Is that why you are here?"

"Do you always answer everything with a question?"

"Who me?" mocked Tony.

Both men now laughed.

"Tony, I came here because my Archbishop told me to. I serve God wherever it takes me. So, that is my reason. No mystery. So, what is yours?"

Tony sipped his coffee.

"Well, do you want to share your story?" asked Tom.

"You mean like a last confession to cleanse my soul?"

"If you like. We have all sinned. It is nothing to be ashamed of, especially if you seek forgiveness. Here, let me top you up."

Tom reached across for the whisky bottle.

In this man's gentle company, Tony suddenly felt the need to unload the burden that he had carried on his shoulders for so long. As he began to tell his story, Tom listened intently. By the time he was finishing, he noticed the older man had nodded off to sleep. Whether it was his illness or the whisky, Tony was not sure.

He rose from his chair, reached over and took the empty whisky glass from Tom's hand. The man did not stir.

Tony smiled and left. How much Tom Gwynne would remember when he awoke was anybody's guess.

But he felt better for telling him. He knew this conversation would go no further.

As Tony shared his past with Tom Gwynne, Joe guided his boat into the jetty and tied it off. The passengers began to disembark. The attractive brunette passed him and asked, "Is there a pub on the island?"

"Indeed, there is, just the one. *The Smuggler's Haunt.* You can't miss it. Just follow the pathway here straight up to the front."

The woman flashed him an engaging smile.

"Thank you very much... I am sorry, I didn't catch your name."

Joe returned the smile.

"Joe. Joe Williams."

The woman extended her hand.

"Susie Rawlings."

Joe shook it. Her skin felt soft and cool.

"Are you an islander, Joe?"

"Yes, born and bred."

'I work for a newspaper. This is my colleague Matt. I would love to do a story about the island from an islander's point of view. Would you be interested in talking to me?'

Joe became wary.

"I don't think so. I am a busy man."

Susie smiled her best smile once again.

"I am in a position to pay you for your time. What do you say?"

The mention of money changed Joe's mind.

"Okay, you twisted my arm. I finish work early evening."

"Great," replied Susie, "I will be in the pub, say 6.00pm? See you later."

Joe watched her go. He admired her disappearing shapely figure. He was roused from his thoughts by the man with the goatee.

"Excuse me, pal. Do you have a hotel on the island?"

"No," replied Joe, "But there are a couple of B&Bs. Just follow on pass the shops and you will come to them. Both are good."

The man nodded.

"Thanks. Have a good day."

The man lightly jumped off the boat and made his way up the cliff path.

Joe still had an uneasy feeling about him.

D.C.I. Wyatt and Sergeant Richmond sat back in the dockside café they had been in earlier. They were waiting for the *Mermaid* to come back from Graig o Mor. It was due within the hour. They were both in high spirits.

Their chat with Jim Edwards had proved most helpful. Edwards had been at the job for years and knew the comings and goings of everybody on the dock.

He told the police that he made trips to Herring Island and Great Stack for a bit of fishing. There was not much else on them of interest. Graig o Mor was the main island.

He went on to tell them that most of the big boat franchises had the major trips covered there, but apart from him, there was one local man still trying to give them a run for their money. That man was Joe Williams who ferried the *Mermaid*. Jim had also told them that he was an islander, but had served his time in the army.

That was the link that they had been looking for between this Joe Williams, Doug Jacobs and Tony Slade. The final piece of information, though, had been the icing on the cake.

When probed further, Jim revealed that for the past three or four months, Joe had another man working the boat with him, although he had not seen him today. His name was Tony Swan.

When asked for a description, the old man had pretty much described Tony Slade. They had finally found the bastard.

Jim asked if Tony was in some sort of trouble, but Wyatt assured him that he was just helping with enquiries. This seemed to satisfy the man that he had not got anybody in trouble.

They thanked Jim for his help and let him get on with his work.

Back at the café, Richmond ordered two coffees and returned to the window table that Wyatt and himself had chosen.

"So, how are we going to play this, Gov?"

"We take the ferry with this Joe Williams when it gets here, and we lay it on the line for him. We want to know where Slade is. Then, you and me will surprise him."

"What about the local boys?" asked Richmond.

"I don't think initially we need to worry them unless Slade tries to make a break for Cardiff. Then, we can get them on standby to pick him up."

Richmond smiled.

"Sounds good. We don't need anybody else stealing your thunder, Sir. This is going to be your collar and rightly so."

Wyatt nodded.

"Indeed. I have lay awake many a night waiting for this moment. I don't want any fuck ups now."

"Talking of fuck ups. What about Rawlings and Sloan?"

Wyatt was about to answer, but paused as a young girl brought their coffees to the table. When she had gone, he continued.

"As promised, we will give them their story, but only after we make the collar."

Richmond looked out the window.

"I don't expect Slade is going to come quietly, do you?"

Wyatt smiled ruefully.

"I don't think so, Steve."

Richmond took a sip from his coffee.

"Good. I wouldn't want it any other way."

Wyatt regarded the younger man.

"Do not underestimate him, Steve. If you poke an old lion, it will still bite."

The D.C.I.'s phone sounded and he answered. Richmond watched his boss as his features registered disbelief as the person on the other end spoke.

"Right, give me his number."

A few seconds later, Wyatt pocketed his phone.

"Steve, you are never going to believe this. We have just had a call placed to our Crimestoppers number with information about Slade."

Richmond raised his eyebrows.

"Genuine?"

Wyatt smiled.

"I think so. The caller was a Joe Williams."

"Your joking, Gov."

"No, I am not. But what intrigues me is why is he giving him up now after all this time?"

Wyatt pulled out his phone again.

"Time to find out, I think. I have got his number here."

Joe watched the last few passengers leave his boat. His mobile rang. He did not recognise the number but answered. He knew who it would be.

"Mr Williams. This D.C.I. Wyatt here. I understand you have information about Tony Slade?"

Joe paused for a second. This was it now. If he carried on, there was no turning back.

"Yes, that's right," replied Joe.

His throat felt dry.

"Well, Mr Williams. You may not believe this, but I am sitting at Cardiff Bay waiting for your ferry service. So, how about coming over and we can talk face to face."

When Joe got off the phone, he felt sick. The cops had somehow found the lead to the island and the connection between him and Slade. It had all gone too far now to stop. He needed to get back across the Bay and finish this.

As Joe prepared for his return trip, he spied another small vessel dock close to him. Three men disembarked rather awkwardly and walked towards his boat with purpose. He knew straight away that this was, as promised, Coates' 'business associates' coming to visit. He ran his eyes over them appraisingly.

The man in the lead was suited and booted smartly. Designer sunglasses hid his eyes. He looked to be in his sixties and carried a briefcase. Joe presumed he would be the talker.

Behind him were two big men. Both had shaved heads and sported leather jackets. Joe estimated both were in their thirties.

As they got closer, he noted one of the men had a nose that seemed to have been broken a few times. The other man had a pair of cauliflower ears which suggested he may either have rugby or wrestling experience.

"Mr Williams?" the older man called.

"Yes" replied Joe ignoring the extended hand.

"I am Harry Webb. I work for Mr Coates. I take it he told you we were coming."

Joe jumped down from his boat and stood in front of the man named Webb.

"Yeah, he did. I wish I could say I am pleased to see you, but I am not."

Webb spread his arms.

"I understand Mr Williams. These things are never easy. If we could just look over your boats as a way of valuation, then we will be on our way."

"And what if I refuse?"

Webb glanced around at the two big men behind him.

"That wouldn't really be in your best interests. Plus, I would hate to have to take another route."

Williams smiles ruefully.

"Who are these guys? Your public relations officers?"

Webb smiled.

"This is Mervin and Colin. Let's say they deal in insurance."

Both men regarded Joe stony faced.

"Look, Mr Webb. If you just give me another forty-eight hours, I will have the money and there will be no need for any of this."

Webb shook his head.

"It is far too late for that. You have become a liability that we no longer want. You have taken advantage of Mr Coates' good nature for too long with false promises. Therefore, we are here. Now, if you will just step out of the way, please."

Webb went to move past Joe. Joe immediately blocked his way.

"Sorry, but you are not going to set foot on my vessel until I speak with Mr Coates and explain the change in my circumstances. It's as simple as that."

"Oh dear, Mr Williams. I am sorry you feel that way."

With this, he nodded, and Mervin and Colin moved forward menacingly. Joe braced himself and spread his legs for better balance. He could handle himself, but two of these goons might be a step too far. Whatever the outcome, they were not coming on his boat. The man called Mervin produced a heavy looking cosh from his pocket.

"Get the fuck out of the way while you can still walk," he growled at Joe.

"Everything alright here, Joe?"

The voice had come unexpectedly, and Joe glanced over the shoulders of the two thugs to see Tony Slade standing there.

"Friends of yours?" asked Tony.

"Not really, no," replied Joe.

"Thought as much."

By now, the two big men had turned their attention towards Tony.

"Why don't you fuck off, Dad? This hasn't got anything to do this you," snarled Mervin.

"Yeah. Well, as it happens, it does. I work for this man and he is my friend. So, why don't you all crawl back under the stone where you came from?"

"Fuck you, wise ass."

Mervin moved towards Tony brandishing the cosh. Tony was way ahead of him. He had been here a hundred times before. He thrust-kicked the big man hard in the solar plexus. This took the wind completely out of him and put him in the dock. The man thrashed around in the cold water trying to get his breath.

Colin made his move, but Joe grabbed him around the neck in a choke hold. The man went ballistic trying to get out of the hold, but not before Tony steamed forward and slammed two brutal punches into Colin's balls.

He sunk to his knees with a grunt of pain. This gave Tony the chance to bring an edge of the hand chop down on the back of his neck that had him sleeping like a baby.

Harry Webb stood rooted to the spot in shock. Tony moved towards him and he suddenly flinched in fear.

"I take it this situation is about Mr. William's temporary cash flow problems to pay his outstanding debts?"

Webb nodded still dumbfounded that his two colleagues had been dispatched with such ease like cattle in a slaughterhouse.

"Well, tell your boss that he will have his money in the next day or so just like the man told you. Understand?"

Webb nodded dumbly.

"Now get your two gorillas on your boat and get the fuck off this island whilst I am in the mood to let you."

Webb went to their aid. While he did this, Joe took Tony to one side.

"Thank you, Tony. That situation could have got tricky if you hadn't shown up."

"Well, I had just finished a little afternoon's Irish coffee with Father Tom and after he had given me his daily blessing, I thought that I would seek out my good deed for the day."

Joe smiled.

"Well, thank you.

"No problem, my friend. You would have done the same for me."

Joe was momentarily silent. Guilt washed over him as he thought of his phone call to the police.

"You okay?" asked Tony.

"Yes, yeah, I am fine."

They watched as the boat with the three men left the dock. They all looked a sorry sight.

From the safety of the boat, Webb shouted, "You haven't heard the end of this. We will be back."

"Ok, Arnie," quipped Tony as the boat sailed away.

He then turned back to Joe.

"I don't think they are going to try anything again today. Look, when you are finished, can you pop up to the cottage this evening?"

Joe nodded. He felt a tightness in his stomach.

"Yeah sure. Any reason?"

"Just something I would like to run by you. That's all. I am planning to leave the island next week."

Joe's eyes widened.

"You are. When exactly?"

"Not sure. Look, we will talk later."

Joe tried to remain calm but inside his stomach was churning. He regarded Tony.

"Okay. And thanks again. I have got to go. I have got one more run to do today."

"You sure you don't want me to come with you just in case."

"No, no. I am fine, honestly. Like you said, they won't be back today."

Tony thought his friend was a little anxious but let it go. He made to go back up the jetty, but then stopped.

"Joe, just a quick question."

"Yeah, shoot. What is it?"

"This morning when you ferried customers over here, was there anybody unusual that stood out from the normal onboard?"

"Well, there was an attractive brunette newspaper reporter doing a piece on the island."

"Oh yeah. Female, I take it?" quipped Tony.

Joe laughed.

"Yes, female. In fact, she wants to meet me for a drink a little later and have a chat."

"Does she now."

Tony knew it was too much of a coincidence for this brunette reporter not to be the meddlesome Susie Rawlings.

"What was her name?"

"Susie. Susie Rawlings. Why do you ask?"

"No reason. Anybody else?"

Joe thought for a few seconds.

"Just a creepy guy with a goatee beard and an intense stare. Unnerved me for some reason."

Tony felt a tingle of adrenaline run through his body.

"Do you know where he is now?"

"Not really, but he was asking about a B&B."

Tony nodded deep in thought.

"Everything okay, Tony?"

Tony scanned the surrounding area.

"Yeah, everything is just fine. I will see you later. Like I said, I want to run something important by you."

With that, Tony turned and walked back up the jetty. He was now on red alert. From Joe's description of the man, it could only be Roth. He was here.

Chapter Twenty-One

Andy Roth settled into the small but comfy room in the *Harbour Lights* Bed and Breakfast. It was run by a nice old bird named Mrs McGrath. Call me Peggy, she had told me as she went through the house rules and breakfast times.

Roth mused that it was not dissimilar to prison, but he did not plan on spending too long here. He had introduced himself as Graham White and had paid cash up front for a few days.

He opened his holdall, searched beneath his small pile of clothes and smiled as his hand wrapped around the handle of a wicked looking 10" matt black Bowie knife.

He would wait for evening to come and then go on the hunt for Slade. The island was small, and he knew he would find him sooner or later, but ideally, he wanted to catch him unaware. He wanted to see the fear in the bastard's eyes. He had waited so long for this moment and he meant to savour it.

Roth was also no fool. He knew Slade would be no pushover. He could not afford to underestimate him. He would have to use guile and cunning to cut down his prey. A sudden knock on the door drew him from his thoughts.

"Yes?" he called.

"It's only me, Mr White. Peggy. I have some clean towels here for you. I will leave them outside your door. Is everything alright with your room?"

Roth stood looking at his reflection in the full-length mirror on the wardrobe door. He brandished the Bowie knife menacingly.

"Everything is just perfect, Peggy. Thank you."

The *Mermaid* sped across the waves. Joe stood at the helm. The boat was empty.

His mind was in turmoil. He felt bad about Tony, especially after his timely intervention back on the island with Coates' thugs. He thought about turning back and not meeting the policemen, but that would not change anything. He would still be up to his neck in debt.

Tony had probably prevented him taking a beating, but he knew Coates would be more than pissed at him and they would be back with reinforcements and more interest to pay on the loan. Then he also had the debt collectors connected to the online gambling habit breathing down his neck.

Every time his phone rang these days, he expected the worst. The reward money would go a long way to buying him some more time.

He had two choices open to him. He either jumped off the cliffside on Graig o Mor and let the ocean claim him and all his debts or he took the reward money like a Judas from the police and live to fight another day. The die was cast and there was no going back now.

As his boat approached the Bay, he saw two men waiting at the quayside. He knew, without doubt, by their clothes and demeanour that they were police. He docked his boat and his passengers got off. He then roped off the entrance to the *Mermaid* and hung a *Not in Service* sign off it. He regarded the two men.

"D.C.I. Wyatt, I presume?"

Wyatt flashed his warrant card.

"Yes, it is, and this is Sergeant Richmond. And you must be Joe Williams?"

Joe nodded.

"May we come on board," gestured Wyatt.

"Help yourself," replied Joe.

Both men boarded.

"Okay, Mr. Williams. You left a message for me saying that you have information on Tony Slade. So, what have you got?"

Joe sighed and sat down on one of the benches. The two policemen joined him.

"If I tell you, nobody must ever know where this information came from. I do not want my name mentioned. Okay?"

Wyatt nodded.

"It will all be confidential."

"And the money. The reward. That is guaranteed, right?"

"If the information you give us leads directly to Slade's arrest, then the £25,000 will go directly into your bank account. You have my word. Now, what have you got?"

"Tony Slade is on Graig o Mor and has been for nearly six months. He worked on my boat. He pretty much kept himself to himself. He was recovering from gunshot wounds, I believe."

"Did Doug Jacobs organise this?" asked Richmond.

Joe remained quiet, reluctant to drop another friend in it. Wyatt sensed this.

"There is no point in covering up for Mr Jacobs. Unfortunately, he passed away a few days ago."

"What!" exclaimed Joe in horror, "How?"

Wyatt went on to briefly explain about Roth and how he was also tracking down Tony. Joe now realised why Tony had been so paranoid about not being seen. It was not just the police that he was running from.

"Yes, Doug arranged it. He is… was a friend of mine and asked me to look after Tony, no questions asked. That's what I did."

"And you didn't question any of this?" enquired Richmond.

Joe Williams regarded him.

"No. We were all ex-army looking after each other. You never question helping a brother in arms."

"So, why come forward now with this information?" asked Richmond.

Joe looked him in the eye.

"It's personal. I need the money. That's all."

"Care to share it with us."

Joe shook his head.

"Does Slade have any inkling that we are coming or that you may have shopped him?" continued Wyatt.

"No. Not as far as I know. I have said nothing. But he did tell me earlier that he was planning on leaving the island soon."

Wyatt stood up and took a deep breath of sea air.

"Where does he live on the island?"

"In a fisherman's cottage at the top of the cliffs. It's named *Seaspray*."

"Does he live there alone?" asked Richmond.

Joe nodded.

"Yes, just him and his dog. A Jack Russell."

"Take us to the island, Mr Williams," said Wyatt

"What will happen to him?" asked Joe.

The D.C.I. turned and looked out towards the distant rocky crags of Graig o Mor.

"That will depend on Slade."

Wyatt felt a tingle of adrenaline in his belly as the boat engine started up.

Andy Roth left his room and went downstairs. Mrs McGrath was polishing the hallway furniture.

"Hello, Mr White."

Roth flashed his best smile.

"Graham, please Edith."

Edith blushed slightly.

"Okay, Graham."

"Where is all the action on this island then, Edith?"

Edith laughed lightly.

"If you came here for action, then I am afraid you are in the wrong place."

Roth faked mock surprise.

"What? No casino, lap dancing club or drug den?"

"Sorry. We have a pub though."

Roth checked his hair in the ornate hallway mirror.

"That will have to do then."

He stepped closer to Edith.

"Seriously, Edith. I am here to visit an old buddy of mine, Tony Slade. We served in the parachute regiment together many years ago. We lost track of each other, but recently, a mutual acquaintance of ours told me he was living here. A bit unusual for Tony,

I must say. He was always such a livewire. No disrespect like."

"None taken, Graham. Our little island isn't exactly Las Vegas."

"Do you know Tony then?" asked Roth.

"Well, not to speak to, but I know he lives in the *Seaspray* cottage up beyond the cliffs and he has been working for Joe Williams on his boats. He came here about six months ago. Keeps himself to himself really. Seems nice enough though."

Roth contained his excitement.

"He's a real diamond, our Tony. I am here as a surprise so I would appreciate you didn't mention me or anything to do with me being here for now. I am trying to arrange a big army reunion."

Edith returned to her polishing.

"How lovely. Don't worry. I won't say a word. He will probably be in *The Smuggler's Haunt* at this hour. I expect he will be surprised to see you."

Roth headed to the front door.

"Yes, I expect he will. See you later, Edith."

"Oh, Mr White. You might want to bring a raincoat. I heard on the local news that a storm is heading this way tonight. Very heavy rain and sea mists."

"Thank you, Edith. I will try and be back before it comes."

Roth disappeared into the night.

The *Mermaid* docked into its usual spot on the jetty and Wyatt and Richmond disembarked.

"Right. Thank you, Mr Williams. I will be in touch very soon. Just keep your head down and all will be okay. We will get Slade and you will have your money."

Joe nodded. He did not feel good about himself.

"His cottage is at the top of there, you say?"

Wyatt looked up to the cliffs.

"Yeah. You cannot miss it. It has a *Seaspray* name plaque on the outside wall above the door."

"Nothing unexpected we don't know about up there?"

"Not that I am aware of. Like I said, he has a dog, Skipper. But it is a Jack Russell, not a Doberman, so you should be safe."

Wyatt laughed. His face then returned to be serious.

"I don't suppose you might know if he in is in possession of a firearm?"

Joe looked surprised.

"Shit! No, I don't. I have never seen one and he certainly hasn't mentioned it."

"Right. Thanks. Oh, and by the way, I would appreciate that you kept our presence on the island just between us."

"Of course, Detective Chief Inspector. I have as much reason to keep this quiet as you do."

Wyatt nodded in acknowledgment and both policemen walked up the pathway away from the jetty.

Joe looked at his watch. It was nearly six. Time to meet Susie Rawlings and see what she had to offer. If there was money on the table for a story, he would give her it. He felt bad about what he had done, but he now knew that he would be able to save the family business and that was all that mattered to him.

When his girlfriend Marion had left him, it was not just because she could not handle island life. She had also told him that she was carrying his child. A son.

She had said she did not want a baby growing up on this godforsaken island and had asked Joe to sell up the business and move to the mainland. But he was reluctant. Employment was tough and the business was or had been his safety net. They argued daily about this with Marion threatening to leave with their unborn son.

Joe got stubborn and dug in his heels. One day, he had returned to their home after work and found her gone. A note explained that she could not stand another day on the island and that she could not face bringing up her baby on it. That was it. She was gone with no forwarding address.

But Joe hoped one day that he would meet up with his son. He did not have anything of worth in his life except his boating business. Maybe he could leave the business to his boy. That is why it meant so much to him and why he could not risk losing it.

Tony Slade watched Roth leave the *Harbour Lights* B&B from the cover of the bushes and trees of the front garden.

It had not been hard to find him. After all, there was only this B&B and the *Waterfront* a little further down the hill.

Roth was heading down the hill, probably towards *The Smugglers Haunt*. Tony watched him go and then stealthily made his way back up the hill and headed back to his cottage.

It was time to prepare for Roth. He knew when Roth did not find him in the pub that he would come to the cottage. Tony was going to be ready for him.

Chapter Twenty-Two

Joe headed towards the pub. He was running late. As he neared the entrance, he saw Susie and her colleague sat at a window seat. She waved and he acknowledged her. Just as he was about to enter through the door, his phone rang. He took it out of his pocket and saw it was Tony calling. Now what?

"Hello, Tony. Everything okay?"

"Joe, I need you to get up to my cottage right now. I will explain everything when you get there, but I haven't much time. Can you come right away?"

Joe could hear the urgency in the other man's voice and this concerned him.

"Yeah, sure. I am on my way."

The phone went dead. Joe slipped it back in his pocket. He cursed under his breath. This was all he needed. He glanced towards the window and saw Susie Rawlings watching him.

Joe needed to find out Tony's plans, as he could not risk him slipping off the island; otherwise, that was the end of his reward money.

He made his decision. The journalist would have to wait. He headed away from the pub in the direction of Tony's cottage.

Susie Rawlings saw him turn and walk away. This puzzled her. She got up from the table and told Matt

Sloan to wait there for her. She ran outside and shouted Joe's name, but he just carried on walking briskly and did not acknowledge her. She watched him disappear over the brow of the hill.

He was certainly preoccupied and it must have been something to do with the phone call he had just received. He was in a hurry and this intrigued her. Just as she was about to follow him, she heard a familiar voice call her and she turned to see Wyatt and Richmond approaching.

"Slade is on the island. The boatman Joe Williams confirmed it," said Wyatt.

"Really?" replied Susie. "Well, I was just about to have a meet with this Joe Williams, but he received what looked like a rather urgent phone call and he just disappeared up the hill leading out of town."

"Gov, that's the way to Slade's cottage. You don't think he has changed his mind, do you?" questioned Richmond.

Wyatt looked momentarily concerned.

"Only one way to find out. Let's get up there and see. Susie, get Sloan and follow us. This could be our big moment. Steve, radio the police at the Bay and tell them to get a boat with back up out here and keep an eye on the dockside just in case he slips the net again. Also, tell them to do nothing without my say so."

Susie regarded Wyatt and saw the glint in his eye.

"Shouldn't you wait until back up gets here? Slade may not come quietly. And don't forget he is a trained soldier."

Wyatt looked at her. His face was a mass of grim determination.

"This is my case, my collar. Fuck any of the Welsh boys getting credit for this. I am touched by your concern, Susie. I know what Slade may or may not be capable of, but I am going in."

He turned to Richmond who was just finishing his radio call.

"All set, Gov."

"Right then. Let's nail this bastard. Yes?"

"Totally," grinned Richmond.

Wyatt looked back at Susie and Sloan.

"Keep your distance. Once you get to the cottage, you both stay outside. Don't get in my way and you will get what you need."

With that, he turned his back and started walking.

Joe knocked on the door of Tony's cottage. He felt uneasy about the visit. He saw the curtain of the front window part slightly and then he heard the front door being unbolted. Tony appeared in the doorway and gazed momentarily over Joe's shoulder into the gathering dusk. Skipper scuttled around his feet excitedly.

"Come on in," he said.

As soon as Joe entered, Tony shut and locked the door and drew across the bolt. This did not go unnoticed.

"Everything alright, Tony? You look a little spooked."

Tony turned towards Joe.

"Sit down. I need to talk with you urgently."

Now it was Joe's turn to feel spooked.

"Here, let me put Skipper in the bedroom out of the way."

Tony ushered the Jack Russell into the bedroom. The dog reluctantly complied. Joe walked to the kitchen table where he spied a bottle of whisky and two glasses sat on it. He also saw the gun.

"What's with the shooter, my friend?" he asked warily.

Tony sat down and poured two generous measures of whisky into the glasses.

"I will come straight to the point, Joe. My past is about to catch up with me."

Joe accepted the offered glass and took a sip from it.

"I don't understand."

"The man sporting the goatee beard you had on your boat earlier. His name is Andy Roth and he is here to kill me."

Joe was genuinely shocked.

"Shit, Tony. Why?"

Tony went on to briefly explain the reason why he was really there on the island and the accident that happened that resulted in him being there.

Everything was falling into place now as Joe got the full picture of what had happened in the coffee shop in Bristol and why the police were so anxious to catch Tony.

"I now need to get off this island as soon as possible. I am in no doubt that the police are probably due here at any moment also. My time has run out here. But before I go, I must finish off Roth. Once I do, then I need you to sail me out of here up to North Wales. I will then cross over into England and head for Liverpool and get a flight out of there. Will you do me this last favour?"

Joe was silent. His thoughts were running riot in his head. If he agreed to get Tony off the island before Wyatt found him, bang went his reward money and so too his business. But seeing Tony so desperate, he also felt for his friend. Tony sensed Joe's apprehension.

"Look, I know it's a big ask, but I have something for you."

Joe snapped back to reality.

"Something for me?"

Tony got up from his chair and walked across to the sideboard and opened the top drawer. From it, he produced a large brown paper bag.

"When the incident with Robbins went down, I obtained some money that was originally his. Its untraceable. Nobody knows I have it. It was meant to be a nest egg for Annette and me."

Tony paused for a moment.

"Anyway, that's over now, and I will have more than enough money to disappear, so I want you to have this."

Tony handed the bag to Joe who took it.

"What is it?" he asked.

Tony smiled.

"It's the answer to all your problems. There is £40,000 there. More than enough to save your business and pay off the fucking sharks."

Joe stared at the bag and his heart sank. He had been a fool, a judas. The man he had chosen to betray. A man he had called a friend was now offering him a lifeline amidst all the shit he was facing.

"I can't accept it, Tony."

"Yes, you can. It will save that business you love. I want you to have it for all that you have done for me. You earnt it, my friend."

Joe drained his glass and stood up.

"No, I haven't. I am a complete bastard. A waste of space."

Tony looked puzzled.

"Hey, where is this all coming from? Take the money and get on with your life."

Joe raised his head and looked Tony in the eye.

"I have done something unforgivable. I am so sorry. I was desperate."

Tony began to feel unease creep into his body again.

"What do you mean, Joe? What have you done?"

Joe swallowed hard struggling for the words.

"The police were offering a reward of twenty-five grand for your whereabouts. I was in dire straits. I wasn't thinking straight. I…"

Joe's words trailed off as Tony was hit by the full impact of what Joe was saying.

"Are you telling me that you sold me out to the cops? Is that what you are saying, Joe?"

Joe hung his head. When he spoke, it was barely audible.

"Yes. I sold you out for the reward money. I…"

Tony cut him off.

"When are they coming, Joe?"

Joe stumbled over his words.

"I said, when are they fucking coming?" shouted Tony.

"Any time now. They are already on the island."

Tony stood rooted to the spot, his mind working through the possibilities.

"Is it D.C.I. Wyatt and Richmond?"

Joe nodded.

"What about the newspaper woman. Is she in on it too?"

"I don't know, maybe. I am sorry, Tony. I truly am."

Tony moved to the door and unbolted it

"Take the money and get out, Joe. Just leave."

Joe moved to apologise again. Tony grabbed him and pushed him out of the door.

"Have a good life, Joe. Now get out of mine."

He threw the bag of money after him.

"Tony, please listen. I will sail you off here, I promise.'

Tony looked at him as if he was a stranger.

"Forget it. It's too late. The trust is gone. It's done."

Wyatt and the group had taken a wrong turn and had ended up at a dead end. They now stood in front of a five-bar gate that led into a field. In the gathering darkness, they could make out the outline of cows or was it sheep?

"Shit, we will have to go back. This is obviously the wrong road. Come on."

As they turned around, they felt a drop of rain on their heads.

"Bollocks, that is all we need," stated Wyatt.

"A storm is coming according to the weather," said Sloan.

Nobody bothered to answer.

Joe stumbled down the porch steps.

"Tony, please. I am sorry."

The cottage door stayed firmly shut. Joe just stood there. He had fucked everything up and made a right mess of his life.

"Tony, open the door. I want to make amends. Let me help you."

He was only greeted by silence. Wearily, he turned to go and that was when he became aware of a man coming up the garden path. He was moving fast. Joe recognised him immediately. He also saw the knife in his hand. He turned back to the front door and started banging on it frantically with his fists

"Open up, Tony. Quick. He's coming…"

The words got cut short as Joe was grabbed tightly from behind before he could react. Roth clamped the man's mouth shut with his hand and drove the knife blade into his right kidney.

Roth vaguely recognised the person as the boatman who brought him across to the island. No matter though. He was now just another obstacle in the way of him getting to Slade. He pulled the knife out and plunged it in again only deeper. He viciously twisted the blade as he looked towards Tony Slade who was now framed in the doorway of the cottage. A look of shock was upon his features.

Tony watched Joe Williams dying in front of him and there was nothing he could do. He saw the evil glint in Roth's eye and then heard his voice call.

"You're fucking next Slade!"

This spurred Tony into life. He drew his gun and aimed it at Roth. Roth saw it and pushed the dying body of Joe into Tony. The gun discharged harmlessly as Tony fell onto his back with Joe on top of him.

Roth moved forward, but Tony managed to free himself and level the gun on him again. This caused Roth to come to a standstill. Both men stared at each other. Time seemed to stop. Finally, Roth spoke.

"Is this how you want to end it, Slade? Shooting me? Come on. That would be too easy. It wouldn't satisfy a man like you. No, you want to make me suffer for the death of your friends. You want something a bit more drawn out."

Tony regarded Roth with hate in his eyes.

"Is that right? Why should I give a fuck how you die, Roth?"

Tony scrambled to his feet after disentangling himself from Joe. His eyes never left Roth.

Andy Roth smiled malevolently.

"Because you do. You are a fighter, Slade and deep down, you need to see me suffer for my crimes. Yes, you were a soldier, but I know you prefer your hands to guns. So, how about it? You and me. No weapons. Let's settle this the right way."

"Alright, Roth, you piece of shit. Why don't you move out into the garden? Drop the blade and I will put down the gun."

Roth nodded and backed out of the porchway and down the few wooden steps into the garden. The rain was now torrential and he was careful not to lose his footing. Tony stepped over the body of his dead friend on the doorstep and followed him.

His adrenaline was pumping, and he now knew why he had been spared in the shooting. It was to rid the world of scum like Roth.

"Come on then, Roth. Let's do it. Let's see if you are man enough for a straightener face to face or have you only got the balls with a knife in your hand?"

"Well, at last I get the chance I have been waiting for, Slade."

Tony smiled grimly.

"They say be careful what you wish for, Roth. I sense you are only good for creeping up on people and stabbing them like the cowardly shit you are. Facing me one to one could be a big mistake."

Roth sneered back at Tony.

"Don't be too sure, soldier. A man of your advancing years and recovering from some serious injuries. I think I have the advantage."

"Well, let's put down the weapons and find out then," replied Tony.

Just as he said this, he caught the movement of flashlights piercing the darkness and voices. A voice echoed out from the darkness. It carried a distinct Bristolian accent. He had forgot about Wyatt and his little search party. Roth also noted it.

"Both of you, stay where you are. Don't move. Armed Police."

The voice was still a short distance away and the visibility was poor due to the rain. Slade knew that time was now of the essence. He looked at Roth.

The policemen and the two reporters had finally got back onto the right track to the cottage when a gunshot had echoed through the night.

Trudging through the appalling weather conditions, a cottage had loomed out of the darkness up ahead. Through the sheeting rain and darkness, D.C. I. Wyatt saw two figures in the garden of the cottage that they suspected was Slade's. Although he could not identify them fully, he was sure he saw a gun in one of their hands. It had to be Slade. Was the other Roth?

The visibility was minimal as the sea now began to bring in a mist to add to the rain.

Wyatt looked at Richmond.

"We need to get closer, but be careful. One of them is armed, maybe both. Approach with caution. Understood?"

Richmond nodded his reply.

After hearing the approaching voices, Tony spoke quickly.

"It's the police coming, Roth. They are coming for me primarily, but finding you here is going to be a bonus. The trouble is we will never get to do the dance together. So, I suggest you get out of here and I will meet you in ten minutes up by the old lighthouse."

Tony pointed up in the direction of the cliffs.

"We can settle things once and for all there."

Roth looked at him and then again at the advancing flashlights.

"How do I know you are telling the truth? Maybe you are going to run again?"

"I could have shot you a moment ago but chose not to. You are right, Roth. I want this moment as much as you. Shooting you is not enough. You will have to trust me on this, Roth, as we have only minutes before we are both nicked."

Tony saw Roth thinking it over.

"Right, I will see you there. You better show up."

"I would not miss it for the world. You murdered two of my friends and you will answer for that, I promise you."

Without another word, Roth turned and disappeared into the night. Tony moved quickly back towards the cottage stooping momentarily to pick up the bag of money on the porch steps dropped by Joe. He knew that he had very little time left before Wyatt would be on him.

He now came to the motionless body of Joe. Bending down, he turned the man over and checked his pulse. There was nothing.

Joe had come good for him in the end warning him of Roth's presence, but it came with a hell of a price. His money problems were now gone forever.

He got up to go, but on impulse, he searched Joe's pockets and found a key fob which had the keys to both his boats on it. He slipped them in his coat pocket.

A voice shouted again. It was just about audible above the incessant noise of the rain.

"Slade, it's time to stop running. You can't get off this island. The police have it covered. Give yourself up now."

This sounded like Richmond. Fuck him.

Tony hurried into the bedroom. As he opened the door, Skipper shot out and jumped excitedly around Tony.

Tony moved to the wardrobe and removed an old army rucksack. It was already packed with essential belongings and the rest of his stash of money. He opened the rucksack and pushed the paper bag of money inside and strapped it back up. He looked around the cottage that had been his home for a short while. Time to move.

Tony heard voices outside again and the garden gate banging open. Wyatt's voice called out this time.

"Slade, give yourself up now."

Tony swung the bag onto his back, tucked the gun into his waistband and slipped through the kitchen and out of the backdoor. Skipper followed. The night swallowed them both up.

Chapter Twenty-Three

Richmond swung the front gate to the cottage open. He cautiously moved up garden path. Wyatt was right behind him. The D.C.I. looked around at the two reporters hot on his heels.

"Stay here. Don't come any closer until we have secured this area and I know it's safe. That was a gunshot we heard a moment ago."

They both complied.

"Gov, look."

It was Richmond and he was pointing to the prone body on the doorstep. Both policemen drew their firearms and moved cautiously until they were stood over the body.

"Fuck, it's the boatman," hissed Richmond.

"Do you think Slade did this?

Wyatt regarded the body.

"Don't know."

"Is that Slade's body?"

It was Susie Rawlings' voice right behind him. Wyatt turned around.

"Christ, I told you to stay back."

"Is it Slade?"

"No, it is the ferryman, Joe Williams. Looks like he has been stabbed not shot."

Susie brought a hand to her mouth in shock. It had only been a short time ago that she was going to be meeting this man for a drink. Yes, it had been work related, but she had also sensed an attraction towards this stranger. Who had killed him and why?

She turned to Sloan. His face was barely visible inside the hood of his raincoat, but she thought that she saw fear in his eyes.

When he spoke, his voice was a whisper.

"Roth. It has to be Roth. The bastard's here."

Susie was not sure whether it was the damp or not that sent a sudden shiver up her spine. She looked around the garden at the deepening shadows and wondered if they were being watched. Wyatt eyed the area warily.

"You two, go back to the gate and wait there."

Wyatt looked towards the cottage. A dull lamplight illuminated from its interior. Richmond reached in his pocket and produced his phone. Wyatt saw this.

"What are you doing, Steve?"

"Calling for back up, Gov. God knows what has gone on here."

Wyatt grabbed his arm.

"Remember, Sergeant, I am the officer in charge here and I will make that call if needed."

"But, Gov, it could be dangerous. Slade is an unpredictable character. Plus, if this Roth bloke is lurking around as well…"

Wyatt pulled Richmond close to him.

"Get a grip, Steve. You know I am near to retirement. This will probably be my last major arrest. I haven't been answering any of Hardwick's phone calls or texts, so I suspect I am already off the case. I don't give a fuck.

I deserve it, Steve. I need it. I want to be the man to bring in Slade. Do you understand?"

Richmond looked into the eyes of his superior and saw a crazed determination in them that he had not witnessed before. Slade had become more than just another collar; he had become an obsession for Wyatt.

He knew he owed his boss so much, particularly as he had recently put him up for promotion. He could not let him down now.

"Okay, Gov, we play it your way."

Richmond felt the older man's grip relax on his arm. Wyatt nodded.

"Good man. Once we have him, then we can call the reinforcements in. I will take full responsibility, Steve. You will be okay."

Richmond nodded in agreement. Both men approached the cottage giving the doorway a wide berth. Once they were positioned either side of the door frame, Wyatt called out, their guns held high.

"Tony Slade. This is D.C.I. Wyatt. Time to stop running and come quietly. I want you to step out slowly now and no tricks."

There was no reply. In fact, there was no movement at all. Wyatt nodded to his sergeant. Richmond positioned himself and kicked the front door open. In they went.

A quick scan of the main room saw it empty.

A brief search of the kitchen and bedroom made it clear that Slade had gone.

The open back door confirmed this.

"Right, he can't be far. Let's go."

Susie Rawlings and Matt Sloan saw both policemen come out of the cottage and gesture upwards towards them. Sloan looked puzzled, but then it was past his supper time and his belly was rumbling.

"What are they up to now?"

"Looks like Slade has done a runner. We need to get some photos of the body and anything else of interest, then we follow Wyatt."

As they moved forward, the rain came down heavier.

Tony moved through the undergrowth like a panther. His senses were on full alert. He knew he could not trust Roth. He was a psychopath and did not play by the rules. A psychopath had no emotion or conscience.

Slade had underestimated another psychotic bastard in the past by the name of Don Frasier and it nearly cost him his life.

Frasier had worked at a gym owned by gangster Kenny Robbins. He was an ex-marine and a steroid monster. When Tony came to train at the gym and Frasier had found out that he was an ex para, macho banter soon turned to hate and loathing.

In a showdown, Tony had been lucky to live. Frasier had not been quite so lucky.

Tony would not make the same mistakes again.

He knew he would have to kill Roth. A man like him just kept coming. That did not bother Slade unduly. He had killed many times before in the line of duty. He knew he had it in him. His only concern was that he had been recovering from gunshot wounds and his body was not used to the rigours of combat as it had been in the past. He did not know how it would hold up.

All his early talk of Roth being a coward had been bluff to psyche him out. He knew deep down that Roth was going to come at him like a madman.

The heavy rain made visibility in the darkness difficult. The ground had also become a slippery muddy mess unsteady under foot. But Tony had walked and ran this path so many times that he knew every inch of it. Wyatt did not and it would slow the search party down, which was good news for him.

Tony was used to dealing with hostile terrain. He was at home out here and that might just be all the edge he needed. He dropped his head against the driving rain and ploughed on.

Richmond cursed as he slipped on the muddy incline.

"Fucking hell. I nearly broke my ankle."

He steadied himself.

"You okay, Gov?"

Wyatt was puffing a bit. Too much time sat behind a desk these days. He was not in the best of shape.

"Yeah, I am okay. Just keep going, son. I am right behind you."

Both men were soaked to the skin and even with their torches on full beam, they were finding it difficult to follow the rough dirt pathways. Not being familiar with the territory was a massive handicap.

What lay beyond was unknown to them, but they did know that there was only one way up and down this hill. So, they kept going, knowing Slade and probably Roth were somewhere up ahead. There was nowhere else to go.

Tony had now seen the lighthouse up ahead. Its beam shone out to sea. It partially lit up the surrounding area, but there was no sign of Roth. Tony lay his rucksack down by a large rock and scanned the darkness. He was breathing heavily.

In normal circumstances, the climb would have been a walk in the park, but his fitness was not on point and he knew it.

The automated beam of the lighthouse swept out across the angry, dark ocean. The sea mist was getting thicker, but the rain had lightened. Tony shivered in his wet clothes.

"Roth, where are you? Get the fuck out here now," he hissed.

He turned 360 degrees looking through the eerie tendrils of mist floating in the air. Suddenly, the lighthouse's automated foghorn sounded. It broke the silence with a huge bellow that made Tony flinch.

In that moment, Roth came out of the mist and rushed Tony tackling him to the ground. The element of surprise was enough for Tony to land heavily. Roth was on him like a flash throwing punches.

Tony composed himself and from his back, he wrapped his legs around his assailant's waist and fended off his attacks. With his extensive Jujutsu knowledge, he was comfortable to fight on the floor. Tony was rusty and out of practice, but knew he held the cards here.

He grabbed hold of Roth's coat collar and attempted to pull him down closer for a choke hold. Roth gouged at Tony's eyes and throat. Slade shuffled his hips back and as his attacker leant further forward to rip at his face, he hooked a foot inside Roth's legs and turned him up and over unto his back.

Tony came up on top of Roth and smashed punches and elbows down into his face. He was already breathing heavily from the exertion.

The blows contacted with brutal force, but Roth just screamed and laughed like a maniac, spitting blood out through broken teeth.

"Is that all you got, Slade? You pussy."

Tony realised that Roth must have taken some sort of substance and was as high as a kite and freakishly strong.

Tony now smashed a headbutt down into his attacker's face. He went to throw another, but had been unaware that Roth had reached down to his boot and palmed a small combat dagger. The first Tony was aware of it was when he felt a sharp sheering pain in the back of his left buttock. He howled in pain and surprise.

Roth tried to stab again but missed and grazed Slade's hip bone. But the first stab was enough to wrestle Slade off him and get back to his feet.

As Tony tried to scramble to his feet, Roth drove a kick into his chest. The pain exploded like a grenade inside his body. The trauma of the gunshot wounds were protesting.

As Tony had suspected, a long absence from any form of combat had taken its toll on his reaction time and stamina.

Roth lunged in with the blade raised high above his head.

"You are done, Slade. You are mine."

Tony rolled onto his back, his feet held high ready to lash out at Roth's knees.

Then, something black and white rocketed out of the undergrowth and sunk its teeth into Roth's leg. It was Skipper.

Roth growled in pain and kicked his leg out trying to shake the little dog loose, but it held on gamely. He slashed blindly at the dog, but missed it.

Tony now saw his chance. He got to his feet. Pain shot through his leg as he did this, but he blanked it out. Storming forward, he was on Roth before he realised it.

Wary of the knife, Tony slammed the 'v' of his hand between his forefinger and thumb into Roth's windpipe. With the same arm, he brought his forearm up with force into the elbow of the knife arm dislocating it. Roth howled in pain.

Then Tony drove his knee into the injured man's groin and pulled down his head into a guillotine choke. He cranked on Roth's neck and throat in a vice-like grip.

Roth grabbed at Tony's balls in an attempt to break the hold, but Tony defended it and squeezed more tightly.

Roth was flagging and in a last-ditch effort to escape, he reached for Tony's legs and drove him backwards towards the edge of the cliff. He was prepared to take both Tony and him over it to certain death.

Tony glanced back and saw the edge of the cliff rapidly approaching him. He knew what he had to do. There was no other option.

He squeezed as hard as he could on Roth's neck and then fell backwards to the grass, projecting his enemy over his head in a Jujutsu rolling rice bale throw. This also resulted in projecting the screaming Roth over the cliff's edge into the darkness and the sea and rocks below.

Tony lay on his back breathing hard. He was getting too old for this action man shit. His whole body felt like it had been run over by a truck.

He suddenly felt a wet tongue lick his face. He reached out and hugged Skipper.

"Good on you, buddy. You saved my bacon."

Tony lay with Skipper at his side looking up at the lighthouse as his heartrate settled.

Voices nearing prompted him up onto his feet and he retrieved the rucksack. He felt at his waistband for his gun, but it was gone. It must have fallen out in the fight, but he did not have time to search for it. He limped painfully to the cover of the old lighthouse entrance. Skipper obediently followed him.

From the shadows of the doorway, he saw Sergeant Steve Richmond coming out of the mist.

"We'll spread out, Gov. He can't be far. Fuck knows what that scream was we heard."

Slightly further back, he heard the voice of D.C.I. Wyatt.

"Okay. Go steady and keep your wits about you."

Tony waited in the shadows as Richmond neared the porchway entrance of the lighthouse. He registered the gun in the policeman's hand. He knew what he had to do.

"For Christ's sake, Matt. Will you move your fat ass? We will lose them at this rate."

Susie Rawlings was trailing way behind Wyatt due to her colleague's complete and utter lack of fitness. Too many years of sitting at a computer eating junk food and smoking cigarettes had already taken its toll on thirty-three-year-old Matt Sloan's body. He looked up at Susie as he leant against a granite rock halfway up the hillside gasping for air. Mud splattered his clothes and caked his shoes.

"I'm fucked. You will have to give me a moment to get my breath."

"We haven't got a moment, you prat. I am on to my biggest break ever and I am lumbered with Mr Blobby. Now fucking move will you or I will take the photographs myself."

Sloan pulled his bulk up and began to follow the departing figure of Rawlings.

"Bitch," he mumbled under his breath.

"I heard that, Sloan," answered Susie as she threw a handful of mud in his direction.

"Bollocks," he retorted and began climbing again.

Tony waited until the last moment and when the foghorn sounded again, he sprang on the unsuspecting figure of Richmond. He clamped a tight sleeper hold strangle on the hapless policeman. Resisting was futile. Slade was an expert in this field, even when he was not firing on all cylinders.

As Richmond attempted to fight back, his finger involuntarily pulled the trigger on his gun and it harmlessly but loudly discharged into the night sky. It had sent out a warning signal to the others and it set Skipper off barking loudly. Tony cursed under his breath as he lay the sleeping body of Richmond onto the grass. Wyatt's voice then sounded close by.

"Steve? Steve? Are you okay? Answer me."

The policeman only answered with the pattering of raindrops. He knew something had happened to his sergeant.

"Slade, give it up. The place is surrounded and there is no way you will get off this island. You are done running. Hand yourself in and we can talk. You are digging yourself a bigger hole."

Tony's voice sounded eerily out of the mist.

"Are you alone, Wyatt?"

"Yes. Well, apart from Sergeant Richmond, but I sense your paths may have already crossed."

Tony smiled to himself.

"Very astute of you. But don't worry, he is only temporarily indisposed."

"I am glad to hear that. You are in enough bother as it is. So, how about it? Come out and show yourself."

"Nice try, Detective Chief Inspector, but I know you have that nosy newspaper woman with you looking for the big scoop and unfortunately, I can't afford to let certain parties know that I am still alive. So, I am afraid it's no deal."

"You mean Andy Roth?" asked Wyatt.

"Not anymore. We have met up already. He is dead. The scream you may have heard earlier was him. The cowardly piece of scum took an unscheduled swim in the sea."

Wyatt could not blame Slade for that.

"Did he murder Joe Williams?" he asked.

"Yes, he did. He got what he deserved."

Susie Rawlings and Matt Sloan had arrived in time to hear the end of this conversation.

"You can't run forever, Tony" shouted Susie.

"Ah, at last, you have spoken and confirmed my suspicions, young lady. Don't be too sure about your last statement. I have been running all my life one way or the other."

"Then tell me your story. Tell the world. If you have nothing to hide, then what are you running for?"

"Sorry, pet, I am not ready to spill my guts to somebody who doesn't give a fuck about me, just their career. And I don't fancy spending my golden years in a cell courtesy of her Majesty who I ironically fought for on many occasions."

"Then tell me," said Wyatt.

Susie Rawlings looked at him in disgust.

"John, you promised."

Wyatt raised a hand for silence.

"Why don't you and I have a chat and clear the air? If you are innocent, I can help you."

"Listen, Wyatt. I appreciate what you are trying to do, but it wouldn't matter what I told you. As I said, there are a network of people out there that would like to hunt me down as Roth did if they suspect that I am alive. I have done my utmost to disappear and hide my identity. That is the only way I can stay alive. Just let me go, Wyatt. I will disappear for good and you will never hear from me again."

"You know I can't make that promise, Slade. Look, whatever happened in that coffee shop that day you can tell me. I will bring you in unharmed. You have my word."

"Sorry, I can't."

Wyatt cursed under his breath.

"So be it then, Tony. But as I said, the harbour police are already on the dock side and members of the firearms team will join them soon. On my say so, they will be deployed. It won't end good for you, Tony."

"Neither for them, Wyatt. I know this won't make any difference, but please don't follow me. I don't wish to harm you."

"It's my job, Tony. As I told you way back in the hospital, I am relentless. I do not give in."

Wyatt was only greeted by silence. He shook his head.

"Shit."

He reached for his phone and made the call to the police in the harbour.

"So, what now?" asked Susie.

Wyatt looked out into the darkness.

"We keep going and hope we find him before the rest of the police."

"The story, John. Am I in or out?"

"You have always been in, Susie. I wouldn't have got this far without your help. You have waited as long as me for this and we both deserve a break. I was just spinning Slade a line a moment ago. Come on. Let's crack on. I think this mist is beginning to lift."

Susie nodded. She looked at Sloan.

"Time to move again, big boy."

"Great," mumbled Sloan.

The three of them carried on forward. It was not long before they came across Sergeant Richmond who was sitting propped up against the edge of the lighthouse. In the beam of Wyatt's torch, his face was a pasty shade of white. He looked up sheepishly as his boss approached.

"Sorry, Gov. He jumped me. I didn't see him coming."

Wyatt regarded him. Richmond hung his head.

"Come on. Get up," exclaimed Wyatt.

"Right. Let's stick together whatever. We can't let him off this island."

Tony knew his only hope of survival was to get off the island as the net would be closing fast. If the armed response unit caught up with him, they would not be asking too many questions.

He needed time to think and regroup, so he moved through the darkness until he reached the old gun fort and slipped in between the ruined stone walls and found a sheltered corner. Skipper, ever faithful, was by his side.

Tony needed to treat his wound before he could go any further. He had lost some blood and could not afford to lose anymore. He already felt thirsty and slightly light-headed. Luckily, the blade had missed any vital arteries or nerves.

Reaching into his rucksack, he dug down and produced a hip flask. He took a swig of scotch from it. He dropped his trousers and hoped to God that he did not get shot with his pants down. How ironic would that be after all he had been through.

He proceeded to pour a generous amount of the scotch over the wound. The stinging pain hit his senses hard, but he grimly overrode it. It was not the first time in his life that he had had to apply a field dressing.

He tore a long strip off a spare shirt and pushed it on the wound. Then he used a roll of surgical tape to bind it as tightly as permitted.

In the side pocket of the rucksack, he found a bottle of water and he sat down with his back to a wall and greedily drank it down. He felt better for doing this and it helped him think more clearly.

Tony felt in his pocket and his hand touched Joe's key fob. He thought about the possibility of getting to the harbourside and on to one of Joe's boats, but he knew the police would have them both covered. Going back was not an option. Was he destined to never get off this bloody island?

He looked up over the walls of the fort and saw flashlights. He had to give Wyatt his due. He was not lying when he said that he was relentless. Then he suddenly remembered something.

He moved quietly over the grass until he came to the dolmen stone. He got down on his knees and ran his hands over the wet mud until he found the old grill in the ground. Was this just a drainage tunnel or could it possible lead down to Buccaneer Cove? If it did, then he knew Tom Gwynne's dingy was down there. This just might be his escape route.

Whether there was a tunnel that led to the cove was a matter for debate, but he had run out of options.

He shone his torch on the padlock that held the cover in place. It looked newer than the grill. He dug into his rucksack and pulled out his fishing knife. He worked the tip skilfully into the lock. He soon had it undone. The grate protested with a screech as he pulled it open.

Tony shone his torch into the hole and saw a ladder attached to the wall. It was covered in green mould and rust from the sea air ,but hopefully, it would take him to the bottom safely.

He attached his rucksack to his trouser belt as he could not get into the hole with it on his back. Then he climbed in and tested his weight on the ladder. It held firmly.

Skipper investigated the hole and yelped excitedly. Tony looked up at the dog.

"I am so sorry, boy, but this is the end of the line for you. I can't take you any further. I don't know what I am going to encounter down here. You go back to the cottage. Somebody will find you. I am sure Annie will look after you."

The dog just stood there looking at Tony.

'"Go. Go, Skipper. Before it's too late."

He pulled the grating down in place and started carefully ascending downwards. Skipper let out a whimper as Tony disappeared from his view.

Wyatt and the others reached the fort ruins and shone their torches around. The rain had now stopped as the storm had moved on and the mist had lifted enough to see a watery moon ironically filtering through the breaking clouds. It cast a ghostly silver glow over the silent buildings.

On further investigation, Wyatt found traces of wet blood on the grass and stone floor by one of the walls. So, Slade was hurt.

"He was here, Steve and it looks like he was injured."

A sudden movement in the bushes nearby caused both men to level their guns. They, then saw a black and white Jack Russell come running out towards them. Both men lowered their firearms.

"Hello, boy," said Wyatt. "What are you doing out here on your own?"

"It must be Slade's. We can't be far from him now," said Richmond. "He is running out of ground unless he wants to take a dive off the cliffside. There is no way out for him, Gov. He is ours."

Wyatt would have loved to believe this, but something told him that Slade was not running blindly. He had proved time and time again to be more than resilient.

Chapter Twenty-Four

D.C.I. Wyatt had climbed to the highest point of the island beyond the fort and found no trace of Slade. He radioed to the harbourside and spoke to a Sergeant Greg Bush.

"Any sign of Slade? We have lost the trail up here."

"Nothing, Sir. But we have now got a satellite image of the whole island. I will send it over to your phone. It will give you a better idea of the island's layout. Having studied it, there are quite a few inlets and coves hidden around its perimeter. Slade may well have headed for one of those. Where is your location at present, Sir?"

"We are at the old army fort," answered Wyatt.

"Well, Sir, there is a small cove about a mile north of there."

"Is it accessible on foot?"

"Unfortunately, Sir, I can't ascertain that from the image. But if he hasn't doubled back, it is a possible way back down to the sea. But the cliffs look treacherous. I think you would need climbing gear to descend them."

Wyatt pondered this for a few seconds. Slade had the advantage of knowing the lie of the island intimately. Plus, he was an ex-paratrooper trained to overcome such problems. Did he have an escape planned at the cove or could he have doubled back without him noticing? He didn't think so... yet.

"Sergeant, are you still there?'"

"Yes, Sir."

"Right, listen. Get your men to a boat moored up. It's called the…"

He looked around to Richmond, Susie and Sloane.

"Joe William's boat, what was it called?"

They all looked blankly for a moment and then Susie pulled a small notepad out of her coat pocket and flipped through the pages.

"Here we are. It called the *Mermaid*."

Wyatt spoke back into the radio.

"The boat is a passenger ferry, a lightweight sloop called the *Mermaid*."

"We have already seen that boat, Sir. All is quiet on it," replied Bush.

"Shit," cursed Wyatt.

Sergeant Richmond now spoke up.

"Gov, remember when we were trying to locate Williams. The harbour authority also said that he owned a fishing trawler."

It was now Richmond's turn to consult his notepad.

"The *Gipsy of the Waves*. A beam trawler."

Wyatt nodded his head in acknowledgement.

"Sergeant Bush. There is another boat owned by Williams. A beam trawler named the *Gipsy of the Waves*. Check it out. The bastard might just be going for it."

"Right, Sir. We are on it. I will keep you informed."

"Also, Sergeant, I believe Andy Roth is here on the island and after Slade. Put the word around and keep an eye out for the bastard as well."

"Will do, Sir."

Sergeant Greg Bush switched off his radio and pulled out his mobile phone. He headed to a quiet spot on the harbour away from his colleagues and pressed speed dial. A voice answered immediately. Bush spoke quickly.

"I believe they are heading for Buccaneer Cove. It's a small pebbled beach on the north side of the island. I would get there as soon as possible."

He rang off and pocketed the phone.

Wyatt switched off the radio and regarded his three companions.

"Do you really think he could have doubled back down to the harbour?" asked Susie.

"I don't know, but I am running out of ideas."

"I am more inclined to think that he is still up here. Remember, he's ex- army. He is used to this terrain. I bet he has an escape route in mind." said Richmond.

Sloan regarded the policemen.

"So, do we go on or back or not? I am getting well pissed off with all this?"

Wyatt regarded the man with a glint of malevolence in his eyes.

"You can stay here on your ass if you want, son. It's up to you if you want to be part of this. If not, fuck off now. We go on."

Susie also saw the wild look of determination in the D.C.I.'s eyes and the harshness of Wyatt's tone. She realised this was now his last throw of the die. He was a desperate man.

"We are coming, Inspector. Aren't we, Matt?"

She pushed her colleague to his feet who was still protesting. Sergeant Richmond suddenly called from the darkness up ahead.

"Gov, I found something. Quick."

They moved towards Richmond.

"What have you got?" asked Wyatt.

"The dog led me to it. Look."

Under the looming shadow of the dolmen, they all regarded the grill in the ground and the open padlock.

"This looks like it has been recently opened. I am betting he has gone down here," exclaimed Richmond.

Wyatt and Richmond lifted the grating together and shone their torches down into the darkness and saw the ladder.

"It's some sort of tunnel. It could lead down to the sea," exclaimed Wyatt.

"What do you want to do, Gov?" asked Richmond.

Wyatt shone his torch down into the blackness again.

"Get down there and stop him before he reaches the sea."

Tony had reached the bottom of the ladder which must have been about 30 feet in length. He was now walking through a descending tunnel carved out from through the rock. The walls were damp with sea water and some stretches of the ground were ankle deep in it.

His powerful Maglite torch beam cut through the gloom and illuminated the pathway twisting away to the left.

So, the smugglers tunnels really did exist. It was not just legend. They also looked like they had been used more recently than suggested. Maybe a bit of smuggling was still done to the island. Maybe drugs instead of brandy and tobacco? He suddenly thought of Tom Gwynne and Jim Edwards down on the cove.

"Shit. No way. Could it be?" Tony muttered to himself.

Too late now to ask him. Anyway, Tony had more pressing matters to deal with. Good luck to whoever it may be.

If there was truth in the stories, this tunnel would take him out onto Buccaneer Cove and Tom's waiting boat.

As he carried on, the pathway began to slope even further downwards. Further back, Tony heard voices echoing. As he had suspected, Wyatt had found the tunnel. He now began to pick up the pace the best he could on his injured leg. He tried to blot out the pain.

The further he travelled, the rougher and wetter the terrain become. As he rounded another bend, he could now smell the salty tang of the sea more strongly. This spurred him on.

His four pursuers had all negotiated the ladder, even Sloan, and were now walking into the tunnel. Their torches picked up wet muddy footprints which encouraged them.

Wyatt now led the group. His gun was drawn and ready. Behind him, Richmond also had his weapon at the ready and was watching his governor's back. Susie Rawlings followed next. Her stomach tingled with excitement. She was already thinking about how she was going to write this up. Jameson would be drooling when she slapped it on his desk.

He would be putting her up for promotion. There might be a book in it. A journalism award maybe? TV appearances. She would be headhunted by the tabloid giants. Her mind ran riot with possibilities.

Sloan, as usual, brought up the rear gasping and wheezing. His thoughts were not so lofty. He was wondering when he would get his dinner if at all and also what a nice ass Susie had.

Tony followed another twist in the tunnel and saw a dull grey light ahead. He could also hear the sea. He hobbled as quickly as possible as the grey light became brighter and then he was out of the tunnel and stood on a craggy ledge about 20 feet above what he presumed was Buccaneer Cove.

This was the entrance to the sea cave. The rock face was wet and slippery. It was going to be a hard climb down, even without his injury, but Tony was confident. In his army days, he had negotiated bigger and more dangerous heights than this.

He played his torch over the rocks and quickly made the decision to which path he was going to take. As he swung his legs over the side of the cliff and gripped the rocks tightly, he heard voices echo once again from the cave. Wyatt was close.

Wyatt rounded a bend in the tunnel and saw the opening ahead.

"Here's the way out up ahead. Be careful. Slade could be waiting for us."

The policeman's heart was thumping in his chest. At last, he had tracked his quarry down.

Tony was making good progress. He had had a few scares on the way when loose rock had given way under his feet several times and a startled sea gull who had been guarding her nest had angrily swooped and tried to attack him.

Within six feet of the bottom, he heard Wyatt call out.

"Slade, don't move or I will open fire. I mean it."

Tony looked up and saw four figures on the cave entrance's ledge. He knew none of them would get down the rockface. He called out to them.

"So, what are you going to do, Wyatt? Have me hang off these rocks forever? It's your move. Are you going to come down here and arrest me? If so, then do it."

"Still a fucking smartass, aren't you, Slade?"

It was Richmond.

"Gov, I am going over. I can get down there."

Wyatt regarded the younger man.

"Are you sure, Steve?"

Richmond looked down towards the sea and swallowed hard.

"Yeah. A piece of piss. I was in the Boy Scouts."

Wyatt smiled grimly.

"Okay, I will alert the harbour patrol to get a boat around to this cove as quickly as possible.

Tony Slade watched Richmond begin his climb down. He had to give the bastard his due. He had balls.

In his favour, Richmond's descent had detracted Wyatt and it allowed Tony to drop the six feet to the sand below. He landed as he would have done from a parachute jump, protecting his injury as much as possible.

"Sir, he's dropped to the beach," shouted Richmond.

Wyatt put the radio down and leant over the cliff edge. He saw Tony scrambling to his feet, and he levelled his gun.

"Slade, freeze or I will shoot."

Tony ran in a zigzag pattern across the sand for the cover of more rocks. Two shots rang out into the night and the sand erupted around him.

Tony rolled and made it to a small cluster of rocks. As he crawled in behind them, he saw the black rubber body of Tom Gwynne's dingy. Bingo. He had found it.

Another shot ricocheted off the rocks around him.

"Slade, give it up. You have nowhere to go."

Tony moved to the dingy and slowly eased it out from the cover of the rocks into the cold, inky, black waters. He now waded out into the sea. He felt the coldness envelope his body, but it was nothing he had not experienced before.

He had endured cold water survival training as a paratrooper, having to dive on many occasions into ice holes. Later, as a mercenary in Africa, he had crossed more than one treacherous river that inhabited God knows what.

Stealthily, he pushed the boat out until he was chest deep in the water.

Tony waited until the last moment before pulling himself up into the dingy. Dull pain ached in his muscles. The recent rigours had taken their toll on his still recovering body. Once aboard, he headed to the outboard motor and pulled on the rota cord to start the engine. Wyatt saw him.

"Steve, get down there. He's got a fucking boat."

As Sergeant Richmond turned his head seaward to look for Slade, the nesting seagull again agitated by the intrusion flew at him and flapped around his head. This startled Richmond who lost his footing and fell backwards ten feet down to the beach below.

"Shit," exclaimed Wyatt as he saw his colleague fall.

He looked over the rocky ledge and saw Richmond. He lay spread-eagled on his back. He was not moving.

"Steve, are you okay? Steve, answer me."

He was greeted by silence. Wyatt now turn his attention back to Slade.

"You bastard Slade. You will pay for this."

He levelled his gun once more in the direction of the dingy. Susie Rawlings came forward and gripped Wyatt's arm.

"John, please leave it. Let the harbour boat pick him up. He is too far away. You need to radio for medical help for Richmond."

Wyatt looked into her pleading eyes and then back to Slade battling to start the boat's engine. He pushed the radio towards her.

"You do it."

He took aim and fired off a couple more shots. One whizzed past Slade into the darkness, but the other one struck the dingy puncturing it.

"Yes," shouted Wyatt triumphantly as he fist pumped the air. "He's going nowhere now. He's mine."

He turned to Susie.

"Is the boat coming?"

Susie looked at the ragged and wild features of the policeman.

"Yes, it's coming. There is also medical help onboard."

"Good. Now let's see if we can find a safe way down to the beach."

Tony cursed as the dingy began to deflate and water began to spill into it.

Shit, now he was in trouble. He would not last much longer in the cold sea without catching hypothermia. Swimming back to the beach was out of the question. Wyatt would pick him off. He gripped his rucksack to use as a float and slipped over the side into the water.

His only hope was to try and swim towards an outcrop of rocks he could see stretching out one hundred metres or so from the cove. He guessed a boat would be on its way soon and it would be a matter of getting over to the outcrop before it arrived. Even then, he had no idea if there was any escape route if he got there.

He was feeling weak from all the exhaustion. His energy was sapping fast. His clothes felt heavy and he could not stop shivering. His arms and legs began to feel heavy. He had seen two of his army comrades die from hypothermia in the past. It was almost impossible to battle it by yourself.

He gazed back to land and he now saw figures on the beach. They had found a way down. He could not go back now even if he wanted. He stared up to the heavens as if looking for an answer and then miraculously it came out of the clouds.

Wyatt crouched over the body of his sergeant. Richmond was unconscious but breathing. His left leg was twisted at a nasty angle. It looked broken, but apart from this, he could see no blood or head injury.

"It's okay, son. You will be alright. Help is on its way."

Susie Rawlings was a little further up the beach speaking into her mobile to Carl Jameson, her editor.

"I know its late, Carl, but wait until you hear this. You won't believe it. We have got Tony Slade."

Matt Sloan had taken all the photos he needed and he now sat on a rock. Having fished around in his anorak pockets, he had found an old sherbet lemon sweet. The paper was a bit sticky and fluffy, but when he unwrapped it, the sugary sweet tasted like paradise. He would not be sad to see the back of this island. He was wet, tired and hungry. He glanced towards Susie. That girl put him through hell, but he was glad for her. She deserved the story.

As if she sensed Matt looking at her, she turned towards him and gave him the thumbs up sign.

Tony stared into the night sky as a strong beam of light lit up the sea around him. The helicopter swooped low. He recognised it as a Bell 212. It was normally used for commercial flights and could carry up to fifteen people if need be. The door opened, and a ladder dropped down to within his reach. Was he dreaming? A man he did not recognise knelt by the open door and shouted.

"Get up the ladder, Slade, and in here now."

The Kalashnikov aimed at him persuaded him that he was not dreaming. He slung the rucksack onto his back and grabbed the ladder with numb fingers and began to climb. He prayed that he had enough strength left to make it.

Wyatt and the others suddenly became aware of the helicopter and the thunder of its rota blades. They saw the ladder drop and Slade began to climb it.

"No!" roared Wyatt.

He ran into the water emptying his gun in Slade's direction. The bullets whizzed around Tony. The swaying of the ladder in the vacuum of air created by the rota blades prevented any of them hitting him, but they were dangerously close to the helicopter, so the man with the Kalashnikov machine gun opened fire.

A stream of bullets were aimed in Wyatt's direction. One hit him between the eyes. He was dead before others ripped his chest open. His body dropped to the water like a puppet who had his strings cut.

Susie Rawlings and Matt Sloan froze in shock at what had just happened.

Tony saw Wyatt drop and he turned his head and gritted his teeth. More death. Would it ever stop?

The man with the machine gun reached out and grabbed the collar of Tony's jacket and pulled him unceremoniously into the helicopter. Tony lay on his back breathing heavily as the man loomed over him, machine gun poised. Then he moved away and two other men now stood over him. They had Browning automatics aimed at him. At first, Tony did not recognise them. But it was the strong Geordie accent that gave it away as one of them spoke.

"Well, well, well, Tony Slade. Between you and that prick Roth, you have both led us a merry dance. We are not particularly pleased to have to leave the comfort of Newcastle to come to this shit hole, but needs must. Well, time to answer a few questions."

Tony now recognised the features as well as the voice of Danny Ewan. The other man was his business partner Joe Walsh. The men who now ran Kenny Robbins' firm. They threw him a few blankets.

"Get them around you. We don't want you dying on us."

Tony reached out and took the blankets and wrapped them tightly around himself. Danny Ewan spoke again.

"First, is Roth dead?"

Tony Slade shut his eyes for a moment. Then nodded his head.

"Good. That's one mess sorted. We have some other questions, but you can take your time, Tony. We have an hour or more before we get back to Newcastle."

Tony afforded himself a wry grin. Talk about out of the frying pan and into the fire. He pulled himself up to a seated position. Pain shot through his body again. He looked out of the window. He saw the island of Graig o Mor disappear below him.

Poor Wyatt, he did not deserve what he got, but the truth was it could have been Tony lying dead down there. He regarded the two men. They looked older than he remembered. Both had well-groomed grey hair. Ewan also sported a neatly trimmed beard. They looked like two middle aged businessmen until you looked into their eyes.

"Suppose you wouldn't have a whisky?" he asked.

Ewan looked at Walsh. Joe Walsh reached to his inside coat pocket and produced a drinking flask and handed it to Tony.

"You cheeky fucker."

Tony received it gratefully with trembling hands. He flipped open the top and took a deep swig of the amber fluid. It tasted like nectar. He was trying to act composed, but this was a total surprise and not part of his plans. Danny resumed speaking.

"Been a while, Tony. You're not looking too bad for a man who was at death's door. Much better off than our old Boss Kenny Robbins."

Tony eyed both men warily along with the guns.

"I didn't kill him."

Both men smiled.

"Maybe not, but you were neck deep in the shit with him after stealing his woman," said Danny.

There was silence for a moment.

"So, Roth is dead, you say?"

"Yes, you don't need to worry about that psycho anymore. His body is washing around in the channel somewhere."

Danny and Joe both exchanged a look that did not go unnoticed by Tony. It looked like relief. Joe now spoke.

"Roth was a loose cannon. Didn't obey orders and went off on a one-man vendetta. He has left a trail of carnage after him. We wanted none of it traced back to us or the firm. We have had to clean it up and we aren't too fucking pleased about it."

"Am I one of the details you have come to clean up?" asked Tony.

There was a moment of tense silence.

"No, Tony. You are not," replied Joe.

Tony was puzzled.

"I don't understand. The guns?"

Joe lowered the gun and so did Danny.

"We didn't know how you would react when we found you. It was insurance. The guns were really meant for Roth."

Tony nodded towards the thick set man who sat quietly with the Kalashnikov cradled on his lap next to the pilot.

"Your man there killed a copper back on the beach. He was a D.C.I."

"Collateral damage, I'm afraid, Tony. Being an ex-army man, you can appreciate that," replied Ewan.

There was more silence.

"I still don't get it, Danny. What's going on here?"

Ewan leaned forward towards Tony.

"The truth is whatever happened to Kenny in that coffee shop did us and the firm a favour."

Tony waited for an explanation to the statement.

"Remember the Dutchman Bergkemp?"

Tony nodded.

"When you were working for Kenny, this Bergkemp was about to do a deal and take over Kenny's businesses."

"Yes, I recall all that," said Tony.

Joe continued.

"Behind the scenes, none of us wanted the deal. Danny and me threw our hat into the ring and told Kenny we were happy to run the firm if he wished to retire and move to warmer climates. But he said no. He wanted to get rid of the whole thing and wash his hands with it, which would have resulted in Bergkemp bringing in his own team and us getting booted out.

There was a lot of unrest and then out of the blue came the shootings. As soon as Bergkemp heard about it, he was back in Holland like a fucking shot. He wanted no part of it. He thought that he had triggered some sort of turf warfare.

Blokes like that want to stay squeaky clean. He pulled the deal and with no Kenny around, Joe and I as senior staff took over the reins without any protest and we are happy with that.

We didn't really give a fuck about you, Tony. You were a good bloke when you worked for the firm. I had no personal beef with you. What you did was fucking cheeky and took some balls but when all is said and done, we got what we wanted in a roundabout way with your help."

Tony absorbed this information. They had ironically got what they had wanted. Tony had not. He had lost Annette.

Danny carried on.

"It was all sweet, except for Roth hellbent on revenge. We spoke to Kenny many times about getting rid of him from the firm, but he had this bond with Roth. He just wouldn't hear of it, even though he knew he was becoming a liability.

When Roth came to us saying he was going after you, we tried to put him off and buy time, but he just went rogue.

In the end, we had to come find him. The storm curtailed us a little, but as soon as it cleared, we flew in. It was as much by luck that we came across you as you came across us. Karma maybe?"

"How did you know where to find me?"

"An inside contact in the police down here contacted us. He told us that a D.C.I. from Bristol was down here in Cardiff asking about you and Roth."

"Friends in high places, eh," replied Tony.

"Something like that," said Walsh. "Anyway, we asked him to keep us updated. Today he informed us that this Bristol copper was heading out to an island in the Bristol channel named Graig o Mor. The word going around was that it was suspected that you were hiding out there and that Roth was coming for you.

So, we decided to fly down and put an end to Roth's killing spree. We didn't know if you would be alive or dead when we got there.

As I said, the storm delayed us, but as it cleared, our contact rang us and told us to fly to the cove on the north of the island. We did, and low and behold, there you were up to your tits in the drink with bullets flying at you like the fucking D-Day landings."

Tony regarded both men.

"I should thank you then for saving my life."

Walsh smiled.

"No need, Tony. It looks like we have both inadvertently done each other a favour, so we are quits. You are free to go."

Tony mulled over the irony of the situation.

"What happened in the coffee shop that day was something that you could only conjure up in a nightmare. For all intents and purposes, I should be dead with the rest of them, but I'm not. So, what does that tell you gentlemen?"

"Like I said, karma," answered Ewan.

As the helicopter moved out over the sea, Tony settled back in a seat. He was wrapped in a couple of blankets and feeling warmer. He was heading back to Newcastle. But he knew his future was not there.

Tony Slade was a survivor and he had to move on. He had made it out. This time physically in one piece, but violence and death had come hunting him once again. Another precious friend's life had been snuffed out.

Danny Ewan turned to him.

"Not long to go now. About thirty minutes. What's your plans from there?"

Tony turned and looked out of the window.

"Who knows? We will see what tomorrow brings. Just now all I want to do is sleep. I am too old for all this Rambo stuff."

A heavy fatigue suddenly overwhelmed him. He closed his eyes and sleep claimed him.

About the author

This is Kevin's second fictional novel. The first being *Battlescars* were he first introduced the reader to the character of Tony Slade.

Kevin is a well known and respected Martial artist worldwide. He has trained and taught for some 43 years now.

Whilst training he started to write articles for Martial arts magazines which spurred him on to write a series of Self Defence and Combative instructional books.

His real passion was to write fiction and particularly a novel. *Battlescars* was finally the result in 2018 and now the follow up *No hiding place.*

Kevin lives in Bristol, Uk with his wife Tina. He is a father and Grandfather.

He is now semi-retired from teaching Martial arts and spends his leisure time reading, writing, playing guitar and travelling.

CPSIA information can be obtained
at www.ICGtesting.com
Printed in the USA
BVHW081251020919
557346BV00001B/76/P

9 781786 235633